I0731390

THE WARRIOR'S ECHO

Echoes in Time
Book Three

Paula Quinn

© Copyright 2022 by Paula Quinn
Text by Paula Quinn
Cover by Wicked Smart Designs

Dragonblade Publishing, Inc. is an imprint of Kathryn Le Veque Novels, Inc.
P.O. Box 7968
La Verne CA 91750
ceo@dragonbladepublishing.com

Produced in the United States of America

First Edition January 2022
Trade Paperback Edition

Reproduction of any kind except where it pertains to short quotes in relation to advertising or promotion is strictly prohibited.

All Rights Reserved.

The characters and events portrayed in this book are fictitious. Any similarity to real persons, living or dead, is purely coincidental and not intended by the author.

ARE YOU SIGNED UP FOR DRAGONBLADE'S BLOG?

You'll get the latest news and information on exclusive giveaways, exclusive excerpts, coming releases, sales, free books, cover reveals and more.

Check out our complete list of authors, too!

No spam, no junk. That's a promise!

Sign Up Here

www.dragonbladepublishing.com

Dearest Reader;

Thank you for your support of a small press. At Dragonblade Publishing, we strive to bring you the highest quality Historical Romance from some of the best authors in the business. Without your support, there is no 'us', so we sincerely hope you adore these stories and find some new favorite authors along the way.

Happy Reading!

CEO, Dragonblade Publishing

Additional Dragonblade books by Author Paula Quinn

Echoes in Time Series
Echo of Roses
Echoes of Abandon
The Warrior's Echo

Rulers of the Sky Series
Scorched
Ember
White Hot

Hearts of the Highlands Series
Heart of Ashes
Heart of Shadows
Heart of Stone
Lion Heart
Tempest Heart
Heart of Thanks
Forbidden Heart

CHAPTER ONE

Mercia, England
Winter in the Year of Our Lord, 1017
Under the rule of King Cnut of Denmark.

CHIEF ULF KRISTIANSEN had his man down in the span of three breaths. With eyes the color of a Norse river in winter, he looked up to the heavens, lifted his sword, and brought it down into his enemy. Blood spurted onto his hide boots and seeped into the snow.

With no time to waste, he yanked the blade out and looked around for the next man to fight. He killed seven more before he lost his sword. After which, he had to use two short swords from two of his victims. He used them to take some heads and fought for another hour. In that time, he saved two of his men from death at the end of a Saxon blade. He wanted no accolades for it. Every chief should keep the men who fought for him or their king safe. And he did, often reaching his men just in time. They followed him loyally because they knew he would give his life to save theirs.

Fin, his second in command. followed him because he was Fin's brother. Fin could save his own life. Still, the chief looked for his brother on the field often. He didn't have to, for Fin was more savage than he. Ulf looked for him because whatever troubles they had between them, Ulf loved his younger brother, and it comforted him to see him among the living.

When there was no one else to fight and only he and his men survived, Ulf stopped and dropped his weapons.

Covered in blood, he picked up one of the heads by the hair and called out to his men in the native tongue of his people while snowflakes fell on the dead. They were victorious. They always were.

"King Cnut will be passing through here in a few hours with his men," he called out. "He will know his warriors are unstoppable."

His men cheered and then dispersed. They would return to camp on foot, a mile to the west.

Returning, he washed in icy cold water from a nearby brook. He was used to the cold. Every Dane was. They'd grown up in it. He fought without his fur cloak so that he would not overheat. When he was done, he retrieved his cloak and went to the fire.

He was the king's most loyal, most skilled warrior, but he didn't want to do it anymore. He was tired of fighting. He'd lost enough of his blood in the last decade. He wanted to go home to Denmark and continue building his longhouse, farming his land, taking a wife, and starting a family.

Nevertheless, what he wanted didn't matter. While he was here in England, with its new Danish monarch, Cnut, he would continue to end uprisings that sprang up in different territories. This month, he was in Mercia. Last month, East Anglia. If that meant killing some Saxons who thought they could beat the Danes, he had no trouble with it. He would show them who was the mightier people.

"Lord!" a young Dane called out, running toward him. "Those Saxons' village is a short distance away. There is food!"

Food. Ulf, or Wolf as he has been known to be called, rubbed his palm over his belly. He was hungry. "How many villagers?"

"About two dozen," the young man reported. "Mostly women and old men."

"To the horses," Wolf called out to his men. They obeyed without question.

He quickly found a shield and a spear, then mounted his horse. Like the Saxons, they used horses to ride, not to fight. The beasts were built for travel, not speed. He commanded his men to follow and get the nets ready.

"Can I ride with your group?" the young Dane asked.

Wolf examined him with a gaze that could stop his enemies and send them running. The young man smiled and shifted under the chief's scrutiny. "What are you called?"

"Akkar, Lord. I came to this land with my family to farm, but I want to fight."

"Stay with your family," Wolf told him and rode off.

Akkar followed him. "Then just let me come with you to the village, then I will return home to my father. Please, Lord. The Saxons killed my mother and my sisters."

Many young men abandoned their farming to fight for reasons just like this. Wolf wouldn't be moved by this one's story.

He nodded though, following the young man's direction to the outskirts of the Saxon village. He didn't waste any further time thinking about Akkar or his father. His belly was grumbling. He was cold. He wanted to conquer and eat and make camp for the night. If there were any more uprisings between where they were and Wessex, his scouts would discover them and report to him. He and his men would defeat them all. For King Cnut. For the Danes…and for Akkar's family.

When they reached the village, Wolf stayed out of sight while six of his men stole into their market and blended in…for about ten breaths. The rest of the soldiers took positions around the perimeter of the marketplace and drew their weapons. The villagers screamed and tried to run but there was no place to go. They were herded like sheep to the center, where nets were cast over them.

"Who is the leader here?" Fin demanded in the language of the Saxons.

When no one answered, he pulled a sword from its sheath on his belt and raised it high.

Wolf raised his hand for his second in command to wait. Fin obeyed and lowered his weapon.

"By decree of England's King Cnut," Wolf told them from his saddle, "I give you a chance to live if you obey. We can cut each and every one of you—"

"Help!" a woman screamed from the trapped crowd. "What happened? Where am I?"

He followed her shrill voice and found her clawing at the netting. She was…rather beautiful. He hadn't seen anyone like her in all his years. She wore her long, golden hair loose and flowing just over her dainty shoulders. Her large eyes were wide with terror and panic. They were painted in dark shades of blue and gray, like a storm filling the sunlit sky. Their shape, like his cat's eyes at home. The top half of her was covered in a puffy red coat, cut to her hips. The bottom half of her was most intriguing in black hose and furry boots. Wolf had never seen garments like hers before. What was it she was screaming?

"Let me go! Is this some kind of sick joke?"

Was it the language of the Saxons? He spoke it almost fluently. This sounded somewhat different.

"I demand to speak to the person in charge!" she screamed out.

He rode to her, stopping before he trampled through the crowd. They scattered, but she did not. The net sank around her. She held it up in her fingers and glared at him.

"I am the leader," he told her, staring into her defiant gaze.

"I'm going to have you fired for this."

He couldn't help the crook of his mouth rising with amusement at the venom of her threat. "Fired in what?"

"What?" She went a little paler than she naturally was.

"You will stop speaking now," he commanded after his head cleared. "I will not be seduced by your witchery."

"Witchery?" She managed to sound indignant instead of afraid. "What is this? Who are you? You don't get to tell me what to do. Do you know who I am? Let me go!" By now, she was screeching and paining Wolf's ears. "The joke is over, and it wasn't funny!"

Fin came forward on his horse and rode the snorting beast so close to her that she had to step back lest she be trampled underfoot. "Do you disobey our chief?"

Though the blood drained from her delicately cut face and her eyes appeared glassy and deeper blue, less gray, the haughty tilt of her chin and the pert lift of her nose proved her foolish courage. Who was she? Wolf wondered. Where had she come from around here, where women were so bold? Or garbed themselves the way she did, with her beguiling curves almost bared before all?

She was terrified, yet—

"Are you all supposed to be Vikings?" she managed to ask.

Fin lifted his sword to her face. There was blood, still wet from his many victims, on it. She looked at it, covered her mouth, then her eyes, and then fell backward into a dead faint.

"Bring her to me," Wolf commanded, then looked out among the crowd. They were mostly women and children, some men too old to fight a war but too young to be called old men. "If any of you are the wives of the fighting men, you are now widows. I am remorseful for your sakes—for how you will now live." He stopped and waited while wailing filled the air and brought with it dark, dreary clouds. "I want food and lodging for me and my men. You will serve us from now on and will be provided for."

Silence, save for some weeping, but no one defied him.

He turned his horse and was about to ride toward one of the huts for some shelter, when someone rose up to defy him yet again.

"I'm not serving anybody! Um, I'm Camelee Pendrey!" She gripped her head. "I think I need a doctor."

He turned to look at her. He knew it was a mistake. The men were lifting the net while she awoke from her faint and sat up. The netting pulled and tugged at her hair. Her color had returned. Pale pink with darker contours masterfully applied with some kind of magical paint. He couldn't take his eyes off her.

Camelee Pendrey.

"You are now my servant," he corrected her. "Bring her to me."

He was patient while Fin and Akkar dragged her from the center of the market to him.

She resisted every step, even after he found a smile within him and let it shine on her.

"Seriously," she pleaded when she reached him. "What's going on here? Please. What's going on?"

He understood enough of the Saxon's language to know what she was asking. He understood that she was pleading for something. That was a little more like it. She was finally understanding that being subservient would get her more—

"Where. Am. I?" she asked carefully. "Who brought me here?"

"You are in Mercia. In England," he added when she still looked lost. "Were you hit in the head?"

She shook it and tried to fight when Fin and Akkar tried to tie her to his horse.

"Stop resisting," Wolf warned her. "Or you will discover what happens when my patience wears thin."

She stopped resisting. Clever woman. He would have hated to go after her.

She walked at his side while he trotted slowly to one of the huts.

"I can't be in Mercia, England, wherever that is. This is New York! This is some kind of sick reenactment thing and you've kidnapped me!"

"Call it whatever you wish," he replied. He looked down at her and lifted his brow. "You will do what I ask or suffer the consequences."

He almost heard her tight growl. Storms brewed in the ominous depths of her eyes. But she followed him. When he dismounted, she stepped aside just in time to avoid colliding into his body.

"I'm hungry," he said, untying her from the horse.

"Okay?" she asked, as if she had no idea why he was telling her such a thing.

"Make me—us," he corrected, looking behind them at the men "—something to eat."

She laughed, tossing back her head with a dramatic flair. An instant later, she settled her darkening gaze on him. "I don't know how to cook, and this isn't my house."

He tried to ignore the lock of her hair falling over her right eye. "What do you mean you don't know how to cook? You are well past marriageable age."

A flash of crimson brushed her cheeks. "*Well* past?"

He snapped his mouth shut, realizing the insult he'd given her. He looked over her shoulder at the other women following. "Do any of you know how to cook?"

They all nodded their heads and stared at him with fear and hatred in their eyes.

He'd have to keep his eyes on them. Men or women, none of them could be trusted. "Feed us," he ordered.

"What's to stop us from poisoning you?" Camelee Pendrey threw at him.

"Well, I will be stopping you by keeping you with me." He flashed a stiff grin at her, and then found Akkar in the sea of faces entering the hut.

"The men need barracks."

The farmer's son nodded and ran off.

He took a step into the nearest hut and waited for her to follow. When she finally did, he stared into her eyes. He saw the hint of terror there, the battle she fought with herself to not fall at his feet and weep.

Wolf kept his gaze locked with hers. Or was it she who held the power of *his* gaze?

"Why are you not wed?" he asked while women went to

work around her.

"How can this feel so real?" She fell into a chair and closed her eyes.

"It is real," he assured her. "Are you possessed by a demon?"

She opened her eyes and gave him an impatient look. "No. I'm confused because a little while ago I was in some guy's office in the city holding a brooch I inherited and then I was here, being captured by you! One second my whole world, my life changed." She snapped her fingers, which Wolf noticed were each tipped with red paint or dye on her fingernails. "My bag is gone. My phone was in it, and my vape, credit cards. I don't have any money, so you're not going to get anything from me. Is that what this is? Are you holding me for ransom?"

"No," he scoffed. "Is there someone of means who might give up their valuables for you?"

"No."

She was lying. "Where is your husband? On the field?" he demanded to know.

"I'm not married."

"Expected, since you cannot cook," he murmured, and without waiting for her reply, he went to speak to Fin, who was waiting at the door.

"We need a bigger hut," his brother suggested. "Everyone will not fit in here."

Wolf nodded in agreement. "Find out if there is a town hall or a great hall nearby. Keep me apprised."

A short while later, the men all piled into a large town hall at the north end of the market, near the town church.

Wolf decided to remain in the hut, without all the noise, and in the company of Camelee Pendrey—and two of the women who were cooking for him. Normally, servants did not sit at his table, but Camelee had already been sitting there from when she fell into her seat earlier.

So, he sat opposite her. He wanted to see her, though he did not stare, and when he looked, he was quick to look away before being caught.

"Are you from this village?" he put to her, accepting one cup of whatever they drank here and taking a sip. She stared at the cup and cleared her throat. He observed her glancing around the table for her cup. And then at the other two women, who'd served him. When she realized she wasn't getting anything to drink, her heated gaze found his.

"I'm thirsty."

He handed her his cup. She stared at it as if were a dead herring.

She turned away toward the women. "May I have some water?"

"Camelee," he said keeping his voice low. He still held the cup out to her.

"You are tempting them to defy me. Is that truly your desire?"

She went pale, but only for a moment, and then she fumed at him. "What is this? Who are these people? End this now and I won't have my lawyers destroy you!"

"Why do you speak like a madwoman? Are you?"

"I wasn't mad this morning. But now I don't know."

He pushed the cup closer. She finally accepted it and brought it to her nose. "You don't understand—at home, I'm an actress. I'm famous. I am treated very well. I—"

"Where is your home?" he asked her, not knowing, or caring what an actress was or why she was famous. If she was treated *very* well, that was going to change.

"New York. Manhattan."

"York?"

"New York," she corrected. "New York," she said again when he gave her a curious look. "The city that never sleeps. Home of the Yankees."

"Yankees?"

She laughed a little. "Oh, come on, you don't know who the Yankees are? Every guy knows—" She stopped and looked at her surroundings, at the two women cooking, the large stone oven, the bed a few feet away. The fear, so carefully concealed throughout most of her capture, became suddenly clear. The truth of her demise was difficult to ignore. Her tears welled up along the brims of her eyes—but they did not fall. She drew in a deep breath and patted her cheeks.

When she set her glassy gaze on him again, she wore a well-practiced smile. "Where did you say we are?"

He didn't answer. He should have sent the two cooks away. Word moved swiftly around kitchen fires. A chief who had taken an interest in a captive? A servant? And a mouthy one at that? Who cared if she was mad in the head? All the more reason for her to not be sitting here.

He glanced at the two women cooking. "Stop asking questions. If you must speak, show gratitude to me for letting you sit at my table."

She smiled, but her beguiling lips were pulled tight against her teeth. "Well then," She gave him a pitiful look through her flaxen locks as she stood up. "I think I'll be leaving now." She tilted her chin and tucked her hair behind her ears. "And there's no reason to answer my question. I already know I'm in hell."

She turned to leave. He called her name to stop her. "You will remain here and wash the dishes. If you cannot cook, you will wash. That is it. It is done. Do you understand?" He believed she did.

She stopped and swung around to look at him. Still smiling, as if *he* were the mad one. "No, I don't understand."

His smirk widened. "Let me be more clear then. If you are not here to do these dishes, I will give you to Fin."

Her eyes widened with pure terror. "I am not your property to give away!"

He nodded to disagree. "You are the spoils of war. My side won, yours did not."

"But," she said, returning to the table. "I don't have a side."

"How can you not have a side?" he asked, genuinely curious.

"Are you a traitor to your countrymen?"

"No!" she answered without haste. There was at least that. "Don't try to put words into my mouth. Now tell me, what are the sides?"

"Danes against the Saxons."

"A re-enactment," she said in a low voice, almost a whisper.

"What is a re-enactment?" he asked. "You have strange speech."

"But this can't be real. It's impossible!"

The two women, whom Wolf learned were called Brigid and Alison served him turnip and mushroom soup with carrots, and onions, and butternut squash. He tasted it and smiled. "It is real." He invited the cooks to eat the rest before his men came looking for him. Camelee refused but he warned her that he didn't know when her next meal would be. So, she ate.

"Now tell me," he said after he asked Brigid and Alison to leave, "why do you keep saying this cannot be real?"

"Because I…I was in New York City this morning. I inherited some brooch and—I don't know, I rubbed it. I felt compelled to rub it. A name appeared. *Pendragon.* I said it just like that—" She stopped and looked around as if expecting something to happen. "I said it and then I was here, under your net somewhere in England—"

"Mercia," he reminded her, enjoying her tale and how she sounded telling it.

"Mercia." She scrunched up her face. "How old is—" Her gaze roved over the room. "It may seem odd that I don't know, but what year is it?"

It was odd. What was her ailment, he wondered? "It is one thousand and seventeen."

Her mouth fell open a little. He was admiring it when she fell over once again into a dead faint.

With a sigh, Wolf rose from his chair, walked around the table, and scooped her up in his arms. She had opened her coat and he looked at the shape of her as it fell open. She was slight, thin, but curvy. He felt a bit out of breath. He didn't know why.

He stretched her out on the table near his food and sat down to finish his meal.

He would decide what to do with her later. For now, though, he wanted to keep her.

CHAPTER TWO

AMELEE'S EYES FLUTTERED open. For one blissful instant, the memory of where she was eluded her. What was so hard beneath her? Where was Karen with her coffee?

No coffee.

Everything came back, not in a rush, but slowly, taking its time to lengthen the time of her torture. Dear God, no. Vikings? Was this a dream she was stuck inside of? An acting job on the series with that gorgeous blond? Whatshisname? She was afraid to open her eyes. What if she didn't wake up? She couldn't go on, *acting* like she wasn't afraid because she didn't want to give some maniac the satisfaction of seeing her crawl.

Screw that. She was terrified. So afraid, in fact, that she'd fainted twice. But fainting was beyond her control. She wouldn't tremble or fall apart. She just couldn't. It wasn't in her nature. Still, she didn't want to face the Viking reality. He'd said they were in the year one thousand and seventeen!

Please, God, please, don't let it be real or some cult group preparing to kill me.

"Are you going to pretend you are asleep for much longer?"

His voice rolled across her ear like a deep, ancient drum. The sound of him called to her and startled her. In fact, she was sure if it was possible to jump out of one's own skin, she would have done it. She gave herself a moment to slow her breath and not throw up. She almost couldn't do it. She was still here. Wherever or *whenever* here was. She was in trouble—about to lose her mind and her life. Either this guy was the leader of a whole bunch of maniacs who went around acting like marauding Vikings in twenty nineteen where they belonged, or she'd traveled back in time to–God forbid—ten seventeen to a Saxon village just taken over by Vikings, and she was now a slave.

If so, she seriously considered opening her eyes and cursing him to his face and letting him kill her.

"Camelee."

Oh, why had she told him her name? The sound of it from his mouth sounded possessive, sultry, and almost oppressive.

Since the idea of time travel was ridiculous, the only other possibility was that she'd been abducted. She had to escape and find a phone.

She was drowning!

Choking, she bolted upright. She took a moment to note that she'd been lying on the table. She coughed, and then glared at him holding a jug of water he'd just poured out on her face.

If he were anyone else, she would have smacked the jug out of his hand and then slapped his face. But her captive was a big guy with broad shoulders clad in fur. His dark hair flowed past his shoulders, braided at the temples, and pulled away from his face. He looked deadly, in a beautifully, soulless kind of way. His face was scarred on both sides. Nothing hideous, but he'd definitely been sliced up. He had faint lines around his icy blue—no wait, were they pale green eyes? They changed when the firelight hit them a certain way and were the color of lagoons on a brochure of Fiji, but unlike the brochure—or the island, there was nothing inviting in them. He had a well-groomed mustache beneath his nose, with a bare space just above the dip of his bow-shaped upper lip. She forgot to breathe looking at him. Of course, this nut would have to be the best-looking guy she'd ever seen.

"I was praying you and this horrible place weren't real," she told him, clearing her eyes.

He knit his dark brows. "To which god do you pray?"

She knew what these Vikings believed. She'd watched the show. She held up her finger. "There's only One."

He didn't argue. "But I am real. You are mad."

"And you're a real piece of—"

He stared at her, horrified. "What is the black liquid coming from your eyes? Are you possessed?"

"What?" She rubbed her fingers under her eyes. "Oh, it's mascara. It's not waterproof, sorry."

His expression darkened and it was a frightening thing to see. "Wipe it off before someone sees you and thinks you are melting."

She snatched the hand towel he offered her.

He snatched it back and seemed to grow right in front of her.

She hesitated, but only for a moment. No one ever treated her this way, and this bastard wasn't about to start. She yanked it from his fingers and leaped from the table, wiping her face. He didn't chase her or try to take it back.

"Are all the women in the next centuries as bold and willful as you?"

"You believe me?"

"No, of course not." His lips tilted into a smirk. "Do I look like a fool to you?"

She tried not to stare at his lips. They were carved in the shape of a cupid's bow on top, with a full, succulent lower lip. Both were perfectly accentuated by his facial hair.

"Please don't make me answer that." She smirked back.

"Why do you pretend not to fear me?" he asked, silkily.

"What would you like me to do? Beg you for mercy?"

He shook his head. "No. I prefer your trickery."

"Really? I would have thought a guy like you would lavish in someone else's fear."

"Because I am a Dane?"

"Because you're a misogynist, and probably a rapist."

"No, I am not a rapist. I do not know what the other thing is, so I cannot agree or disagree."

"Look, if you let me go, I promise not to say a word."

"Where will you go?"

She shrugged. "Back home. I won't go to the police, I promise."

"All right," he said, leaving his chair. "Go. You are free."

Was he serious? Just like that? He was letting her go? She hurried for the door, pulled it open, and ran outside. There were a handful of old men roaming about. Some women were balled up in their doorways, wailing. Everything looked so real.

She heard raucous sounds coming from down the road. The town hall. She ran the other way—straight into someone's arms.

Oh, no! The really mean one. Fin!

"Well, well. Are you escaping?" he purred above her ear.

"No! He let me go!" she argued.

He took her by the hair and dragged her back. "If you are trying to deceive me—"

What if the leader lied and said he didn't set her free? She fought back, trying to dig her heels in, but it was no use. Okay, this just left the possibility of it being a prank, or a movie set. He was hurting her, pulling hair from her head.

"Get your hands off me!" She'd never been treated this way before. She was having a hard time believing it.

He gave her hair another hard yank. Her anger and reflexes took over and she kicked him in the calf. He raised his hand high over his head and was about to bring it down on her. She closed her eyes, too afraid to move. She'd never been hit by a man! She wanted to scream but something stopped Fin's hand. Camelee had to open her eyes to see what it was.

"Fin, let her go."

It was the simplest of warnings, but there were a thousand threats behind it.

Fin lowered his hand and released her with a slight shove.

Camelee was shaken to her marrow. Whatever century they were in, she'd been about to get hit by that piece of trash.

She was saved by another one.

She was spitting mad! She was Camelee Pendrey! She—

"You should come back with me," he urged in a hypnotically low voice.

Right. He knew what was behind the door when he'd told her she was free. She felt sick. She looked around at the multiple tents and thatched-roof huts, the snowy paths toward a horizon with *nothing* in the distance. She bent over and clutched her belly. No help was coming.

If she was in ten seventeen, no help was coming.

If she was in ten seventeen, she'd gone mad, and no help was coming.

She felt him near as she hunched over and threw up her breakfast of coffee. She still had the hand towel he'd given her. She wished it had been a knife so she could end it all right now. She almost sobbed when he laid his hand on her back to comfort her.

He removed it when someone passed by. She straightened and wiped her face then handed him back his towel.

He motioned for her to follow him. She was his prisoner without using any restraints. She'd like another chance at that knife, so she could bury it into him. But she breathed and patted her hair. She wasn't a complete fool. This one seemed to like her. He wasn't as barbaric as the others. She needed to stay close to him while she was here. Yes, she still had hope of being rescued from this place, whether by a doctor or by the police once she was reported missing.

She followed him back to the hut and almost ran inside after him when three of his men came traipsing out of the larger town hall. They were laughing and pulling three weeping women behind them.

Camelee stopped at the door and then stepped back out. Were those men going to rape those women? No! She headed toward them.

"Camelee."

She heard the leader call her name and was tempted to forget what was going on and return to him. How was he already familiar? Was it a part of a victim's psyche? You latch on to the one who shows you kindness?

Well, she'd be aware of it. Right now, though, she wasn't about to let three women be raped. "Hey! You there!"

The men stopped laughing and squinted to have a look at her. "Let them go!"

They began to laugh again. One of them released a woman and moved toward Camelee with naked male intent in his eyes. He said something in a language she didn't understand. The other men laughed.

Her captor paused at her side and then approached them. He said something to the men and they bowed their heads.

"Are they going to violate those women?" she asked her rescuer.

He set his gaze on her and studied her thoughtfully for a moment. "Most likely."

"You're their leader. Tell them to let the women go. Please."

He smiled and stared at her. When he realized she was serious, his smile faded. "Those women are the bounty of war. They—"

"They have nothing to do with your war," she told him. "They simply don't all have you to protect them." It was a line from *Stand by Her*, a movie she'd starred in last winter.

He stared off in the direction the men had taken. She could almost see him trying to decide what to do. She realized that the more he did for her, the more obligated she would feel to him. But right now, the women here needed help.

"They are human beings, made in God's image," she told him. "They're afraid, just as your sister, or mother, or wife, or someday your daughter, would be."

His expression darkened. She'd hit a nerve. He pushed her aside to head off toward his men. She heard him shout something and then watched the women running back to a hut. She wanted to thank him but when he returned, walking briskly toward her, he passed her without a word and headed for the town hall.

This time, she followed him, though she didn't want to be in a room with his men. She thought it best to stick close by him. She might be a pampered actress, but she was a tough New Yorker, too. But again, she wasn't a fool to pick a fight with any of these men.

Most were big and blond or ginger. They wore furs and hungry smiles as the women served them. Her captor was dark-haired and a bit smaller, smaller than 6'3" that is, more athletic. He didn't smile often.

He leaped onto a table and called for what she guessed was attention when they all turned to him. He spoke in his language, which Camelee suspected was Old Norse. She didn't understand it. Many of them set their gazes on her as they let go of the women they were groping.

Her gaze softened on her captor. He went against what they wanted, to do what was right. He also caused her to have many enemies. But then she heard him say something that sounded like mother. They all looked remorseful, their gazes even warming on her.

But the gentleness didn't last long. He pulled her forward by her shoulder, said something that included her name, and then pushed her behind him.

"You are serving," he told her over her shoulder. "Go find out what is needed of you."

"Serving? Oh, but I don't serve."

"Now you do," he answered woodenly and turned to look forward once again.

"That's it? You're abandoning me?"

He smiled and she knew she had to put away her thoughts of how good-looking he was.

"I will be sitting just there, with those men. I would hardly call that abandoning you."

"Fine," she brooded. She didn't want to serve. She was used to being served. "Do whatever you want."

He did, disappearing to another table where a group of savage-looking men sat drinking in their animal skins. He didn't spare her another look. She cursed him silently and went to seek out a woman who could help her.

Serving wasn't horrible—no, who was she kidding? It was repulsive. Not only did she have to serve the men, she had to serve Fin. She kept her gaze locked on to her captor's while she served.

His furtive gaze found her more than once, but no one else saw him looking. He neither smiled nor frowned when a few fights broke out, possibly about her. Maybe they were fighting over who would get her after their leader died. She didn't understand what they were saying. She thought it was just as well. She didn't want to know what they were talking about.

She hated it here. With them.

Her eyes settled on her captor. With him.

Chapter Three

CAMELEE WASHED THE last plate and fell into a chair in the candlelit kitchen of the town hall. The skin on her fingers was white and water-logged. She'd been at the dishes for the last hour.

He waited for her there in the kitchen, with his hand on the hilt of his sword and his diamond-hard gaze on her. He wasn't altogether unpleasant to look at.

Where the hell was she?

If she thought serving was repulsive, washing dishes was doubly so. She never wanted to eat again.

"Tomorrow, we leave for Wessex for the Christmas festivities," he informed her. "After that, I will have an audience with King Cnut."

She looked at him coming closer. "And then what?" she asked nervously.

He sat in a chair next to hers. "And then we shall see. I would like to go home to Denmark."

"What of me?" Why did she ask him? She hated that she needed his protection. But for now, she did. She would play along with whatever this was.

"You will come with me, of course."

To Denmark? She almost laughed out loud but she felt too sick to her stomach. How long would she have to stay with him?

"Have you sailed upon a longship before?" he asked her.

She blinked. "What?" She knew what he was talking about. No, she'd never been on a longship before. If there was a longship, did it mean they really were in England, pre-William the Conqueror? No. Impossible.

"I assume you have not. You will be ill for the entire trip, no doubt."

Wonderful. More fun to look forward to.

"What are you doing here? Waiting for me?" She didn't want to ask, but it was late, and she was tired.

"I do not let what is mine get ravaged by the dogs."

She wondered if pulling out a club from behind his back and hitting her over the head with it was next. "How sweet," she seethed. "And is it just me you think you own? I would have thought you had a flock of women."

He crooked one edge of his mouth into a smirk. "One is difficult enough, but when I return home, you will be the first of my servants." He said it happily, as if it were the most natural thing in the world and she should be happy, too.

She was tempted to poison his food.

"Come," he said standing up from his seat. "It is late."

"Um…" She stayed sitting. "I'm not going to bed with you, so forget it. I'd rather you just kill me now and get it over with."

His smile turned into amusement. He wore it so well it made her blood bubble. "I was going to offer to walk you to the hut. I've procured a bed for you. You. I will not be with you. But knowing you would rather be put to death than give yourself to me is well noted."

Good. Good, she was happy it was well noted. She wanted to tell him that it was because of the way he bossed and tossed her around. He was playing this whole chest-beating, authoritative jerk to the trillionth degree. She thought of Fin…and probably all the rest of them. Maybe this one wasn't the worst of them.

"What's your name anyway? I'm Camelee," she added when he gave her a confused look. "You are?"

"Ulf Kristiansen. I am called Wolf."

"Of course you are," she said, looking him over in the soft candlelight. He was, in fact, positively wolf-like in his furs and hungry, piercing eyes.

"I didn't mean I would literally rather be dead than—"

"Do not trouble yourself with what I think," he overrode her. "You will address me as lord in the presence of others."

"I will?" she scoffed.

"You will, either freely…or not."

How could he threaten her and his voice sound so velvety and sultry that it made her mouth go dry? She was afraid of him. But for some crazy reason, she trusted him not to hurt her.

"Okay," she said softly and stood to her feet, close to him. "What do I call you in private?"

He stared down into her eyes, and she was sure she could read some of his thoughts. Thoughts of them together…

"Wolf."

He seemed to be the powerful one among his men. Maybe she was looking at this all wrong. If she was going to be here any longer, she was going to need someone powerful behind her. If she made him her lover, would that give her power, too? What about contraception? She suddenly felt lightheaded. This was real.

He caught her in his arms, seeming almost familiar with her form. But then, hadn't he been the one to set her on the table when she'd fainted?

"What is it?" he asked behind her, against her ear.

"I…I must be more tired than I thought."

"Hmm, not used to working is my guess." He leaned down and, in one fluid motion, scooped her up in his arms to cradle her against his chest. "I could tell from a league away that you had no idea what you were doing."

So, he'd been watching her.

"I told you I didn't. Now, please, put me down."

He shook his head. His braids fell against her hands as they locked at his nape.

"Put me down. What will your men think if they see you

carrying a slave?"

"That I am a considerate master, and—"

"Master?" she asked with distaste.

"That is correct."

"No. It's *not* correct. Slaves are no longer a thing to want or need, okay? We've become a tad bit more civilized."

"All right," he said softly. "I stand corrected."

The sound of his steady heartbeat in her ear resonated through her body. She felt weightless in his arms. And safe. His chest and belly were rock-hard, proving that he spent time in a gym. His shoulders were wide above her.

"Thank you." She closed her eyes in his arms and promptly fell asleep.

SHE AWOKE THE next morning in a straw bed that didn't smell fresh. She leaped out of it and made a soft squeak when she saw Wolf in the bed with her.

The lying bastard. Did he want to see angry? He would see angry now. She looked down at herself. Thank God, she was fully dressed. Had they done anything? She clutched her belly. Did they have plan B here? No. This was real. She didn't have a purse anymore. Or a phone, or any identification.

Had they made love? Wouldn't she remember doing it with him? She stared at him asleep in the bed, covered from low on his waist, down. His chest was bare and carved with hills and valleys, harder than granite. His belly was tight like a trampoline, ready to be jumped upon.

She tried to lift the thin woolen blanket to see if he was naked underneath.

"What are you doing?"

His voice startled her enough to make her jump away.

But why should she feel ashamed? "You lied to me! You told

me you procured a bed for me!"

"I did not deceive you, Camelee," he let her know from the bed, barely opening his eyes. He kicked off the blanket and before she could close her eyes, she saw that he wore short white breeches of sorts. But he was covered.

"When I arrived at the hut with you, the woman of the house advised me that thanks to my men, several of her neighbors were now widows and were staying with her. She could not give a bed to a stranger over a friend. I thought of commanding her to give up a bed, but I am not a cold-hearted beast. Not all the time, anyway. In the end, I had nowhere else to put you but in my own bed in this cottage."

She listened, afraid to ask him if they had done anything. "Where can I use the restroom?"

"The what?"

She drew out a long sigh. "Where can I go to relieve myself?"

"Oh. Just out back."

"Out back. Of course. You do know it's winter, right?"

"I did not build this place, Camelee," he called out. "Someone else did."

She hated when he was logical. He was supposed to be the kidnapping, marauding maniac.

A cold dread washed over her that had nothing to do with the weather as she slipped on her jacket. The longer she remained here, the more real it became. She hadn't heard a plane or helicopter all day yesterday.

But how could she have traveled through time? She thought about that while she found the outhouse, which was a hole in the ground.

She wondered if anyone back home missed her. Did her parents? Did they even know she was gone? She spoke to them once a year on the phone. It didn't matter if she never called them. She was their perfect daughter who could do no wrong. As long as she was successful, they were happy. They weren't her biological parents. Those two dropped her off at an orphanage downtown and never looked back. She grew up the daughter of Henri and Claire Pendrey and studied to be an actor since she was five. She'd done some commercials and a soap until she was ten. She'd scored a bunch of minor things, but finally after a "masterful audition", she was hired to play the lead role in an original series on cable. That was eight seasons ago. Life changed after that. Money was good. She had a penthouse in Chelsea. She was waited on hand and foot on set. She rarely had to do anything or pay for anything. People adored her. Men fawned all over her. Everyone wanted to be her friend.

But she felt more alone than ever. She cried herself to sleep every night. No matter how much her fans loved her. Her mother and father by blood, and by choice, did not love her. They'd abandoned her. She hated them for it. Every time she saw a baby being loved and adored by its parents, she couldn't understand what had been so bad about her that both sets of hers couldn't love her enough to make it work. It was the only role she had trouble playing. A mother.

She thought that if she was loved by the masses, it would fill the emptiness—but it didn't. Forget a serious relationship. Men wanted to have sex with her and then move on, as if she were good to have on a resume of women they'd screwed. Or they wanted to worship her and then became bored.

What about Wolf? Did he have sex with her while she slept? No way. No one slept that deeply. She felt relieved, finished, then frowned when she realized there was nothing to wipe with.

Oh, how she hated it here.

Chapter Four

WOLF WATCHED HER from the small window while she hurried to the well, filled a cup of water, then ran back to the outhouse.

He liked looking at her in her hose and short, heavy woolen shirt. Her hose hugged her arse quite nicely, better than any skirts. Where had she gotten such attire? Where had she learned such boldness? Of course, it wasn't possible for anyone to travel through time. Who would believe such a mad tale?

She was a mystery. He'd asked many of the women in the town and all denied knowing her. Who was she? Where had she come from? He wondered if she was completely mad or if there was a part of her still sane. She intrigued him with her strange words and even stranger clothes. He wanted to know more about her. He shouldn't have stayed with her all day and all night though. Sleeping with her was nicer than he'd expected. He didn't put his hands on her, but he could smell her. She smelled like flowers. Not one, but many. It was faint. He had to move closer to get a better whiff. He could hear her breathing. He liked listening to it, learning her rhythm. It made him feel closer to her in a different way, like…he should be with her.

No. She was his captive. His servant. Chiefs, especially soldiers under Cnut, did not lose their hearts to their slaves. He could take her to his bed as often as he wished, without her consent, but because he could, didn't mean he would. He might be a barbarian on the field, but he wasn't one in the bedroom—except if his woman wanted him to be.

His woman…

"It's disgusting," she grumbled, coming back in. "I need a bath."

He grinned at her, raising an eyebrow. "There is a stream—"

"Ha! You're kidding right?" The sound she made was something between laughter and a growl.

"Then, no bath."

"Dear Lord, help me," she prayed as she fell onto a chair at the table.

She opened her eyes and stared at him with a pleading urgency. "I'm not cut out for this kind of life. I want to go home. And it's got to be pretty bad here if I want to go home."

She'd shown strength and fortitude since she'd been captured. She was saucy and spirited, and through all this, she had not wept.

He kept his eyes on her. He wanted to know more about her. "What is so terrible about your home? Do you have a husband who beats you?"

She shook her head and shrugged her delicate shoulders. "There was no husband, and it wasn't completely terrible. There was coffee."

"What is coffee?" he indulged.

"It's a drink made from ground up coffee beans. It smells like nothing you've smelled before. Slowly pouring boiling water over it makes it a strong hot or cold drink. I like mine with cream and sugar."

He watched her eyes close with delight while she thought of her drink. He suddenly wanted to be the one who brought such delight to her face. He felt ill, a little lightheaded. "Camelee," he interrupted, unable or unwilling to stop speaking. "I will try to have a hot bath prepared for you when we reach Wessex."

She opened her eyes. "You will?"

He nodded. "Anything you wish if you will just try to make

me something to eat. We can have bread and butter, but I was thinking—"

"Eggs and bacon." She looked around. "And we'll see what's in the cabinets, eh, cupboards," she corrected, looking around again.

Did she smile at him? Why did it make his belly tighten and his heart feel weightless? He'd seen men who had fallen in love, Odger Ragnarsen, one of his men, and Rune Aethlesen a chief from East Anglia. They became mindless, thoughtless, senseless, everything helpless there was. He would not become that over any woman.

Or so he'd always thought.

But Camelee was different. He wasn't sure he even liked her. He knew beautiful women. None of them had ever affected him the way she did. He tried to stop it. He had to. He was a warrior. He would likely die young. Though he wished for more in his life, he didn't want to leave his woman and his children behind, unprotected.

"Fine." He gave her a stiff smile and rose from his seat. "I heard a rooster. I will go check for chickens and eggs."

"Okay," she mumbled while she rummaged through jars of jam and spices.

He left the cottage with a slight smirk on his face and then followed his ears to the henhouse. He liked this feeling of waking up with someone…her and preparing to eat with her. He was thinking how foolish and pitiful he must appear. He had to exercise more control. He—

He looked up. What was that? He didn't wait to find out but ran back toward the cottage. He paused to take his knives out of his boots and flip them in his hands before he listened at the door. He heard men's voices. Camelee's muffled cries.

"Are you here alone?" one of them demanded to know.

Saxons! Wolf was going to kill them! He opened the door as slowly and as quietly as he could. He could see one of them holding her, one dirty hand over her mouth and the other caressing her bosom!

Wolf felt his blood boil. In less than a breath, he noted three other men standing around the kitchen, and positioned his knives. He aimed and let one fly. It flew into her assailant's temple. He let her go and sank to the floor. Camelee turned to look at her latest captor, dead and bleeding around her.

She cried out.

He felt his eyes go wide. They hurt her. He was going to destroy them! But no, he couldn't lose control now.

"Camelee! Get behind me," he commanded as he sent the second knife into another man's neck.

He released the two axes from his belt before the second man's body hit the floor.

With Camelee at his back, he hacked at the last two men, swerving and pulling her down to duck. He groaned and swiped at them with all his might. Their meager blows could not keep his axes away until he left them both dead.

He moved with the strength and purpose of a feline predator despite her clumsy steps and her fingernails digging into his back and shoulders. They moved through the cottage, with Wolf ready to kill at a moment's notice. They checked outside for more men but found none.

When he deemed it safe, he put away his axes and turned, but she didn't let go of him, so that he was in her arms.

"It is over. It is over," he assured softly. "You are safe."

She let him hold her for a while. He could feel her heart beating hard and fast, like his.

"This is horrible," she said, finally breaking away. "I cannot live like this. I'm trying to act brave, but this place is breaking me down. It's breaking me down."

"Will you just give up then?"

"No."

He liked how quickly she answered. It was instinctual. She would not give up. But what did she mean *acting* brave? "You will make it through whatever it is you are suffering. I will protect you. You see that I can."

What was he doing? This was marriage talk! He was not offering himself to her. He wanted to laugh. He would admit, he was drawn to her, but it was nothing serious.

He took a step back. The danger was over. "We need to go. We will eat some of the food the men have collected from here."

"Wolf," she said softly. It was the first time she'd said his name. "Please let me go. Take me back to the city, and I'll take it from there."

"Travel with me, and if you find a place you wish to stay, I will see to it."

"Okay," she agreed and turned away.

His smile faded. He didn't want her to choose to go. Would he let her? She was his, after all.

They went to his horse and rode it together back to the town to gather the rest of the men.

"You took a chance sleeping alone so far from help," she told him, riding uncomfortably in his lap.

"Did I?" he said over her head.

"What if there were ten men?"

"I would have fought differently, but I would have saved you," he promised her.

She dipped her head and laughed softly. "Okay, I believe you."

He didn't seek out another horse so she could ride separately. It was Fin's suggestion that she ride a horse of her own to keep Wolf's horse alive.

"I've never ridden a horse before," she told Wolf. "But I'll give it my best shot."

He looked at her with curiosity, not war, in his eyes.

"I'll try to ride," she explained.

It took nearly an hour to get all the men outside and at their proper stations. No one had eaten, so they all partook of some bread and sweet butter. There was also dried meat and semi-fresh berries.

Fin kept his massive warhorse on the other side of Camelee. Wolf didn't like it. He needed to watch Fin around her. Fin possessed something cold and savage. Wolf didn't want it set loose on Camelee. He might have to make it clearer to Fin that Camelee was his.

He thought nothing of the way he saw her, as his. He felt protective of her, amused by her, curious about her. He thought about her *coffee* and the other things she'd told him about her home. It was all quite magnificent.

"May I come with you, Chief?"

Wolf flicked his gaze to Akkar's. The chief clenched his teeth. "I would not keep you from helping your father."

"He does not care if I go. It would be an honor on my family name to fight at your side."

"Well, I do not know about fighting yet," Wolf told him.

"Then I may come?" Akkar's dark eyes opened wider, his smile did, as well.

"You may come," he allowed and ignored the young man's happy grin. He wasn't a friend. He was their commander. If they didn't obey him, they could die or cause the rest of them to die. Akkar's duty was to do whatever menial task Wolf needed of him.

They set out, bringing with them some of the widows and their children. A few men to work fields.

Camelee rode close to Wolf, clenching her jaw with every bounce of her horse. "What's going to happen to them?"

"They will be coming to Denmark in the spring," he answered, keeping his gaze steady on the road.

She waited and watched him to see if he would look at her. He wouldn't.

"How many of them?" she asked.

"As many as the longboats can carry."

She gave him a horrified look. "How do you know how many that is? You have many different weights here."

"If the boat does not sink, we can set sail."

"Wolf!" she snapped her mouth shut and then corrected herself, as they weren't alone. "I mean, Chief! What if you take on water and begin to sink?"

"Then," answered Fin, "we begin to throw some of them overboard." He smiled, amused by her horrified shock when she turned to Wolf.

"Is that true?"

He didn't answer. He didn't have to.

"What is the matter, Chief?" Fin sped up his horse a bit so he could see Wolf and smirk at him. "Why do you use caution with her?"

"Fin," Wolf told him slowly. "For the sake of our blood, I will not bound over these horses and remind you who asks the questions here."

"Understood, Chief." Fin lowered his gaze and slowed his pace, then finally broke off and rode with the others.

"I do not want to hear your womanly sensibilities about how I was too hard on him," he told her. "Fin is fortunate I did not kill him. I must command the respect of every man, or woman here. If just one of them thinks I am weak, it could become disastrous."

"I understand."

"You do?"

"Yes. You're the leader. That means they must follow you. I get it. Plus, that one needs to be brought down a peg or two."

He nodded, then stopped, unsure what he was nodding at.

"He must be told that you are mine, Camelee." He expected her to be angry. She was bolder than any female he knew. But he didn't expect her to laugh.

"Okay, okay. Chastise me. I didn't take you seriously in public. I'm sorry, but only delusional men talk like that where I come from."

"Well, we are where I come from now," he told her angrily. "If you prefer to be alone for the remainder of your journey. I can arrange it."

He had been hard on people before. It didn't usually trouble him. But it did now. Still, he said nothing. He led a thousand men at times. He wasn't about to let some woman turn him soft.

"Well?" he put to her. "What will you have?"

"I'll stick with you," she said after a few moments in which he thought she would foolishly tell him she wanted to be alone.

There. He felt pleased with himself for a moment. And then pleased with her for using good judgment, though she was clearly angry. It was the sign of strength, the sign of a leader.

"Tell me again what you did in this other life of yours?" he asked her, keeping close while they rode.

"I am an actor."

"But what do you do?"

"I…" she paused and looked off to the side a little as if something had just occurred to her. "I pretend. I get a script, I memorize my part. I, along with the rest of the cast, rehearse it and then we perform it as perfectly as we can, and it's recorded and edited for the movies. There's a lot more I'm leaving out because you're looking kind of lost, but that's the gist of it. I don't usually have to lift a finger for myself."

He blinked and kept riding, regretting that he had asked.

"What about you?" she asked. "What do you do when you're not raiding? And what are you fighting to claim now, Viking?

"We fight to hold our claim over England and King Cnut's throne. As for when I am home, I farm my land. We grow wheat and oats and barley. I built my own longhouse and am trying to add to it. I tend to my animals and livestock. It is a hard but satisfying life."

She nodded. "So, England is in the hands of the Danes?"

"That is correct. The Danes are unbeatable."

"That is because you're all so barbaric," she told him with distaste tainting her voice.

"Civilized people aren't prepared for the likes of you."

"It is war, Camelee," he defended, not understanding why he did. "We do what must be done to win and to stay alive."

"You've made many widows," she pointed out.

"I am called to fight by my king," he told her, keeping his horse at a slow pace. "Should I disobey him? Should I not practice my skill and become a master at it so that I am not killed on the field?"

She nodded. "Yes, of course. My brother was in the military. He died four years ago."

Wolf lowered his head. Her brother was a warrior. He gave the man the respect he was due with a moment of quiet.

When he looked up, he found her smiling at him. He doubted the good of his senses when every part of him grew warm, and he smiled back.

CHAPTER FIVE

CAMELEE BIT HER bottom lip every time her horse set its hooves on the ground. It had been six hours since they'd left the town. She thought her thighs must be bleeding. The pain was almost unbearable. Except for when Wolf asked her if she was all right and she said yes because Fin was listening. She didn't want to come off as helpless—but at this point, she feared falling out of the saddle.

"Chief—" Ugh! How she despised calling him that! She understood they were supposed to be in the eleventh century and women were subservient. She hated having to pretend. But like any other acting job… "I need—"

"Chief," Akkar called from his horse, pulling up close so they could see him in the dim light. "There are women with little ones. They need to rest. Can we stop for the night?"

Camelee shut her mouth and prayed Wolf would agree to stop for the night.

He was looking at her, waiting for her to finish what she was going to say. His expression told her that he might understand what she was going to say but didn't. His eyes warmed for a moment. "Very well, Akkar. We will stop here for the night. Tell Bjorn to prepare a fire."

"Thank you, Chief," the young soldier said and hurried off.

Wolf nodded and then glanced at her. "You will stay with me."

"No, I won't. I'm going to sleep with the other women." She didn't wait for his approval but started after Akkar.

"Camelee," he called.

She sighed and looked up, then at him.

"Good dreams."

If she didn't feel like she was going insane, she would have smiled at him. "Good dreams to you, too, Chief."

She rode her mount after Akkar and followed the other women when he gathered them together. He spoke even less Saxon than Wolf, but she managed to settle down amid other women.

She soon regretted her decision to stay with them as most of them cried themselves to sleep. She wanted to join in right along with them. Of course, she hadn't lost her husband. But she did lose everything else, including her mind. She felt the burning behind her eyes and bit her inner cheek to keep from crying.

"Mumma."

She heard the low, pitiful cry a few pallets away and opened her eyes. A child. She closed her eyes again. She couldn't comfort a child. What did she know about such things?

"Mumma!" The crying grew louder.

Camelee put her hands over her ears and tried to block out the sound. Where was the child's mother? The weeping grew louder. Had one of the men taken the mother? She sat up.

"There, there, now, Treasure," soothed a woman's voice beyond the firelight. The comforting sound of her seeped through Camelee's bones and warmed her blood. For a moment, and then it turned her cold.

Finally, the mother had returned. She seemed to be just fine. Had she been off giggling with one of them, at the cost of her child? Camelee threw herself back down.

The child began crying again. "Mumma!"

"Miss?" someone asked, approaching her.

It was the woman. The mother.

"Yes?" Camelee asked.

"You…ehm…know the chief? The little girl's mother was taken away by one of the men and the child needs her."

"What?" Camelee sat up again. She wasn't the child's mother? "Someone took her?"

"Correct," said the woman. "You know the chief. Please, help her."

Camelee left her pallet. "Bring her."

They followed her by the light of campfire until they came to Wolf's side of the camp. He had his own fire close to his pallet. He was awake and staring into the flames when they stepped into the light.

He stood up when he saw them. "What is it?"

He appeared concerned and she was grateful once again to be in his care.

"Sir, the mother of this child has been taken by one of your men," Camelee informed him, then waited for him to rise up and find the—

"How do you know she did not go of her own accord? I heard no screaming."

No, she wouldn't claw his beautiful eyes out in front of a little kid. "This woman says the child's mother would never have left her."

"Is that so?" he asked with a scowl as he turned to the woman. "And who are you?"

"Genevra, my lord."

Camelee turned to her and saw her for the first time in the firelight. Her hair was blonde, a shade lighter than Camelee's and piled atop her head with a few strands hanging down the sides of her beautiful face. Her eyes were silvery-blue and her skin, golden tan and beginning to show signs of her age. Early forties. Something about her looked too well-bred to be wearing tattered skirts.

"Where is your husband?"

"I have never taken a husband, my lord."

He quirked his mouth at her and turned to the little girl holding Genevra's hand. "And what are you called, Child?"

"Hild."

"Hild, did you see the man with your mother?" When she nodded, he asked her to describe him. But the little girl was young, about four and didn't know what he was asking.

"Hild," Camelee bent to her. "Did he have hair like mine or like the chief's?"

"Like you," Hild told her, wiping her eyes.

That describes almost all the men here, Camelee thought miserably. She narrowed it down until they both realized she was describing Fin. Wolf bolted across the campfire. He reached an empty pallet and then stormed for his horse.

But as he was beginning to mount, Fin sauntered back into the camp.

Wolf went directly to him. "Where is the woman you took to your bed tonight?"

"I took no woman to my bed," Fin told him, sounding insulted. "She refused and I obeyed your order not to force myself on her."

"Well, then where is she?" Camelee demanded, stepping forward.

For an instant, Fin looked so angry that Camelee thought he would strike her. She was about to take a step back, but Wolf moved in front of her, blocking Fin's view of her. "Let us go find the child's mother," he told his brother and waited for him to go get his horse.

"I will return as soon as I find her," he told Camelee and Hild.

He shook his head, scowling at Camelee and muttered under his breath something about why was he doing things to please her. It made her heart sing when she thought about him doing things to make her happy. It made her want to smile at him, and even blush.

He was a big brute, who looked at killing as if it were a sport. His ideas were ancient and misogynistic. How could she entertain any kind of pleasant thoughts about him?

As soon as he was gone, and the reality that seemed to be happening to her returned, her thoughts switched to Fin. Fin didn't seem like the kind of guy who respected a woman's "no". He was lying. If he'd been with Hild's mother, he'd had sex with her, whether she wanted to or not. Maybe he'd hurt her after that, to keep from Wolf finding out what he'd done.

She glanced at the little girl, who'd been watching her.

Genevra set her jewel-like gaze on hers and swiped away a stray lock of golden hair from her eyes. "You are not from Bristolton. I do not remember ever seeing you."

Camelee smiled at her, as if she could not help herself, also glad for the change of topic. She had a dreadful feeling in her guts about Hild's mother. "I arrived this morning."

"Just in time to be captured by the Northmen?" Genevra asked, her eyes going wide. "You poor dear. Let me tend to you."

At first, Camelee didn't want a stranger trying to "tend" to her, but Genevra was a kind woman with a compassionate ear. And there was something about her, something Camelee couldn't put her finger on. But it made her feel comfortable, comforted, and they'd barely said a word to each other.

"Goodness, what did you say you are called?" Genevra asked, bringing her fingers to her forehead. "Did you already tell me and I…oh, if you did tell it to me, it is only because there is so much going on with the poor babe that I—"

"No, no, I haven't given it yet. I'm so sorry. It's Camelee."

"Camelee! What a lovely name!"

Camelee offered her a warm smile. Genevra was a kind person. It was nice to find one, even if Camelee had to go back a thousand years to do it.

"Mumma!" Hild took up crying again. She yawned and closed her eyes as if she just couldn't hold them open another second, but she needed her mother before she could relax and rest. Camelee wanted to comfort her. She understood that feeling. She also remembered giving up hope of her mother—her true mother—ever finding her. And then giving up trying to find her mother. She learned how to go to sleep on her own.

"There now, little one," Genevra cooed, sitting by the fire, and pulling Hild into her lap. "Remember what the chief said, he will try to find her and return her to you, aye?"

Hild nodded and rested her head on Genevra's bosom, and then finally closed her eyes.

Camelee sat near them, looking at the little girl. All the emotions she'd been holding back for the dozen or so hours came like liquid fire to the back of her throat and the brims of her eyes.

Genevra said nothing but reached out in the fiery light to hold Camelee's hand.

"I'm sorry. I don't usually cry, but I'm just thinking of her future," she confessed, heedlessly wiping her eyes.

"We do not know what the years hold for her," the older woman offered.

"But we do, Genevra. And it isn't good. Unless you consider a hard life of work, I mean toil, fun."

"We are not promised a *fun* life, Daughter."

"Don't call me that," Camelee scolded, her expression going cold. "I'm not your daughter."

Genevra smiled gracefully. "But you could be."

Camelee stood up. "But I'm not." She marched off without another word, not understanding why she was so upset, just knowing she was.

Mothers couldn't be trusted.

SHE OPENED HER eyes to the low, morning sun, and the two Viking warrior-looking men returning on their horses. She sat up on her pallet. They were alone. Hild's mother was not with them. Her heart sank.

And then hardened on Fin. On all of them for raiding and killing these women's husbands, for making Hild an orphan in this crappy world of theirs, if, God forbid, she was truly in it.

The chief's cerulean gaze found hers. Before she let him bewitch her again, she turned and went the other way. Why did this have to happen? He would never believe her over his second in command. Why should he? She had proof of absolutely nothing, except Fin's confession of being the last person to see her alive. Not only that, but Wolf hardly knew her. Even if she had proof, he probably wouldn't believe her.

Fin wouldn't be punished, and she couldn't stand the thought of it. She wouldn't forgive Wolf for letting it go.

She disappeared into the bushes to relieve herself, on this, her second day here. She wiped miserably with snow and then cleaned her hands with more snow, and a few tears.

Instead of returning to the camp, Camelee realized that no one had been following her. The chief and Fin had gone to Hild. She was alone. She didn't have much time. She didn't think about possibilities or consequences, just about escaping.

She ran. Soon, her Uggs were soaked through with freezing boggy water. Tall reeds grew all around her. This didn't look like anywhere in Manhattan that she knew of. New Jersey maybe? Pennsylvania?

This time yesterday, she was in Manhattan. What happened? She woke up in her bed. Karen brought her coffee and a blueberry scone, pulled open her bedroom curtains, and turned to smile and tell her about her day. Yesterday, they were filming the last episode of the first half of the season. She missed it. Would they sue her? Not if she'd been abducted. But she was beginning to believe that she hadn't been abducted. In that case, they really couldn't sue her. She almost laughed. She was going out of her mind. How did they treat mental disabilities in the eleventh century? She was guessing not too good.

She thought she heard him calling her name. She stopped and looked around. There was nothing, not a tree, not a house, a stone, a marking of any kind. There were only reeds as far as her eye could see. She panicked. How would she ever find her way out? She turned around. Was that the way she'd come?

She heard him again, resonating, agonized, urgent. "Camel-ee!"

The hairs on her arms and the back of her neck stood on end. "Woman, answer me!"

"This way! I'm lost!" she cried out to ensure his leniency when she explained what she was doing here.

"Thank you, God," she heard him say when she burst through the towering reeds. She ran through the water, pulling up the reeds that tangled around her ankles, and almost leaped into his saddle.

He pulled her up by the arms and let her sink onto his lap. He wrapped his arms around her. "Where were you off to?"

"I had to go, and I was so sad that Hild's mother wasn't with you that I wasn't thinking about which way I was going. Next thing I know, I was lost. Oh, Wo—Chief," she quickly corrected when she saw Akkar.

She wouldn't tell him she was terrified to gain his pity. If he had a brain in his head, he would know that she wouldn't tell him if she was afraid. "How big is this bog?"

"You would come to its end in one day. Or go around it in two days," Akkar answered her.

Wolf grinned at her at Akkar's expense.

"I was not intending to take us through the bogs," the chief let her know as they made their way back to camp.

"Good news to my ears."

"I also have bad news," he said regrettably.

"Hild's mother," she guessed.

"Frida," he told her. "Some of the women know who she is…was."

"What happened? And don't tell me Fin had nothing to do with it," she added softly and tilting her head so that only he could hear.

"She was mauled by a bear. She is…" he paused trying not to be too candid. "Hardly recognizable"

She blinked up at him. "Where was she and what was she doing there?"

"Perhaps she was lost," he answered. "Same as you."

She grimaced at how that excuse had turned so quickly against her. "So, you're not going to question him any further?"

"Camelee, she was mauled by a bear. I saw the body."

She wanted to tell him that maybe Fin had raped her and then left her for dead. But he wouldn't see it.

"What did you tell Hild?"

He shrugged his shoulders and Camelee was once again reminded of how mighty he looked and how strong he was. He was real. He was a Viking warrior and a chief, though she wasn't sure what the latter was.

"Genevra asked me to let her tell the girl," he said. "I allowed it."

"Genevra is a kind soul. I must apologize to her for my flash of anger when she called me daughter."

"Why should that anger you?" he asked.

"I just have this sour part of me about mothers."

"You will be one someday," he pointed out.

"No, I won't. I don't want children. I never want to be a mother."

The slight smile he usually wore when he was around her faded. "You sound certain."

"I am. I will not be a good mother, and I won't take the chance of screwing someone up."

"Very well," he said, "first of all explain what you main by *screwing someone up* and then tell me how you know what kind of mother you will be?"

"Because I...why all the questions?" she argued, stiffening in his arms. "Why don't you question Fin like this?"

"Because I was not thinking about having children with Fin."

"What?" She was already staring at him, so when he spoke, she was watching him. He was serious. He was also insane. Stark raving mad if he thought—he could force himself on her and get her pregnant. Oh, no! What if he tried? What if that was his intention all along? She should have kept on running. So what if she was in a bog? It had to end somewhere.

"Wolf, I would prefer not to ever be a mother, and I certainly don't want to be forced. I don't love you. This is not my home. I will not settle here."

He folded his arms across his chest like a shield against her and scowled. "Do you know how to get back to your home, Camelee?"

For some crazy reason, she didn't want him to put a shield between them. She wanted to run her fingers over the steel muscles shaping him, kiss along his granite jaw until it softened toward her.

"Help me find a way," she said in a low voice facing his chest.

"Is that what I am here for?" he asked, looking down at her.

She wanted to close her eyes against him. The truth was she'd been afraid out there alone in the bog. She was relieved he had come for her. She was afraid here, wherever here was. She was thankful for his consideration and kindness toward her.

They rode until they reached the camp. Fin was there to greet them. He smiled, like some dashing rogue. But he didn't win her over. She didn't care if they'd found Hild's mother mauled by a bear. If Fin had something to do with it, she didn't want him to get away with it.

She dismounted and hurried to the little girl, mostly to be away from Fin's watchful eyes. When she reached her, she saw another woman with her.

"Where's Genevra?" she asked Wolf when he dismounted and reached her.

"Genevra has a master," he told her. "Lord Alfred of Bristolton. He asked for her attention."

"Of course." Camelee grumbled under her breath. "*He* wanted her attention, instead of her giving it to an orphaned child."

"Would you prefer I killed him?" he asked, unruffled, as if he could go do it and come right back to finish their conversation.

"Of course not!" she breathed, horrified at the suggestion. "We don't go around killing people because we disagree with their stance on certain issues."

He knit his brow while he studied her, and then he smiled. "I had my tent set up for the girl. I think she will be more comfortable."

Camelee looked around at the large tent, made of sewn animal hides. She swallowed. It was about the size of a city bus. A tent like this would take a long time to make, many animals…

"Are you unwell?" he asked, laying his hand on her shoulder. "Come, inside where it is warm."

"This is *your* tent? You sleep here alone?"

"I rarely stay in it," he told her. "We do not usually put it up. I made an exception for the girl."

She marveled at it. "It's—"

"And for you," he added quietly.

Her belly flipped as she stepped inside. For a mad moment, she celebrated his fondness for her, but reality settled quickly over her—along with blessed heat from many candles lit on stands and hanging from rafters, precariously close to the top.

She was no longer afraid of having been kidnapped by a cult of maniacs in the twenty-first century. No. She was convinced more fully that she had somehow, magically been sucked through time and entered the horrific eleventh century—when a Dane was seated on the English throne.

As impossible as it all seemed, they had traveled long hours and not once had she seen anything in the sky except for birds. They'd traveled far and she'd only seen one or two houses. No buildings in the distance. New York City wasn't this big. The English countryside in the eleventh century was. There were hills everywhere, most were blanketed by a thin sheet of snow.

This morning was especially cold, making the tent—*his* tent, well appreciated.

The skins held the warmth inside. It was cozy, bathed in golden light, but there was an underlying smell of gaminess. Hild was uncovered and afraid and sitting on a bed made of skins. The thought of it turned Camelee's stomach.

"This woman," he announced, motioning with his chin to Camelee, "will watch over the child from now on. You may go."

"What? No!" Camelee refused.

His eyes smoldered like storm clouds over turquoise seas. "You cannot refuse."

"I just did!"

He shook his head and left.

Bastard! Camelee wanted to go after him. How dare he just walk away? She wanted to tell him what she thought of him ordering her around. Ordering her to take care of this little girl. Camelee didn't want to be a mother, and he knew it!

She tightened her jaw. Well, she guessed that was that. She couldn't leave now.

"Mumma coming home soon," Hild declared happily when Camelee went to her.

Camelee squeezed her eyes shut. No! She wanted the girl to know the truth. Why have the child wait for someone who was never coming back? Yes, it hurt, but not telling her the truth hurt her more and for a longer period.

She bent to the child. She didn't know what else to tell her. She had been given false hope as a child, and when her biological mother never came for her, it devastated her.

"No, Hild," she said as gently as she could. "Your mumma is gone. She has died. She's not coming back."

As she suspected, Hild's smile vanished, and tears quickly filled her eyes. "Yes. Mumma coming back."

"No, little one, she is not coming back. We will take care of you—"

Hild began to wail for her mother. Camelee didn't know what to do. She'd never been around kids before. Not alone and in charge. What should she do? She sat down next to the girl on the skins. "Hild, everything is going to be all right. Mumma is watching over you from Heaven, and we will all take care of you and love you."

The child continued to cry. She was so pitiful that Camelee began to cry with her. The poor girl had lost her mother. It was terribly sad. Camelee hadn't cried in years. Not real tears. Both her and Hild's lives had completely changed in the space of a breath. She understood, so she cried.

She felt a warm hand rest on her shoulder. She sniffed and wiped her eyes before she turned to look behind her.

"It is as you told her," Wolf's heavy, quiet voice swept across her ears. "All will be well."

"How do you know that?" she asked, turning to face him.

"Because," he said staring into her eyes, tender, and yet feral with his flowing braided hair, "if anyone tries to make it unwell, I will kill them."

◆•• • •••◆

CHAPTER SIX

S HE PULLED BACK, out of his reach. He was tempted to grasp for her. *Stay near.* He wanted to tell her. But she wouldn't obey him.

He watched her put her arm around the girl. "She needs to rest."

He pulled off his fur cloak and yawned. "So do I." He crossed the tent in three long strides and fell onto a long, folding bed covered in furs. This is what he needed. To sleep. His lack of it contributed to his latest line of thoughts. Constant thoughts of her.

He opened his eyes. Camelee hadn't moved from her spot. She said nothing but stared at him.

He was surprised that his disobedient servant was learning subservience so quickly. He smiled at her. Slightly. "You may come."

He threw down his blanket on the girl as a sign that he cared about their well-being, and then closed his eyes.

"Excuse me!"

He opened his eyes and looked at Camelee. He tried not to scowl at thoughts of how enticing she looked with her hair disheveled and her cheeks flushed. "Woman, why are you raising your voice at me?"

"Are you serious?" she barked. Then, before he could even ask her what she was saying, she continued. She looked at the child sitting up, leaning her back on the bed, close to him, and lowered her voice. "You're serious about this whole slave thing, is that it? She's beneath you so she sleeps on the floor? I bet we're supposed to be thankful to you for it, too, huh?"

He sat up. "Huh?"

She threw up her hands. "Oh, for goodness—"

"Camelee." He cut her off. He'd been patient long enough. He didn't like the way she was making him soft. He had to stop it before his men saw it. "You will cease this," he warned. "We are weary."

She was obviously too simple-minded to recognize when a man had had enough, for she raised one eyebrow and put her hands on her hips, ready to fight. "Oh," she contended, "so now it's *we*? Good, then you don't need me."

"No." He glanced down at the child, sucking her thumb, and trying and failing to keep her eyes open. "Not now, it would seem. You are free to go."

She gasped. He thought it a strange reaction—as if she had never been spoken to like that before. Impossible if she came from this time…or if she was royalty. Was she some princess escaping an unwanted, upcoming marriage? She looked as if she could be royalty, save for her red, puffy eyes. He'd walked in on her and the child weeping. Camelee had gathered herself though and stopped when she saw him.

She was a curious thing. Why had she been weeping? She had said she had no husband so what was so terrible about going with him? Had he not treated her well from the beginning?

"I—"

She held up her hand. "Good day," she said, then disappeared through the flap.

"Mumma coming back?" the little girl asked him.

It both warmed his heart and worried him that she thought of Camelee as her mother already. Camelee said she didn't want to be a mother. It seemed her mind was made up. She left the child with him to go sleep outside in the cold. A mother wouldn't do such a thing. She would lay on the floor with her child and keep her warm. Good thing he'd been thoughtful and gave the girl his blanket.

He hopped off the bed and reached for his fur cloak. He returned to the girl and took the blanket from her. He rolled it up and put it under her head. Then he covered her with his cloak and looked down at her. He wondered what truly happened to her mother. Should he leave Camelee out there with Fin?

"Mumma coming back?"

"Yes, Hild," he said softly. "She is coming back."

Where else was she going to go?

➤➤➤❌◀◀◀

CAMELEE STORMED OUT of his tent, wishing there was a door she could slam. She wanted to scream and rant and rave, but that wouldn't help her here. Besides, what kind of example would she be setting for Hild? Not that she cared about how the girl saw her. He thought to throw the child at her in the hopes of what, she wondered angrily; convincing her that she did want to have his children and without pain killers? Because you know, she did things the old-fashioned way now.

She hugged herself while she crossed the camp and fell onto her pallet. She didn't need his stupid tent. She certainly wouldn't lay on the floor by his feet like a loyal dog! She'd rather freeze.

Someone dug his boot into her side. "Up now. There will be no sleeping all day around here. Get with the others and start making our meal."

"Get your foot out of my side before I hack it off with the chief's axe," she said in her toughest New York accent, a role she did in one of her first movie roles as Josephine, a gang leader's girlfriend in *Silver Bullet*, a crime thriller.

Her attacker wasn't buying it. He pulled back his foot and meant to kick her. Someone stopped him. Akkar.

"Friend," he warned, "she belongs to the chief, Wolf Kristiansen. Harm her and he will surely kill you."

Her assailant paled and ran off. Camelee thought about telling Wolf about him for the way he treated a woman. She didn't care if she was in ten seventeen and things were different. She wouldn't stand by while women were being assaulted.

"Thank you," she said to Akkar.

"For what?"

"For scaring that creep away."

He shrugged. "In truth, I was thinking about *his* life, not yours."

"Ugh, right. For a minute, I forgot that you're a savage son of a—Viking."

"How could you forget that?" he asked sounding serious enough. He looked to be about eighteen years old, with russet hair shaved close up to the tops of his ears. There was a long, single braid swinging between his shoulders in his fur cloak.

"I really don't know," she told him. "Um, where are you motioning me to go?"

"With me. I'll take you to the other women. The men are getting hungry."

What did she care? She wanted to scream it. She wasn't a slave! "There's been a mistake, Akkar. I'm not a slave."

His dark eyes widened. "You are not? What are you then?"

"Do I have to be something in order not to be a slave?" she asked, following him.

"You know, a noble woman?" he went on as if he hadn't heard her. "Princess? The daughter of an important lord?"

She shook her head. "I'm an award-winning actress. I can perform almost any role! Currently I'm—" she stopped when she saw his blank gaze. He had no idea what she was talking about. She sagged her shoulders, weary of explaining everything she said. She realized, too, that she was simply repeating part of her publicity campaign. This wasn't what defined her. Was it? She was more than an actress, wasn't she?

Solemnly, she resigned that she was here, and she might not get home again. She would never be an actress again, just a slave. She would never see her family, or anyone from her past, or her future. No coffee or music. Life here could be extremely hard until she died—or not so horrible with a strong, gorgeous guy in her bed at night. Of course, he was a misogynistic jerk. But he was a lot better than nothing at all. In ten seventeen anyway.

A man was running in their direction. He wasn't a Dane. She knew because Fin was chasing him on his horse. He held a spear in his hand. Just before the fleeing man reached her, Fin caught up with him and ran his spear through the man's back. The bloody tip came out of his chest and pointed at her.

She gasped and in the hopes of not fainting in front of Fin, she spun around and ran into Akkar's arms.

"Bring her to the chief's tent!" Fin shouted at him. "Guard her or it will be your head, Akkar! That Saxon meant to harm her."

"I will guard her with my life, Commander."

Wait. She stopped walking in her soggy Uggs. "Why would he mean to hurt me?" she asked Fin. "I didn't even know him."

"But he knew of you," he countered. "He blamed you for his village being captured. He said you were a witch. He claimed he saw you appear from nothing. He believed as long as you lived, this village would be cursed."

She blinked and a cold thread of fear went through her. She had appeared from an office in a building on West Thirteenth, where she'd held a charred brooch. She wanted to fall to her knees and cry. It had really happened. And that poor man had seen it.

"Come now," Akkar urged her forward.

Was she supposed to thank Fin for his gallantry? What if he'd just murdered that man for no reason other than to satisfy his bloodlust and he made up that story to cover himself with Wolf?

She wanted to run back to the tent. This was all really happening. That man really died right in front of her. She fought to stay conscious.

Was she stuck here? Was there a way back? If there was, the chief seemed powerful enough to help her find it.

They made it to tent with Akkar's whispers of admiration for the temporary shelter filling her ears.

Taking a deep breath to face him again, she pushed the flap aside and entered the tent. She stopped when she saw Hild sleeping soundly and covered in furs.

Wolf had done it. Amid terror and ugliness, his actions, though small ones, shone light bright lights, drawing and attracting her. Her gaze rose to him facedown and asleep in his bed. His ankles hovered in the air on the bottom end. His arm dangled over the side. He was too big for the flimsy bed. She took a moment to take in the sight of his hills and valleys. He had no blanket. She took a step closer. Was that it beneath Hild's head?

He shifted and turned his face, perhaps to breathe. And opened his eyes.

Her heart thumped so hard she was sure he could hear it. What if he was angry for waking him? What if he rejected her? What would she do for the rest of her life here?

"Camelee?" he asked groggily and leaned up on his elbow. "Akkar, what—?" His gaze settled on her coat. "Is that…blood?"

"It is, Chief." Akkar told him quickly and quietly everything that happened, and all that Fin had said about her assailant. While the young soldier spoke, Wolf kept his warming gaze on her.

"All right, Akkar," he said when he was done. "You may wait outside now."

Akkar left without another word.

"Take off your coat," he ordered her gently. "Quietly, for the sake of Hild."

Camelee didn't argue. It had blood on it.

"Have you never seen a man—"

"—with a spear through him? No. I never have."

"You will never forget him, but he meant you harm."

"Says Fin," she pointed out in a whisper. "The man held out no weapon. Was he going to kill me with his bare hands?"

"I will question Fin on this and get answers. Does that help give ease to your thoughts?" She nodded. When she looked at his handsome face, his plump, bow-shaped lips, the set of his jaw, his piercing gaze, she could think of nothing but him.

"I want to remain with you today," she confessed shyly. Goodness, in her world she would *never* admit such a thing to anyone. *Don't be vulnerable.* It was the first advice she'd ever received. And the best. People were fake. Friends were only there to be seen with her. She would get hurt. But she wanted him to know. "I'm afraid here and I feel better when I'm with you."

He motioned for her to come and sit with him and Hild. She wasn't sleepy but the thought of being pushed around by the men, forced to cook for them…no. She wasn't ready for this reality. She didn't think she ever would be.

She accepted his offering and climbed into the makeshift bed on the floor with Hild. The pelts beneath her were kind of soft and warm, but as she feared, there was a stale, nauseating smell coming from them.

She pulled his fur cloak over her. It didn't smell as bad. In fact, it smelled like him.

She pushed it away from her face. She would try to stay close to him—for safety reasons mostly. But not so close that her heart became involved. God forbid. She had never taken the possibility of it happening to her so seriously. She never had to. She found love repulsive. It tricked and fooled. It betrayed and forgot and could not be trusted. If it could accomplish its goal, it would leave people sucked dry of strength and the will to live. No one ever tempted her toward it. But with him…she let her guard down for a moment and let herself feel and hope for something with him. It was instinct really. The fight to survive. She understood what was happening to her. She was bonding to her rescuer. Now that she knew what it was, she knew she had to stop it.

Oh, if she ever got her hands on Mr. Green, who'd given her that accursed brooch, she'd ask Wolf to beat him up good.

"Wolf?"

"Yes?"

"The man Fin killed said he saw me appear from the air. I was appearing from twenty nineteen."

"It is a lot to ask me to believe, Camelee."

"I know." She blushed looking up at him. He smiled and made her nerve-endings burn. "Thank you."

"What for?" he whispered back.

"For not laughing in my face."

"I would not do that," he promised in a sleepy voice.

Would he invite her into his bed? She wouldn't go. Not because she didn't want to. She did. He would get tired of her if she gave him all too fast. As much as she hated to admit it, she needed him. She could debate with herself for the next ten years about if she would need him in the twenty-first century, but what did it matter? She was here now.

"I must go with the men today to scout out the remainder of our route," he told her quietly. "I will take half the men and leave Fin and Akkar here to guard you. You will have to stay with the other women until I return."

"What if you're attacked and you don't come back?" she asked, concerned.

"I will come back, Camelee," he assured her with such confidence, she believed him.

She smiled and closed her eyes, feeling a bit of comfort and relaxation for the first time.

She woke the next morning to the sight of Wolf changing his shirt, or léine, or whatever he was wearing. She watched him silently washing up before a small table with a basin of water and a sponge. His bare back was tapered at his waist and flared at his shoulders. Scars covered most of him. Even with such marks, his body was a carved masterpiece. If he wasn't an eleventh-century Viking, or if she hadn't gone completely mad, she might have thrown all her fears and ideals out the window—if there was a window in the hide tent, which there wasn't. Ideals that she felt at times weren't her own but seemed to have been ingrained upon her from someone, somewhere. They were about as old-fashioned and dated as Wolf. One of which was to seek nothing before honor. She wasn't about to throw her honor to the wind for some savage Viking who considered her his slave. Her fears were a whole different matter.

She could see light coming in from between the stitching of the different hides.

"I sent Akkar for some food for you and the girl," he told her while she sat up and rubbed her eyes.

She turned to the child. Hild still slept. "Should I wake her?"

"I do not know. How long does a child sleep?"

She shook her head. "We should send for Genevra. I should speak to her anyway about—"

"Chief!" Akkar said from outside the flap of the tent.

"Come," Wolf called back to him.

Akkar pushed open the flap and entered. His sable eyes found her immediately. He opened his mouth to speak but Wolf held his finger to his lips to quiet him and looked at Hild sleeping.

Akkar swallowed his words and half-smiled, half-grimaced at her, then looked away.

"Sorry for the delay, Chief," Akkar told him quietly. "Work in the kitchen was slow due to the absence of one of the women. Her master was the man Fin killed yesterday."

"Wolf," she said, rising from her blankets. It was cold out here without his fur. "Fin said that man was running toward me to hurt or kill me. Maybe I should talk to this woman and try to convince her that none of this is my fault."

"And if you cannot?" he asked.

She stared at him and shrugged her shoulders. "What do you suggest? That she also be killed?"

"If she means you harm, yes."

She didn't know what to say to that. He seemed to—

"You belong to me, Camelee. Everyone I took with me belongs to me."

Okay...so that's what she was to him? Just one of his servants? His property? Okay. It was better to have this fact driven into her head. It would keep her emotions at bay.

"Gotcha."

She turned and walked toward the flap.

"Camelee, what are doing? You cannot leave. You need to stay and take care of the girl."

Who was, by now, awake and looking around.

He motioned to Akkar, and the young soldier stepped in front of the flap, blocking her path.

"What? So now I'm a prisoner?" She gaped at Akkar.

"You will do as I say. You are staying with Hild. You will care for her until I return."

No. She would never get used to this. It was bad enough she had to take care of a child, a little orphan who needed a mother, but she wasn't asked to do this. No, she was ordered to do it. Held prisoner and forced to—

He swept past her, grabbed his fur cloak from the floor, giving Hild a smile and a wink before he moved around Camelee.

"Guard her, and get her a cloak," he ordered Akkar and left the tent.

"Ugh! He is an infuriating jerk! I wish I knew martial art so I could kick his—" Her gaze fell on Hild, and she stopped ranting when she saw the little girl watching. "Akkar, please send for Genevra. I need her help with Hild."

He obliged by sticking his head out of the tent and calling for someone. He said something in Norse and then returned his attention to her.

"No matter what skills you possessed, you could not hurt him," he let her know. "I saw him fight on the field. He killed with precision and brute force, taking on two and even three at a time. I have heard tales of him. He is said to be King Cnut's favored warrior."

How could all this be real? But it was. It was.

"I spoke in anger," she confessed, then muttered under her breath, "but if I had a gun, he wouldn't have a shot."

The flap opened and Genevra stepped inside. Her eyes were swollen and red, the tip of her nose was red, too. Camelee felt a little kinship with her because the tip her nose always turned red when she cried.

"Genevra, were you crying?" Camelee went to her.

The woman nodded. "That man the commander killed. He was my master, the man who took care of me these last twenty-six years."

CHAPTER SEVEN

"O H, NO," CAMELEE put her hands to her mouth. The man Fin had killed was Genevra's provider. She almost let out a scream when Akkar grabbed hold of Genevra's arm.

"Let her go!" She tried to remain calm for Hild's sake, and for Genevra's. "Akkar, hasn't she suffered enough? She's lost much today."

He looked torn.

"Please, Akkar."

He let Genevra go but stayed close to her.

"I know what is being said about him," Genevra announced. "It is not true. Aye, he saw you appear from nowhere, but he did not blame you for our capture. He called you an angel. He said you had come to watch over us."

Camelee lowered her eyes, unable to look up. She was no angel. Genevra's master had died because of her. "I'm so sorry. He was running toward me. Fin thought he was going to attack me."

Genevra covered her face in her hands and cried. But she didn't do it for long. Soon, she wiped her cheeks, pulled herself together, and went to Hild. "Are you hungry, Child? Must you relieve yourself?"

Yes! Of course! How could Camelee have forgotten that? Oh, poor Hild if she had to stay with Camelee. She was but three or four years old. Did she even know how to use a –potty?

"I will…what can I do?" she asked Genevra, who seemed more together after just losing her only source of provisions than Camelee did after, well, after losing everything she had and knew.

"I'm so sorry for snapping at you," Camelee told her. "I'm tender about the subject of motherhood, but I had no right to be angry with you."

"Oh, my dear Camelee," Genevra poured out to her. "Forgive me for being so bold as to bring it up."

Camelee stared and studied her. From where did she pull such humility? Camelee knew she, herself, had never possessed such a virtue.

"Come, let us find a hidden place for Hild, and then some food, hmm?"

Hild nodded emphatically, then, "Mumma coming back?"

"Yes, Child," Genevra let her know.

Camelee decided to keep her mouth shut. It really wasn't any of her business what the child believed. She would stay out of it.

Akkar protested when she wanted to go, but she invited him to join them and she did it with a smile that left him blushing and chuckling, like the guys she remembered from her first year of college. Only this one hadn't saved her from that Dane who was about to give her a hard kick. He'd saved the soldier from having to suffer under the chief. But—Akkar was honest. And she liked that about him.

"I have always wanted to be a warrior," he told her while they walked through the camp with her on one side and Hild on the other with Genevra on the outside. "My father was a farmer, and not interested in the fighting. He didn't understand my heart's desire."

"That must have been difficult for you," Genevra said, listening.

He turned to her and his gaze on her softened. "It was."

"Did you run away, Akkar?" Camelee asked him. If he did, he had lied to Wolf.

He shook his head. "I informed my father of my intentions to leave. He shrugged. He did not care."

Camelee clamped down her teeth then fought to open her mouth to bite out, "The love of a parent, huh? What a laugh."

"Though I do not have any children," Genevra told her, "I believe a parent's love is the sincerest, the purest, and given without condition love there is."

Camelee smiled politely at her. "I don't believe that."

"What has caused you not to believe it?"

She breathed in deeply. At first, she was going to refuse to answer. But maybe she was here to learn some sort of lesson and once she learned it, she could return home. There *had* to be a purpose to all of this, a way home when the purpose was accomplished.

"My parents abandoned me to an orphanage when I was a baby."

"Oh, poor dear," Genevra cooed. "You know some parents cannot—"

Camelee held up her hand to Genevra. "Please. I've heard it all. None of it matters at the end of the day. They didn't—" She paused. She didn't know it was going to be this difficult to speak of it, to say the words, or why she was telling them to this perfect stranger. Was it because Genevra seemed like a mother to all? Something about her was comforting and Camelee wanted to tell her everything. "They didn't—love me enough to keep me."

Genevra's large eyes were striking in color. They seemed to illuminate the morning in flashes of silver and blue. "Mayhap, they had to give you up," she said softly and without hesitation, as if the words were there all along, waiting to come out. "If they had not, you might have died."

Camelee stared at her as they stepped beneath another giant tent. This one though, had no sides, only a roof.

"What, Genevra? Like what?"

"I do not know," the older woman said as she smiled regretfully. "I have not lived the kind of life where, if I had a babe, I would be forced to give her up."

"Forced?"

"Mayhap," Genevra answered.

Camelee shook her head, and then turned her wide gaze on the Viking men. All of them were sitting, shoving food into their faces, or covering half their faces with a cup. Both men and women Saxons were serving.

She pulled Genevra and Hild toward another tent, where the women were cooking food. They all greeted Genevra with solemn hugs. Most asked how she was after losing her lord. She assured them all that she was well, though Camelee doubted in her heart that she was.

"This is Camelee of—" Genevra began to introduce.

"New York," Camelee told her.

"York. She belongs to the chief—"

"No. I—" Camelee interrupted.

But Genevra's voice overrode hers and she kept her gaze on Camelee. "So, if anyone harms her, they die."

It was to keep her safe. Yes. She got it. This wasn't her world. In this world, she needed the chief—or to belong to the chief, for safety.

"And this is Akkar," Genevra continued, "the chief's guard, who has been commanded to guard her."

Akkar nodded to them and then sat at the table. Camelee sat next to him.

"So," she said to Genevra now that things had quieted a bit. "Your name is Italian, isn't it?"

"Aye, Italian and Welsh," Genevra said with a smile. "In my case, Welsh."

The others swarmed Hild next. They knew her. They had known her mother. It was heartwarming and heartbreaking at the same time. This entire community offered to raise her. It was good to see, but there was also the fact that their friend was dead, mauled by a bear. She wondered how many of them didn't believe that story.

Camelee had grown up alone. Her parents traveled often on

business. She was raised by nannies most of the time. It was in their care that she mastered the art of pretending to be someone she wasn't. Someone well put together. But the truth was, she couldn't escape the fact that even the parents who'd adopted her had abandoned her.

Finally, Genevra guided Hild into a chair between Camelee's and her own.

They were served, a thoughtful gesture the captives offered to Genevra and Hild. Camelee didn't feel worthy of their servitude and asked Genevra to bring her to the portable kitchen later that night after dinner to help clean up.

It wasn't something she would ever do at home, but she wasn't home. Things were very different here. She must learn to either fit in or die.

"All will be well," Genevra said, smiling at her and reaching across the table to pat her hand.

Camelee knew how to smile while the truth in her thoughts fluttered through her. "We will see."

They ate lukewarm mutton stew with stale bread. They were served a skin of water, cooled in the snow outside. There was also ale for the men. Camelee chose to have the ale.

"Tell me about yourself, Genevra," Camelee requested warmly. "Or tell me about your…uhm…lord if you would like. Some people like that."

Her smile was so inviting that, for a moment, Camelee wanted to fall into her arms.

"I do not remember most of my life."

"What?" Camelee asked, her interest piqued.

"I *woke up* one day, not knowing who I was. I was in my later twenties. In this world." Her pause gave Camelee a thought about what she was saying.

Tears filled Camelee's eyes. She fought not to let them fall. But as waterfalls did, her tears fell.

"Lord Alfred took me in as I was lost and terrified. He kept me under his wing the way he should, and I cared for him as my dearest friend."

Camelee nodded her head, understanding, and thinking about how blessed Lord Alfred and Genevra were to have each other all these years, at least for companionship.

"And you never fell in love with him?"

Genevra shook her head.

"With anyone you knew?"

"No," Genevra told her, straightening her spine, and squaring her shoulders. "My heart belongs to another."

"Oh?" Camelee whispered, leaning in. "Who?"

Her new friend's large eyes widened, and her mouth pouted. "I do not know. I do not remember. But I know that I love him. I have loved him since the beginning of time. At first, I waited for him, but no one ever came. I do not remember who he is or where to find him but I feel his presence. I know he exists. I do not know how I know it, but I do. I wait for him still, even allowing my body to grow old, never having a man in my bed or in my body."

"Maybe the same thing happened to both of us, Genevra," Camelee claimed with a smile. "Half my life, I was somewhere else. But I remember where I came from. And I remember compassion," she added quickly and covered Genevra's hand with her own. "I'm so sorry about your loss."

"It is the way of war," Akkar defended what his kinsmen had done.

"That does not make it okay…all right," Camelee corrected, sitting up straighter.

"What do you remember?" Genevra asked her. "Were you visiting an aunt or uncle in Bristolton?"

"Yes. Aye. I was visiting," Camelee said quickly. "My relatives were killed."

"Such an innocent," Genevra cried. "Would that I could preserve it."

"Hild," Camelee said in the hopes of distracting Genevra. "What is your favorite thing to eat?"

"Scones, Dam," the little girl offered.

"Jam?"

Hild nodded without looking at her. Camelee smiled when their gazes met. In all honesty, she'd never seen such a perfect-looking angel.

Shamefully, she realized that she hadn't even taken a moment to really look at Hild. She had pale blonde curls falling around her cherubic face like a golden halo. Her eyes were as green as the dreams of fairies in the forest.

But the little girl didn't smile back. Three times and nothing. In fact, Camelee was sure Hild slipped her a hateful look. It was because of what Camelee had said about her mother not returning. About the truth.

She sighed. "I would make you some if I could."

Hild ignored her.

No matter, Genevra kept her busy answering questions.

"I haven't had this much interest in me in well," Camelee gave it a few moments of serious thought. "I never have."

Genevra swiped a dainty little hankie she produced from her sleeve across her nostrils. "I am not ashamed to say that I feel a closeness with you. It is as if I have met you before, or I should have."

Camelee felt it, too. She wished they were alone so she could tell Genevra everything about traveling from the future. She knew this woman would believe her. "We should speak more later."

Genevra smiled and nodded. "I agree. We should."

In the meantime, she spoke to Akkar and Genevra and everyone who served them. For the first time in her life, Camelee didn't feel alone. She even laughed when Akkar dropped his drink in his lap and swore.

But in a moment, everything changed. The sound of a commotion drew some of the others to the tent flap. They looked outside. The women screamed and hurried back inside. "Men are coming! They will kill us!"

Akkar leaped to his feet and drew his sword. "Stay here!" he ordered Camelee and rushed for the opening. Was he going to leave them? When she saw him peer out and then hurry back to her, her relief was short-lived.

"They are Saxons!" He yanked at the spikes securing the back wall and pulled them up. "Go! Run!"

But the Saxons were there, too, waiting. They tore through the tent, as the screams of the women inside blended with those clearly heard now from outside.

Everything happened so fast. Three of them broke through the barrier and stepped inside. They looked fierce with wide shoulders clad in animal skins.

One of the men, the biggest of the three, sported a long beard and long, straggly blond hair. He shifted his soulless gaze to Camelee, and then to Hild.

Camelee had the urge to block the girl from his gaze.

"What is going on?" Genevra demanded with all the authority of a queen.

Unfortunately, her countrymen didn't recognize it. One of them came from behind her and struck her in the back of her head with the hilt of his sword.

Hild began to cry.

In an act of supreme bravery, Akkar swung at the three Saxons. One went down. It was the one who'd struck Genevra. But another, just as big as the one who'd spoken first, drove his giant broadsword into Akkar's belly. Camelee watched it come out of Akkar's back, the same way Fin's spear had come from Genevra's lord.

She watched him go down with a horrified scream ripping through her heart.

Fin! Where was Fin!

"Leofric," said the first brutish Saxon. "I wanted him to tell their leader who did this."

Leofric looked around. There was only Camelee and Hild left. "Leave her, Aethelwold." He pointed to Camelee.

They were going to have to kill her if they thought she would let them take Hild without her.

"No," said Aethelwold. "I want them both."

And then her heart went cold when he reached for Hild.

"Don't touch her!" Camelee commanded without thinking or hesitation.

Aethelwold paused for a moment but took hold of the girl. Hild screamed, reaching for an unconscious Genevra.

"Where is the chief?" Leofric, with red braids hanging from his temples, asked. "Is he hiding?"

Camelee wished Wolf was here so he could put an end to this scum who killed Akkar. "He went to meet another marauding band of Danes and bring them here."

"Why are you three females sitting at a table and eating when every other Saxons is serving the Danes?" Aethelwold asked, holding his hand over Hild's mouth. "Are you valuable to the chief?'

"Take your filthy hand off her." She couldn't help herself. She wasn't used to cowering to anyone. Besides, there had to be trillions of germs on his skin.

"A spirited one," Aethelwold remarked with a smirk while stepping out of the tent.

"Aye," said Leofric grabbing her wrists and shoving her out of the tent opening behind Hild. "The kind I like to break."

Where was Wolf? Had he taken Fin with him? Surely these Saxons were more civilized than the Vikings. But no. She thought of what one of them had done to Genevra, and to Akkar. She didn't care if he was a Dane, she liked Akkar.

She looked around and then wished she hadn't. There were dead men everywhere. Women ran every which way, terrified and screaming, not sure where to go. Saxon soldiers were setting fire to everything. Smoke billowed upward, darkening the sky.

Even though, historically, the Saxons were the ones who had been attacked. So, theirs was, of course, the side where her sympathies should lie. But something deep in her bones told her things had just gone from bad to worse. Much, much worse.

CHAPTER EIGHT

F IN YANKED UP his hide breeches and, leaving them untied,
pulled on his boots.

"What is it?" the woman asked, sitting up from her bed in her cottage a half a mile north of the camp.

"You do not smell that?" he asked her, rushing to the window again. "Smoke."

This time, he could see it rising from the camp. His blood froze. He snatched his sword from where he'd set it down in his belt and bolted for the door.

Without a word to the woman in whose bed he'd spent the night, he left the cottage. He ran through the forest bare-chested, but he didn't feel the cold. *She* was there and Wolf expected him to keep her safe while he was away from camp. Fin had stepped away from his post. What would his brother do to him for it? The chief would need to show the other men what became of disobedient sluggards who left their posts.

Fin's chest burned as if someone set fire to it. He huffed and puffed and leaped over tree roots. The closer he got to the camp, the thicker the smell.

He came bursting through the trees and stopped dead at the sight before him. Danes lay dead on the cold ground, their blood soaking into the grass. Twenty men. His heart sank and thundered until he felt ill. They'd been attacked! The men were dead. Who was responsible? He would not stop until he found and killed everyone. He remembered the woman and ran to his brother's tent. She wasn't inside, neither was the child. But his brother's foolish young follower, Akkar was there, dead on the ground, a hole in his chest. Damn it!

He left the tent, not allowing himself to mourn a young man he'd barely known, and searched among the fallen, hoping he didn't find the woman. She caused him trouble when she was here. She might get him killed because she wasn't.

He would admit she was pleasing to the eyes, but she didn't know her place. She was going to make his brother look the fool.

Then again, it didn't appear that she or the child were here. He could see that the women they had taken from the town were gone. Was she with them? He thought of Akkar. Had they been taken?

He saw a woman's silhouette emerging from the flames. Was it…his heart accelerated…Camelee?

"Did you stop them?" her voice rang out when she saw him.

"Who?" he demanded. It wasn't her. "Who did this?"

She paused for a moment, then told him, betraying her people. "The Saxons. They came and killed everyone."

Fin wasn't moved by the tears streaming down her face. She was a Saxon. Why would she give up her countrymen so easily? He asked her.

"We must find her. There is something about her that—"

"You are correct," he agreed. What did he care why the older woman did what she did? "Wolf will return soon. Where do we begin looking?"

"I have been searching. I do not know what else to do, but you should know. You are the commander."

"You are a Saxon."

"You are the Danish sons of wh—"

"Slave!" His voice overrode hers.

"Barbarian!" she shouted just as loud. "They killed your young friend. Do you truly wish to stand here bickering with me when they might have them?"

"Where did they take her?" he demanded.

"I do not know. One of them struck me and I do not remember anything after that. But…"

"But what?" He looked around. He needed to find Wolf's woman. This woman was wasting his time.

"One of them was staring at Camelee and the girl with dark intentions just before I demanded to know what was going on and was struck from behind."

The knots in his belly were growing tighter and tighter "We must find them." He began to turn away to continue his search. They might have struck Camelee and left her here among the bodies. But it was getting harder and harder to see.

"I have told you I have searched," the woman told him. "They are not here. I fear they have been taken captive."

Fin closed his eyes and rubbed his forehead. Wolf wasn't due back for another few hours. He couldn't wait. This woman—what had Camelee called her? Genevra. This Genevra was no spring maiden. She could not keep up. He had to leave her here.

"The chief will return to camp. Tell him what happened, and that I went to find her and bring her back."

"Dane—"

"I must go," he interrupted. "He will not forgive me this—and I do not want to see that in his eyes." He said the last part in more of a mumble and more to himself than to her.

"I just wanted you to wait while I—" She bent to the nearest fallen warrior and removed his jacket and cloak. She hurried to bring them to him. "Put these on before you freeze to death." Her gaze shifted everywhere but to his bare chest.

Her skin looked like the petals of a pale peach flower. Fin wondered if it smelled like a flow—no! She was old enough to be his mother—though he never knew his mother. He'd killed her being born. When he was told the tale by his father's servants, he knew he was cursed. His life and his thirst for war and blood proved it.

"It would be difficult to freeze to death in this heat."

"Heat?" She looked at him as if he'd just grown another head.

"In comparison to Denmark's winters," he clarified and forgot the urgency of what he needed to do.

"Is it desolate and uninviting?" she asked, looking worried. Wolf must have told her his plans.

The thought of Wolf returning home pricked his soul. They would separate. Wolf was giving up. Fin had waited and trained all his life to fight with his brother, and he was already going back?

"No. Its beauty is breathtaking, soul-stirring. It is mountainous, untamed, and uncharted. Winter there is freezing." He set his cool green gaze on her. "Truly freezing. Now I must go."

"Well," Genevra offered him a tender smile and a pat on his bare arm, "take the clothes anyway, please."

He received the offering and left, dressing as he went. He turned to look over his shoulder at her once after he slipped into the clothes. He would have smiled at her, for she was sharp and thoughtful, and oddly comforting. She looked like a slightly older version of Wolf's woman, with the same hair color, and the same spark of life in her large silvery-blue eyes.

He found his horse and searched for hoof prints in the light blanket of snow. It took him some time to find anything, for the snow had picked up and covered the ground and any tracks. His belly sank. They could have gone anywhere.

He felt ill. Wolf left him in charge of the camp. Everyone was dead. The chief's woman was gone. Taken…along with the child. He had left his post for a tumble in the bed of a woman whose name he didn't even know. Wolf was going to be angry. Very angry.

As children, the brothers had gotten along well. Wolf was the oldest by five years. He loved Fin immensely, having raised him alone with their father. Fin worshipped the dirt beneath his older brother's boots. When their father wasn't teaching Fin to farm, Wolf was teaching him how to fight. When Wolf left to fight for Cnut, Fin counted the days, the years until he was old enough to join the warriors.

"Someday, you can be chief, too," his brother used to tell him.

"I do not want to be chief, or anyone in power," he had replied. "Who wants all that on their shoulders?"

Wolf didn't like such talk. "It is not about you, Fin."

To which Fin would often reply with clever words and a playful smirk. But he had grown harder and more serious after twenty-one battles and killing hundreds of men. If a man didn't go hard after living the life he had lived, he would go mad—or maybe he never had a heart to begin with. He lived with the guilt of his mother for as long as he could remember. He was no good. Evil.

Wolf had tried to reassure him that he was not such things, but coming from his brother, whom many thought was a merciless monster, his reassurances held no weight. Still, Fin knew better. Wolf had been a monster only once and he was only merciless in battle with his enemies—and with men who took what belonged to him. When the Mercian army killed their father, Wolf went berserk and killed fifty men with just his sword.

Fin knew many Saxons would die by his brother's hands for what took place today. He might not stop until everyone involved was dead—possibly including him.

He buttoned the jacket to keep the cold off his skin. The icy air was affecting him more today. He didn't care. His only concern was his brother finding him before Fin found her.

"LET ME HOLD the girl," Camelee demanded the Saxon in front of her in the saddle. Aethelwold.

"There is no room in the saddle for me, you, and the girl," Aethelwold answered, looking over his shoulder at her.

She hated when he looked at her for there was no compassion in his gaze. She wanted to inform him that if he jumped off the horse when they reached the next cliff, there would plenty of room.

"Why are you wearing such strange attire?" he asked in his annoying voice that sounded like he was snarling even when he wasn't.

Over thirty men followed behind them on horseback. Another thirty had broken off and gone south with Leofric, who Camelee deduced was Aethelwold's older brother. One of the men who moved with her group had Hild with him. She was crying and wouldn't stop even when the brute gave her a shake and threatened to strike her.

Oh, Camelee lamented, why hadn't she taken those self-defense classes with Karen when she had the chance?

"Because I come from the future," she told him. "A little over a thousand years from now."

He didn't laugh the way she thought he might. He slowed the horse, turned in the saddle, and pushed her out of it. She landed hard on her side in the dirt and gasped for breath.

"Now you can hold her," he offered with a malevolent grin. He motioned to the one holding Hild, and the beast picked her up by the arm and held her over the ground. When he reached Camelee, she grabbed the girl and he let go.

But Hild didn't want Camelee either. She wanted her mother, or Genevra—or even Wolf, but not the woman who had told her that her mother wasn't coming back.

"Please, Hild, you mustn't cry," she begged, catching the many glares headed in her direction. "They will—"

"Shut her up or we will leave her here alone!" Aethelwold called out.

They would have to kill her before she let go of Hild. Oh, where was Wolf? And how could she be wishing for the Vikings to come and save her? Wait. Would they come? They would probably come because of all the men these Saxons killed. She'd seen the bodies when they'd dragged her out of the tent. If they came, it wouldn't be for her and a Saxon orphan. She didn't care, as long as they showed up. She didn't want to be here and every second she was in the eleventh century, she hated it more. But if she had to be here, she preferred to be with Wolf.

Would Wolf save her? She prayed that he would try.

They finally made camp an hour later to eat. Hild had finally stopped crying, but she had been through so much. Camelee set her down in the grass under a tree and sat beside her while the child slept.

The instant her body relaxed, her mind took over and images and memories of what they had done to Akkar assailed her. She'd blocked it out. She'd liked Akkar. He wasn't even a warrior. Still, he had fought well to save her and Hild. She didn't know why she had tears to shed for him. She hardly knew him. She fought her hardest to hold them back. The instant these scabs on mankind saw weakness, they would pounce.

"You!" Aethelwold barked at her. "Get up and serve us! Do you think you will sit on your arse and do nothing?"

"Move," another man called out, "before we wake the other one and have her serve us."

"Wake her and die, Eadric" said Aethelwold, with all kinds of darkness in his gaze. "We finally have peace, and you threaten it?"

"Apologies, Aethelwold. We could leave her."

"I won't leave without her!" Camelee told them in a hushed voice that sounded more like a hiss.

"No. She is to be a gift to my wife," Aethelwold told her, not surprising Camelee that he was married and staring hungrily at her. "She has always wanted a daughter."

"Is the other one for you then?" Eadric asked with a wink.

Aethelwold laughed and then the rest of them joined in. His smile faded when his gaze settled on her, still not moving. Without a word, he rose and went to her, drawing a blade as he went. One of the men giggled with satisfaction.

When he reached her, she called up every ounce of courage she possessed and looked at him.

He pulled back his arm and then swung it hard, striking her in the face with his palm. "Next time, it will be my fist," he promised as she fell to her knees before him. He took her by the hair but instead of immediately pulling her up by it, he pushed her face into his crotch. "Now, get up and serve me before I make you suck me off in the daylight!"

She wanted to pass out, but Hild…she wanted to scream and defy him, but she had no choice. She didn't doubt he would do good on his warning.

She pulled herself up and stepped, a little dizzily, around him and went to the fire where the food was. It was a pot with what appeared to be game and vegetables cut up and cooking over a separate fire.

"Be glad it was not Leofric who took a fancy to you," a young man said, appearing close to her. "He is not called Leofric the Merciless for no reason."

"God help me."

The boy looked up. "Mayhap He sent me to do just that. 'Twas I who has done most of the work. Just add some herbs and water while it cooks—"

"Alric, leave her to her duty," Aethelwold called out. "You are relieved."

"I was simply giving her instructions," Alric said, sounding insulted.

"She will find her own way."

Alric spun on his heel. "You would have her destroy my recipe? 'Tis your palette I worry about, Aethelwold. You know how certain dishes upset your middle."

Aethelwold waved away his concerns and stopped arguing with him, finding amusement in something someone else said.

"Just get on with it," he finally shouted, waking Hild. "I am hungry!"

"I will take care of her while you serve," young Alric offered. He was at least fifteen, so old enough to watch a four-year-old girl. Besides, if he was old enough to cook, he was old enough to babysit.

"Her name is Hild," she told him, accepting his offer. But she wanted to make Hild a real person to him, in the hopes that he wouldn't hurt her or let anyone else do so. "The Danes killed her father, and a bear recently killed her mother. I intend to protect her."

She watched him hurry to Hild and sit beside her. He didn't push his comfort or affection on her, but simply sat there.

Though she felt numb more than anything else, she thought young Alric quite adorable. He was slender, dressed in what looked to be sewn together rags and thin shoes. His wind-burned cheeks were round and red beneath eyes that shone like coffee under the bright lights of Starbucks. She nearly sighed.

Alric looked at her now through a spray of dark curls, then lifted his hand in a pouring gesture.

She snapped to attention, remembering to pour water into the pot. She took hold of a ladle and dipped it into another pot of water. The water seared hitting the stew pot. She knew enough to pour more in.

She finally got it under control and poured whatever else Alric left for her into the pot. There were chopped up leaves. She dumped them in as well. She wished she knew what upset Aethelwold's stomach. She'd put in a double helping.

He'd hit her hard. Her head still hurt, so did her jaw. Piece of garbage. She'd like to poison him. She looked to where he'd been sitting. He was no longer there.

Before she had time to turn, he grabbed a fistful of her hair from behind and yanked her head back.

"I do not like something about the look of you," he growled into her ear, making her cringe and want to scream. "You look down your haughty nose at us."

"A flea would have to look down its nose to see you."

He snaked his arm around her waist and yanked her in. He kissed her neck and cupped her breast with his hand and then squeezed.

"Stop it!" she commanded. Her terrified gaze found Hild's just before young Alric thankfully pulled her away so she could not see.

Aethelwold chuckled at her throat. He was still behind her. "I like your saucy mouth. I'm going to tame you so that you—"

He released his hold on her! Just like that? She was free! She reached for the handle of the pot to fling at him and turned to see Wolf holding him pressed against a tree. Wolf!

Rage burned like heated metal in his eyes as they stared into Aethelwold's.

"My brother is going to hunt you down and kill you all," Aethelwold promised as Wolf drew his knife and without taking his eyes off the man, cut Aethelwold's throat in one quick slash.

Camelee was so glad to see Wolf that she put the blood and violence behind her. This was how these men lived. Aethelwold knew that when he attacked Wolf's camp. She went to him and flung her arms around his neck and held on.

He did nothing to break free. She was gl—Hild!

"Hild! We have to get her," she clutched his cloak. "She's with Alric. Don't hurt him!"

He looked confused but nodded. "Find the girl!" he ordered into the air. Or so Camelee had thought but in another instant the forest around them came alive with fearsome Danes. They were the men Wolf had taken with him today. They appeared out of everywhere, swords and spears held up and ready to swing.

"Kill every one of them," he growled and eyed the bruise on her jaw. "Find the little girl and bring the Saxon who is with her to me. Alive! They are the only two who shall live!"

Camelee's blood ran cold. This was why Wolf was respected as chief. Because he could do the necessary thing when the situation called for it, as it did in this century.

"How is Genevra?" she asked him when he pulled her away from the fighting.

"Genevra?"

"One of them hit her and…" her voice drifted off at his lost expression. "You haven't been back to the camp."

"They took you from camp?" he asked her, his eyes moving over her. He lifted his fingers to her jaw but did not touch her. "How badly are you hurt?"

"Not bad." She smiled to convince him. "How did you find me?"

"I happened upon this camp and when I came closer to consider it, I saw the Saxons. I saw you." He stopped for a moment seeming too angry to go on. Then he finally did. "I suspected they attacked the camp." His gaze peered into her soul. "What happened? Fin?"

"I didn't see Fin, but…Akkar. They killed Akkar."

Wolf clenched his hands into fists. "Akkar is dead? But—he just joined us. He left his father…"

"I know. If it helps, he fought valiantly to protect me and Hild. He killed one of them before they killed him from behind."

The hint of a smile hovered around his lips. "It helps more than you know. His father will want to know of his son's courage. We will send him off according to his belief and tradition."

"You aren't going to fight?"

He looked over her head. "They do not need me. I must find my brother."

"I won't leave, Hild."

"The men will bring her back." He gazed at her and let his much-appreciated smile shine on her full force. "Being a mother has its rewards."

"I'm not her mother."

"You are stubborn."

"I accept that," she replied candidly. "But I'm not her mother.

CHAPTER NINE

WOLF WANTED THIS to be over. He'd fought more battles than he could count and would fight dozens more, but seeing Camelee being manhandled and forced to obey the Saxons, while little Hild lay as if dead in the grass was too much for him.

When he'd moved closer to Camelee and he saw her bruised and swelling jaw, it took every ounce of self-control he possessed not to go berserk. Aethelwold knew somehow that she was his—the child, too. That was why he took them. It was like pissing on him.

Well, now he had back what was his. Aethelwold was dead, and Wolf had looked him in the eyes when he killed the man. His men would take care of the rest of them.

Apart from everything else…Camelee had held on to him, relieved to see him. It was thrilling and refreshing, and bold. Whatever it meant, she was happy to be rescued. And he was happy to be the one who'd rescued her.

"Tell me what took place. Why did my men allow you and the child to be taken from me?"

She cast him a questioning look but said nothing about what she was thinking. Instead, she told him about the noises coming from outside the tent and everything after that. She didn't know if Genevra was alive or if Fin was among the dead littering the camp.

By the time they reached the horses, the other men had almost caught up. It hadn't taken them long to finish off the Saxons.

As ordered, his men had found Hild and the dark-haired boy who carried her and brought them back unharmed.

Camelee ran on ahead and tried to take the child, but Hild clung to the boy. When she finally did let Camelee take her, it was only to be carried to Wolf, in whose arms she practically leaped.

Wolf thought it might be hurting Camelee to be rejected, but neither of them said anything, and neither tried to force Hild to go to her.

Alric wasn't pleased about being in the company of the Danes. He barely looked at Wolf and answered his questions with curt responses. Wolf might have to teach him respect, since he was an experienced warrior, desired in any army and many beds. And Alric was a fifteen-year-old cook who could wield a ladle like a master, but that was about all he could do.

"My father was a slave as was his father before him," Alric told them on their way back to the camp. "I wanted to be more than that, so I became a cook."

"You can understand that, can't you, Wolf?" Camelee asked him from her horse.

"I can if you are a Dane," he said with Hild clinging to him. "We do not enslave our own."

"No matter what you are, no one wants to be a slave," she argued.

"Of course not," he agreed. "But if the Saxon army was stronger, I would be the servant. Is that not correct, Alric?"

"Aye, 'tis," the young man confirmed.

"It is going to happen to someone," Wolf continued. "The only question is, will it happen to me or them? I will do whatever I can to ensure it is not me."

She nodded. Could it be that she finally understood the way of his world?

"Survival of the fittest," she said.

"Yes. Precisely." He smiled at her. "You understand much. It would seem our homes are not so different, after all."

"Your home is my home's history. We've tried to learn from it."

"And have they learned?" he asked.

Riding near him, Alric remained silent.

"Some have. Some haven't. I honestly don't know where humanity is headed."

"Well," his grin deepened, "now you do, at least for the next thousand years."

"I don't want to know," she said with resolute determination. "My place is not here. I was meant for something far better in the future."

His humor vanished slowly until he blinked the last remnants of it away. "I see. Then how do we get you home?"

She stared into his eyes and swallowed. So, she knew she had insulted him. Would she make it right?

"I wish I knew," she said, disappointing him. "More than anything I want to go home."

"Of course."

The warmth in her gaze dwindled out. "Why do you sound angry?"

His grin reappeared but, this time, he could feel it straining. "I am not angry. Why should I be angry? Who would not want to go home?"

"I've been kidnapped twice," she reminded him. "I'm living in the middle of a war, with death and destruction at every turn. I've seen two men get killed right in front of me. I've been hit and had my face pushed into…ugh." She swiped a tear from her eye. "I'm the foster-mother of an orphan. And I've only been here two days."

"I understand," he told her softly, doing his best to do just that. If wherever she came from was safer to live than here, he would not stop her from going back. "It has been a full two days. If there is a way to take you home, we will find it."

"You believe me, then?"

"I have no reason not to."

"What does he believe?" Alric nearly burst with curiosity. "Tell me!"

"That I come from the future," she said.

"Oh. Hmm."

Wolf stared at him. That was it? That was his reaction? Nothing at all? It seemed as if he'd heard of it before. Wolf asked him. "Are you familiar with time travel?"

"No," he assured. "But I once knew a man who called himself a *dentist*. He claimed to be from another time. He gave me something called baking soda to brighten my teeth."

Camelee stopped her horse and turned to him with so much hope in her eyes that Wolf was able to ignore the knots tightening in his belly. "What is it?" he asked her.

"A dentist. It's a tooth doctor. Eighteenth century I believe, but no way eleventh."

Wolf stared at Alric as well. "Where can we find this *dentist*?"

"He is only here in the fourth and seventh months," the young man told them.

"Where is he during the other months?" Camelee asked him.

"Last summer, he told me he'd been visiting the fifteenth century, where for the first time he met another traveler. Kestral was her name. He described her so well I could see her in my thoughts."

"And you believe these tales of his?" asked Wolf.

Alric's only response was a flash of his white, toothy smile.

Wolf nodded, accepting it. "The Roman's calendar says we are in the twelfth month. We will not be speaking to him for some time. Maybe there is someone else."

"What's the name of your dentist?" Camelee asked. "Perhaps I've heard of him."

"Roldan Simeon."

"No. That's a name I would remember." She sighed. "We're right back where we started from. Wolf, you still look annoyed at me. Why would you be? Because I want to go home?" she answered before he could. "Do you think yourself so precious that I should be happy to be stranded in your presence?"

"There are worse places to be," he answered in seriousness, but with a slight smile. "With worse people."

"Leofric," Alric supplied. "Aethelwold's brother." He looked up at Wolf with a dark, pitiful gaze. "He will come for you."

"Did he attack my camp?"

When the boy nodded, Wolf snarled. "I hope he does come for me. He killed many of my men." When the boy said nothing else, Wolf set his gaze on Camelee again.

"You really do think I should be grateful?" she asked him.

He nodded. "The chances of me being someone favorable were slim. Most strangers are not to be trusted."

"Some things never change."

"Even you admit then that I am not half-bad."

She smiled and he felt lightheaded. Was this something ordinary that happened to men when a breathtaking woman was in his presence? He'd never felt anything like it. She made him forget his worst days and the worst things, like was Fin dead?

When he had seen that Saxon bastard's hands on her, he'd thought he would go mad with rage. Part of him didn't like what she made him feel. Another part wanted to explore deeper. He wanted to touch her, kiss her, and make certain no other man ever did.

"I never said you were half-bad."

He laughed softly and unwittingly kissed the top of Hild's head.

"What are your plans for me?" Alric questioned, probably thinking this a good time to ask.

"For now, I would like you to watch over Hild when we stop. I wish to share words alone with Camelee."

"Aye, Chief," Alric replied. "Hild can use as many friends as she can get."

"We shall see about friends," Wolf said, letting him know

that he, himself, would decide who Hild's friends were.

"I have heard much about you, Chief," Alric told him. "Most Saxons have."

"Oh?" Wolf glanced at him. "What have you heard, Boy?"

"You speak our native tongue well."

"I have been fighting here for a long time." How long had it been, he thought? Thirteen years? He'd left Denmark the first time when he was sixteen. He went back five years later and began building his longhouse. He became chieftain after defeating three Norwegian raiding parties. King Cnut I had heard about him and drafted him into his army. Danish forces, already used to the bitter cold and wet weather, swept across England like a plague, devasting Mercia and northern England.

He was almost thirty years old now. He wanted to go home. Soon. He hadn't been scouting the land this morning. He was supposed to be meeting Cnut and his men, but Cnut had never left Wessex. Wolf met with the king's emissary, who claimed Cnut was home with his sick wife, Queen Emma. Emma was the widow of Aethelred, the Saxon king before Cnut. Perhaps she was sick of the man who murdered her husband. Still, Cnut had spared her sons with Aethelred. She was grateful.

The king could not travel but would await Wolf at home for Christmas in Wessex. Nothing had changed, save that Wolf was bone weary. He needed sleep, not a woman and a child, and now a boy in his care. Why was he allowing this? It was his fault. He was taken with a slave! Hild was easy to take under his care. He didn't even have to think about it. But why Alric? Why another soul in need of a happy home life?

He glanced at Camelee and then tilted his head to see her more fully. She was speaking, telling the men a humorous story. Her expressions were full of amusement and the others around her laughed. He looked down and even Hild was watching her from his lap.

He remembered why he'd chosen Camelee. She was full of life and sparks of fire. And like a moth to flame, he was drawn to her. He was a fool. She was a Saxon…or something, but not a Dane. His captive, a servant. And if all that weren't bad enough, she was mad. Wasn't she?

"Some say you are immortal," Alric said from beside him. Wolf had forgotten he was there. "But no one is. Leofric said he was going to prove it by cutting out your heart."

"I do not have a heart," Wolf let him know. "He will find that out."

"Look!"

He followed Alric's finger, looking west toward the camp. Dark smoke rose to the clouds. Fire!

He rode to Camelee and handed Hild to her. "Stay here!" he ordered them and then sped away with his men thundering behind him.

Fin! Was his brother alive? The rest of his men? Aethelwold had done this. Wolf was glad he'd killed the Saxon. He would find Leofric and end him.

He rode hard, reaching the smoky outskirts of the camp, turning on his mount to his men. He pointed right to some, left to the rest. They were too late though. Dead men littered the ground. His men. Some were Saxon, but most were his men. He moved slowly on his horse, gazing through tendrils of smoke at the massacre. The Saxons must have come upon them unaware. Still, the men could have taken the Saxons after gaining their wits. There were more men with Leofric. They had left with him. He would find them.

For now, it looked as if all of them were dead. Was his brother among them? Wolf had left him in charge. He was to lead the men. If he wasn't here among the dead, what did it mean?

"Find anyone alive. If they are ours, bring me to them. Go!" he barked his orders, and his twenty men did as he commanded. He heard a woman's voice. He raked his burning eyes over the bodies. No women.

"Chief!" she called out to him.

"Chief!" one of his men called. "There's a woman—"

"I know. Bring her to—"

"Oh, Chief, I never thought I would say this, but thank God you are here."

Genevra! "Genevra!" He rode his horse to her and dismounted when he reached her. "What happened here?"

"Like I told your commander—"

"Fin? Blond? Nasty?"

She smiled, then coughed, holding her hand over her mouth. "That would be him."

"Then he is alive?"

"Aye. He was not here when the Saxons attacked."

"Not here?" A chill pierced Wolf's heart at the news. "Where was he and where is he now?"

"He was with her." She pointed to a pretty girl with sooty cheeks. She was going through the fallen men's clothes.

Wolf's blood boiled. He released his bow from over his furry shoulder and pulled an arrow from his quiver. "You!" he shouted, nocking the arrow. She looked up from the burned coat of one of his men. "Move away from my men or I will put this arrow through your neck."

She paled and rubbed her throat and stepped away.

"Where were you while this was happening?"

"In my bed. Why? Do you think I had something to do with this?"

"I had not considered you a suspect," he told her with his voice practiced and as sharp as the finest blade. "You protest before I accuse. Come around this way. I have some questions to put to you."

"He was anguished," Genevra told him about Fin. It was a bit shocking to hear. "He left to go find Camelee." Fresh tears filled her eyes. Wolf could see that she'd been weeping by the stripes down her dirty face.

"I found her, Genevra," he reassured her while he looked around. "She and Hild are safe."

"Oh!" She clutched his arm, stopping him. "Thank God! That

is pleasing news to my ears, my lord."

He nodded and gave her a half-smile. Did she care for Camelee and Hild? Well…good. He was glad.

He gave her hand a pat and moved on to the other woman who, it turned out, swore she was with Fin for a better part of the night, though she smiled at Wolf like a hungry feline and licked her lips. She shrugged when he shook his head at her. "He saw the smoke this morn and ran here. He even left me alone."

"I spoke to him after that," said Genevra. "He said to tell you that he went to find her and bring her back. He also said you would not forgive him for this, and he did not want to see that in your eyes."

Wolf stared at her. What? That did not sound like his brother. Maybe the young Fin would have said it, but Fin no longer cared what his brother thought of him. Wolf thought he could be trusted to lead the men. But Fin had been too hard at work in the bed of a woman who robbed the dead to concern himself with the men who were being ambushed and killed.

"Is anyone else alive here?" When Genevra shook her head, he beckoned her to his horse. "Come then, we will return to Camelee and Hild."

"What about your commander? Do you not want to know which way he went, which was obviously the wrong way if he did not find her and you did."

Yes, Wolf thought, unless he had escaped and left Genevra alive to tell him of the noble thing he was doing. Wolf would have scoffed if it didn't prick his heart so much.

"I will find him," he assured her. And he would. But not now. He didn't know what to believe about his brother. Not anymore, and not just recently, but for the last few months. They had grown apart and things had become harder. They had fought about it just last month. Fin knew his brother wanted to return to the north and finish his life there. He was angry about it because he wasn't ready to do the same. But it was time Fin grew up and survived on his own.

If he'd betrayed Wolf in any way, he had better pray to whatever god or gods he prayed to that Wolf did not find him.

The reunion between the women, young and old—or well—older, was pleasing to watch.

At least young Alric thought so—about *him*.

"What?" Wolf demanded, trying to sound firm but quiet after being caught watching her like a lost dog.

"You have a heart, after all." Alric grinned as if he'd just discovered the cure for love. It most certainly felt like an illness.

"The child needs them. It is good to—I like—" It all sounded as if his heart were involved in some way. He was Chief Wolf Kristiansen. He'd just told the brat, Alric, that he didn't have a heart. He—he stopped and ground his teeth, tightening his jaw. "Why am I answering you? Go away before I run you through."

Alric shook his head. "She likes me, and so does Hild, so you will not do that."

Wolf curled his mouth into a snarl. The cold, polished edge of the same blade that killed Aethelwold pressed against the boy's neck before Alric could speak again. Wolf stepped closer, without moving the blade and looked into Alric's eyes. "You risk your life on the belief that I care what either of them thinks."

The boy who thought to stand against him trembled, but his eyes remained steady. "Aye."

Wolf glared at him, but...he was correct. So Wolf left him alone and ordered that they prepare to move out. He didn't let Alric see any trace that he was correct in his assumption. Of course, he wouldn't kill a boy. Threaten him, yes, but not kill him. It showed Wolf, though, how easy it was to recognize that Camelee meant more to him than anything else.

Still, pride could not be allowed to fester. No one was indestructible. He thought of his brother. No matter how much they would disagree, they were still brothers.

CHAPTER TEN

"Y OU DIDN'T RUN away when you had the chance, like the others did," Camelee told Genevra a half-hour later, when they were back on the road behind a small army of men. She thanked God for the millionth time that her friend was safe and alive.

"Where would I go? Who would I care for?" Genevra smiled and looked down at Hild, pressed close to her bosom.

Camelee wasn't jealous. At least the girl's preference for Genevra was a little more understandable. Genevra was motherly. Alric smelled like milk. Maybe that was it.

"I hope our destinies are intertwined," Genevra said, her smile lingering as she set her gaze on Camelee's.

"I don't know if I believe that kind of stuff," Camelee told her, "but if it's possible to be connected to people then I wouldn't mind sharing a destiny with you."

They laughed and then smiled at each other.

What about with Wolf? Would she be willing to share her destiny with him? She let her gaze slip to him riding along the men's flanks. He must have heard them laughing because he looked back.

Their gazes met. She offered him a smile, intact and warmed from someplace deep in her heart. She spared him her glances because there was something different about him compared to the other men she'd met so far. Or from anyone she'd met in the past. Alric was right. He clearly liked her. She knew why he denied it. It didn't make the reason any easier to take. It was because she was a slave.

Ha! He was foolish as well as stubborn if he believed that. She didn't belong to anyone. She didn't care what century she was in, she…her thoughts brought her back to Aethelwold and how dangerous he was. If she hadn't had Wolf in her life, she could have easily been reduced to servitude after he broke her will. She wasn't certain how long she could have lived with him.

It made her see Wolf in a different light. She recognized that she was a psychiatrist's dream, but she didn't care. She would never have given Wolf the chance to see any good in him if she hadn't seen the bad in others. That's just the way it was. She was pampered and spoiled. She might not have ever appreciated this type of guy. Even if this living arrangement wasn't permanent, living in—in the eleventh century—she was happy to have learned from it. Maybe this was all she needed to do in order to go home. Learn something. Well, she did. She closed her eyes and held on to her reins. She was ready.

Wait. Her eyes opened. Was she? What was she going back to? What was the hurry?

She almost laughed out loud. Was she nuts? The hurry was that there were Vikings and Saxons everywhere. She wasn't sure who was more dangerous. Nuts because there were slaves here, no electricity, no phones, nothing!

"Is something wrong?" Wolf's deep voice stole across her ears as he rode closer. "You look troubled."

But the future didn't have him in it.

"No. No. I'm fine. It's just that I don't know why I was sent here." She sounded ridiculous. But she didn't want him to ride away. She liked his company. Maybe she even liked him a little.

"Perhaps," he said with a smile that brightened his compelling eyes and made her want to win his warrior heart. "I am a part of your destiny."

Was it the fathomless, sultry tone of his voice or the possibility that his words were true that made her feel faint? Maybe it was just the way he smiled at her while his hair lifted softly off his shoulders.

"You mean," she managed, fighting his effect on her, "my destiny is to be a slave?"

He didn't take offense at her words or the scathing way she delivered them. He didn't seem to care at all. "You could use some—what is the word the Saxons use?" His smile hadn't changed but what she thought of it did. He was infuriatingly annoying.

"Humility," he said with a wink.

"You are telling me I could use some humility? You? An arrogant marauder?"

"Do I not treat you better than the others?" he asked with incredulousness tainting his smile. "I let you sleep beside my bed and gave you my tent—"

"I sound like your pet dog."

"What would you prefer from me?"

They both seemed to realize what he was saying at the same time. She watched him blink and swallow, as if the truth of him was as unexpected as a summer rain. He'd offered himself up. What would she prefer from him? The possibilities were endless. Umm, how about he appreciate her as a woman, try to see her as an equal? Release all his "slaves"? Help her find her way home and maybe come with her? She wanted to smile thinking of him in New York City. After the initial shock of it, he would like it.

"I would prefer you not speak to me so often."

All traces of humor vanished from his face. "Yes, I would prefer that as well."

He kicked his horse's flanks and flicked his reins. He was gone before she could get out another sentence. What was there left to say? What if she could never return to her life in the twenty-first century? What if this was it? She needed him! But she didn't want to be his servant. Better his than a man like Aethelwold or Leofric, but still a servant.

"You are perplexed about him."

Camelee looked to her left and blushed at Genevra. She had forgotten that she was there, on the other side of him.

"Yes. He does perplex me," she confessed. "He's a nice guy…for a murdering Viking. But I really need to concentrate on finding a way to get home."

"To your future?" the older woman asked, her silvery-blue eyes wide with curiosity and apprehension.

"Yes," Camelee said. "Who told you?"

Genevra's deepening smile radiated with affection. "Alric. But do not be angry with him. It is not easy to keep something like this a secret. He believes you wholeheartedly."

Camelee didn't understand why knowing that comforted her. It was important to be believed. These people had nothing to go on about her. She was different, more likely *not* to be trusted. But Alric…and Wolf believed her.

She wouldn't ask Genevra if she believed her.

"Tell me of it," Genevra said as they rode.

She would be easy to convince. "I live on an island called Manhattan," Camelee began. "It's not too big but almost two million people live on it."

"What is million?"

Camelee smiled and explained the number.

"How do they all fit?" Genevra wanted to know, leaning in toward her in the saddle.

"Their dwellings are all piled atop one another in neat, sometimes quite beautiful buildings reaching toward the clouds."

"How can that be?"

The wonder and amazement in Genevra's expressions made Camelee want to tell her everything.

And she did, for the next four hours, until they reached their destination, a large, fortified fort. There were Danes watching them from their posts on the wooden battlements surrounding the fort.

Wolf called something out in his Norse language and the

thick wooden doors, made of carved branches and thick ropes, were pulled open.

They were allowed passage into the bailey. The reality of everything hit her. It hit her hard. The stench would remain emblazoned in her memory for her life. "What is it?" she asked, holding her hand over her nose.

"The stream runs through here," Alric told her, riding up beside her. "They dump their waste in it."

She gagged. A giant pig strolled in front of her horse and made the beast rear up. She tried to hold on to the reins, the saddle, anything. But she fell to the ground, into the dirt, and whatever else was at the bottom of people's shoes. Oh no, she could never stay here.

She sucked in a breath when a strong arm came around her middle and lifted her through the air…and into his lap.

"Are you injured?" Wolf asked, searching her eyes.

"Just my pride…and my butt." She glanced at him from beneath a long spray of dark lashes and laughed a little.

"I could see to it," he offered with a provocative smile that curled her toes.

She ignored his advance and shifted a bit. His thighs were like sitting on two thick metal poles. "I don't feel secure or safe—"

He pulled her closer. She was sitting with both of her legs hanging over the left side. He slipped his hand beneath her right thigh and flipped it over the other side. She had to admit it was more comfortable and balanced this way.

Chickens squawked as they rushed out of the way.

Camelee looked around. There were various fires burning throughout the courtyard and people standing around them or working at the scattered tents, housing a smith, a tanner, one tent selling wares and another selling fabrics. There was a man pulling a wagon with long loaves of bread hanging over the sides and a variety of different loaves filling the middle.

Flies gathered around discarded food—or who knows what.

"Wolf," she groaned. "I can't stay here."

"You will do fine, Camelee," he tried to reassure her. "I will help if I can, but you must prepare if there is no way back for you."

"No, I can't believe that. I can't stay here," she cried. "Look at this place! It's disgusting and inconvenient."

"Denmark is nicer," he told her with a thread of pride straightening his shoulders. "We bathe once a week."

She groaned louder. "I have to get home."

"Yes, Camelee, you have made that clear. You know, I do not have to let you go."

She turned in his lap to glare at him. She didn't care if she fell. Was he really going to start up with this nonsense? "I thought we established that I am not *yours*. I do not belong to anyone."

"You are mine, Camelee," he said.

It was all he said. He stared into her eyes while he said it like some kind of beautiful wizard who could hypnotize her with the power of his gaze. Possession and…playfulness blended in his voice and it felt like a love potion seeping through her skin when he spoke. She wanted to refute his declaration, but she couldn't form the words. In that moment, she wanted to belong to him in the most possessive way. Sitting against him, she could feel that he was fit.

Images of him naked and in her bed invaded her thoughts. She tried to remember to breathe. She reached for her throat and looked away from him, severing their gazes. As soon as she did, the spell was broken.

"Think what you want," she brooded, folding her arms across her chest. "You and your archaic ideas, which have been at least suppressed in the men of my day. They may still think we belong to them like servants, but we—"

"What is archaic?" he asked her.

She almost made the mistake of turning again to stare at him for cutting her off. But she wouldn't make that mistake again. "Prehistoric. Old fashioned."

He shook his head. He didn't know those words either. And

he didn't seem to care. "Tell me about the men of your day."

She opened her mouth, but nothing came out. "I don't know much about men," she admitted. "Everyone around me, men and women, mostly men, have always been fake. No one really knew me. They just wanted to be around the star of a hit cable series. Most guys wanted to be with my character. When they found out that I wasn't *Illissa D'Angelo*, they left. I had never cared. I'd never wanted any of them to stick around after a date or two."

"Why would they want you to be someone else?" he asked from behind her.

She smiled, forgetting why she'd been angry with him a moment ago.

"They do not sound better than me, Camelee," he told her. "Why do you prefer them over me?"

"I don't," she replied quickly. "I mean, I don't like them either, but at least I can get away from them if—"

"You wish to get away from me?" He sounded a bit hurt or insulted.

"Where would I go?"

"That is not an answer."

She turned her head to look at him over her shoulder. It was a terrible mistake, not because the sight of him robbed her of her senses, but because his eyes, gazing down on her, were so intent. Was her reply so important to him? Why would it be?

"If I must be here," she told him, resting her chin against her shoulder. She knew how to flirt. She apparently didn't know her own mind though, or why she was flirting with him. "I would prefer to be with you."

She didn't expect his face to light up like a kid who'd just found a puppy under the Christmas tree. Vague feelings of regret over missing Christmas in New York were vanquished by the radiant smile of the man who imagined he could tame her, dominate her, make her his. She hated her traitorous heart for actually liking the idea of it, especially in this world.

No. She almost laughed. Let him imagine it. For now, in this cold, horrible era, she needed him to live.

"That doesn't mean I want to be your servant," she let him know, veiling her gaze behind curtains of lashes. She dared not look up because when she did, she wanted to lick his beguiling lips and fall at his feet—if they were walking.

He was quiet, which piqued her curiosity—and paranoia. Was it because of what she said? Or because they were entering the inner yard? She realized it was both when he coiled his arm around her and lifted her out of the saddle and safely to the ground.

"Do not run," he warned and straightened in his saddle. And kept riding.

Oh, she wanted to kill him! He couldn't let his king possibly see him with a slave pressed to his chest. Her head was still spinning at the speed and fluidity he used to get her away from him! She wanted to stomp her foot, kick something, maybe even have a cigarette. Another little light dwindled out inside her. No more smoking, even though she only smoked a pack every two months. No more vaping. No more coffee. No more burgers or diet soda, not including *everything* else! What would she do all day in a place like this? Clean and cook and wait for her husband *or master* to come home so they could make love under his fur blankets, or in the green fields under the stars in the summer.

Danes were practicing everywhere she looked. There were smaller huts and large tents scattered throughout the vast yard. Many were decorated with holly branches over the doorway. There was a tower and a church, also decorated with a wreath, and the main keep, built not only of wood, but of stone. The beginnings of castles, she thought with a chill creeping along her spine.

By the time she reached the regiment of men welcoming Wolf, he was already off his horse and speaking with three men in the lead. One, in particular, commanded respect and honor with his straight, wide shoulders clad in white fur. His hair was pale blond and braided down his back. She couldn't hear what they were saying, not that she could understand them, and when she moved to go toward them, two warriors blocked her path, swords at the ready.

She looked at Alric and Genevra, walking toward her with Hild holding Genevra's hand. What would become of them?

"What should we do?" she asked them when they reached her.

"We are Saxons," Alric reminded her. "They will not believe your story. You are Saxon."

"I could be French," she tried, which brought a smile to his face.

She took his hand to walk inside with him, but he pulled free.

"I have been traveling with Leofric and his brother for some time. Leofric is a formidable warrior and does not go into battle blindly. Remember, he took out half of the chief's army."

"The half without the chief in it," she interjected.

He nodded, giving her the point, then continued. "He learned a few things about his enemy, and I overheard most of it. The Danes see affection as weakness. They will use it against us."

She thought of how Wolf sought to hide his—was it affection for her? He practically threw her off his horse. He even sought to hide it from his men—especially Fin. A chill ran through her. His protection was limited.

"You two!" a man shouted at them.

Camelee's heart thumped so hard she was afraid for a second that it had stopped, and she was seconds away from passing out.

Genevra turned to the man. Camelee did the same. One of the king's soldiers stood behind them. He wore a metal helmet with a piece coming down his nose, a chain mail vest, and a fur-lined cape.

"Chief Kristiansen says you are to come with me," he said to Camelee. "You, your child, and your mother."

Camelee's blood ran like liquid fire through her. Her mother. Her child. No. No. She felt a rush of panic explode within her. She didn't want this. This…this…losing this would end her. She had to keep these emotions locked away. She wasn't loved enough. She couldn't love enough.

"And—" She kept herself from holding on to Alric for support. She stayed up by her sheer force of will. "And my brother."

"The chief did not mention a brother."

"Well, I am mentioning him. We will not leave without him." She knew what Alric had told her about showing affection, but she didn't care. She wasn't a coward like Wolf.

"I do not want to go with them," Alric said, shocking her. "All they do is nag. Take them, I beg you, and give me peace."

The little piece of – oh, he was clever. In her pride, she'd made him a target and he just repaired that. Now, only she appeared to be the weak one.

She looked at Alric. He could take care of himself. He'd already proven that by surviving with Aethelwold and Leofric.

Okay, then. She turned away and followed the man to the rear of the keep and a stairway that led to a two-room chamber off the kitchen. Chambers all to themselves. With one bed.

Leaving them inside, the soldier slammed the heavy wood door shut. The key turned. The lock echoed through the rooms, sealing them inside.

Camelee held her hand over her mouth to keep from screaming.

◆··• •··◆

CHAPTER ELEVEN

"CAMELEE, DEAREST?"

It was Genevra.

Camelee pulled away. Genevra was a stranger, not her mother. She couldn't play this role. She wasn't a daughter, a mother. She would never forgive Wolf for forcing all this on her. She didn't want to be here. She wanted to go home to her fans and Karen, and coffee.

"We must live the life we are given," the older woman said.

"For what?" Camelee argued. "To have it all ripped away from you because of a stupid brooch?"

She didn't realize tears were streaming down her face. She had to have gone mad. She had never cried so much in her life.

"What else is there to do? Give up?" Genevra shook her head. "I will not, and neither will you."

"You can't make me fight," Camelee challenged, but was she sure? When servants ushered in an array of food and left it on the table, she wanted to eat.

"Mayhap not me," Genevra told her and brought Hild to the table to eat.

Maybe not her, Camelee thought and stepped forward to stop the little girl. She took her by the hand and brought her to the basin filled with water and helped her wash her hands first.

Of course, Hild fought against it at first, but Camelee urged her gently and with patience, understanding that the babe didn't know any better.

When Hild was clean, Camelee let her sit and eat. She smiled back at Genevra and sat beside her to eat. Yes. She would fight. She wouldn't give up. But she wasn't Hild's mother.

"Alric."

Genevra nodded and offered her a worried look. "You must speak to the chief."

Yes. He might find Alric and bring him here if she asked. She knew it. She wouldn't pretend otherwise. If she asked, he would do it.

"Yes. I will ask him." She dipped her gaze to Hild eating and smiled with satisfaction. She looked up and caught Genevra smiling with the same satisfaction. They had the little girl in common. Even if Camelee didn't want a child, she had one. And she had Genevra to help her.

"I know you told me," Camelee said, "but help me understand why you have never taken a husband."

"My heart would not let me love someone else," Genevra told her while cutting small pieces of dried meat for the girl.

"Someone else implies there was an original." Camelee didn't know why she was asking. But her breakdown was over. She had to take care of Hild.

"I do not know who he is," Genevra said, sounding sincere. "I have never loved a man that way. 'Tis as if my heart has been reserved for another. I feel my emotions beyond the veil, but it isn't me who must release them."

Camelee wanted to weep for them. Perhaps they were all mad.

"What about you?" Genevra asked. "Why have you not taken a husband?"

"No time," Camelee said with a small laugh. "They are better off, trust me. My standards are too high and, most of all, the thought of love repulses me."

"So, like me, you have never loved a man before."

"Man or woman in a romantic way," Camelee verified.

"Right."

"Our lives do indeed seem to be intertwined."

"Well, not really," Camelee corrected her. "You can't love because some special guy has to come and unlock your heart. Whereas I can't love because my heart has been broken beyond repair."

"It is not too late, Camelee. If you love or care for Hild, it is not too late."

Camelee would have liked to have thought on it more, but the locked clicked and the door creaked open.

Wolf's handsome face appeared on the other side of the door as it opened fully. His shoulders filled the doorway. She wanted to get up and run to him, to feel safe. But he didn't deserve her affections. He was ashamed of his feelings for her. He—

"Are the lodgings fitting?" he asked upon entering. He smiled at her and then at the table of food.

Better now that you're here.

Camelee blinked and then blushed at her thoughts. Was she serious? Really? She was developing attachments to a thousand-year-old man?

"Your kindness is greater than I could have imagined," Genevra sang. Hild smiled at him!

It made Camelee want to cry. Why here? Why now? If she stayed with him any longer…she felt as if she were choking. She couldn't, she wouldn't let herself fall in love with him.

Since Genevra had already said something, she assumed she had to say something, too. She didn't want to throw flattery at him. Sure, he treated them better than some of these other eleventh-century men, but she was still his servant.

Nevertheless, she didn't want him to think her an ungrateful brat. She understood that what he'd done for her already was probably dangerous. The Danes—even the king—would think she was his weakness. Was she?

She looked up at him, and as if he could feel her eyes on him, his gaze slipped to hers.

"Thank you—my lord."

He grinned and raised a sexy brow. "I will see that another bed is brought in."

"Don't go to the trouble," she said and turned to smile at Genevra. "I don't mind sharing a bed with them."

"A bed for me," he clarified in his rumbly low voice when she turned back to him.

"Oh." She forgot to breathe. "You really don't have to." She wanted him to.

"I do," he told her. "There are some here who do not know what I would do to them if they went near you—any of you. All it takes is a few moments for them to hurt you. With me here, I will simply kill anyone who comes through that door at night."

She appreciated why he was staying, but – "You will *simply kill…?*"

He nodded and picked at the bread. "That's correct. You are mine. I have every right to protect you."

She softened her voice, though she wanted to kick him in the kneecaps. "I am grateful that you want to protect us. It's just difficult for me to accept this nonchalance when it comes to taking another life. I understand that as a soldier you obey orders and kill or die, but it's not the last resort here. It's the first defense."

"What would you have me say? That I will leave you on your own? I will not."

She sighed. "Never mind it for now. There is something else I need to ask you."

"What is it?"

"We would like it if Alric was here with us. The guard wouldn't bring him and then Alric started acting like he was fine when he wasn't and—"

He held up his index finger, went to the door, and opened it. His voice was clear and full of authority when he called out orders to the nearest guard to send out men to find Alric.

He shut the door and returned his attention to her. He began to frown and Camelee pondered how anyone could look so good when he was sulking. "You said Alric was *acting*. Is that like pretending, and is that not what you said you do?" His frown grew darker. "So, you pretend you are well when you are not?"

Camelee did some scowling of her own. Oh, now he understands. "It's not the same."

"What is different about it?"

"I pretend to be someone else entirely—" *Usually someone happy and confident.* Her eyes suddenly burned with a rush of hot tears. What? Not now! Oh, what was wrong with her? Why was she so emotional? She turned to look away from him and her gaze fell on Genevra and Hild. Mother. Daughter. She trembled and squeezed her eyes shut to hold it all back.

He didn't try to comfort her—or if he did, he was too late.

"Come and sit, dearest," Genevra comforted at her ear, at her side almost instantly.

Camelee choked on a sob while the older woman helped her to the bed and sat her on the edge of it. She pretended. Her whole life, she pretended.

"I am fine, Genevra," she tried to reassure her. "I'm just a little tired."

When she felt able, she turned to see Wolf pouring some water into a cup. He was the facilitator of it all. It all started with him. Besides, of course, being flung back in time a thousand years, he was the reason she began thinking about husbands and children and mothers…and love.

He came toward her and held out the cup.

She took it, wondering if this was normal behavior for a slave-master relationship.

Hild called to Genevra, and the older woman hurried to her.

"Are you well?" he asked, his voice deep and tender to her ears.

She wasn't sure. "It's been a difficult couple of days."

He nodded. "I will leave you to your bed. I would have you know, there is no need to pretend anymore." He gave her the slightest of smiles and turned to leave.

Insanely, she stopped him with a brush of her fingertips against his hand.

She tried to hold herself together. How could just touching his hand make her want to touch the rest of him?

"How long will we be staying here?" she asked and realized they were alone. Her heart thumped in her ears when he sat at the edge of the bed next to her.

"That depends on the king. But I intend to make my desire known to him."

She tried her best to concentrate on the conversation. It was an important one, but they were sitting on a bed, and she could think of nothing but throwing him down and kissing his boots off. She was having a nervous breakdown. That's what it was. That's how she could be an emotional wreck one minute and passionate for him the next. "What is your desire?"

His gaze pierced through hers and into the deepest recesses of her heart until he found something still burning. "To go home."

"Yes," she said on a breath.

"Tell me everything about how you came here. Maybe we can figure something out."

What? Really? She wanted to hug him, but she didn't dare. She was afraid she wouldn't stop until she had him heaving above, beneath, or behind her.

She told him about Mr. Green and Luke, his bodyguard, the brooch, rubbing it, saying the name Pendragon, and then being here.

"Pendragon?" Genevra asked from the outer room with Hild.

"Yes," Camelee told her, turning to her. "Why?"

"I feel as if I have heard it before."

"It's fictional," Camelee told her. "One of the nannies who raised me read *The Once and Future King* about King Arthur Pendragon and his Round Table Knights. The nannie thought it fascinating that I was named after the king's castle. I studied it all a little further. His wife was Queen Guinevere. Pendrey supposedly is variant form of Pendragon. So, my name could be Camelot Pendragon." She smiled. "It fascinated me. But it ended there. I didn't live in a fairytale."

Wolf covered her hand with his. Her heart felt as if it were melting down to her stomach. How could he not be a complete jerk when he looked the way he did? How could he be a murdering barbarian in battle and a tender protector when he was with her?

"Do you still have the brooch?" Genevra asked her.

"No. It didn't come here with me. Nothing did."

"Do you think Mr. Green is here?"

She looked at Wolf after he asked and felt so fortunate to have found a needle like him in this haystack. Did he trust her instincts so much?

"I don't think he would be here," she told him.

"I will have riders ask around and see if anyone has heard of him, to make certain."

He did so much for her. Was it because, like him, she wanted to go home? It wasn't too much to ask for, was it? "Thank you," she said softly and smiled at him.

Did he appear ruffled? Had his steely resolve just quaked a little—right in front of her? She wanted to stare at him, to watch and see if he came undone if she smiled again. But Hild ran to him and stood before him.

Camelee studied her with her smile growing. She was a cute kid when she wasn't being pitiful. Her eyes were wide and usually haunted, but now they were curious and joyful. She said nothing for an eternal moment and then placed her little hand on his much larger one.

"Uf."

He chuckled lightly and turned to Camelee and whispered, "Is she barking at me?"

Camelee laughed and poked him in the side. "She's saying your name, Silly. Watch the way her nose crinkles after she says it, like someone shook the pepper too close."

His grin remained as he spread his warm gaze over her face, looking at her as if he knew something she didn't.

"Hild," she said, to show him. "Who is this?"

"Uf!" the child exclaimed, lifting off her feet with her expelled breath. A half an instant later, her small nothing-of-a-nose wrinkled at him.

He laughed and took her hand. "What can I do for you, Hild?"

"Uf go outside?"

He looked at Camelee and then at Genevra. "Are you two up for it? I want to keep us all together until I find guards I trust to keep watch over your door."

Genevra agreed to go outside. Camelee would love a hot bubble bath but, oh well. "Of course. Sounds fun!"

They stepped out the door with Wolf going first. No one bothered them or even looked their way. Their gazes were affixed to Wolf's. Some of them wanted to ask him questions about secret southern routes, and northern boats waiting along the shorelines.

But if anyone thought they could leave against the king's orders, they were mistaken. And Wolf told them so. He promised to personally hunt down and kill any deserters.

"How about sharing those three beauties, my lord?" someone called out from a group of men.

Without hesitation, Wolf reached over his shoulder and pulled an arrow from his quiver and his bow from its tether. "Cover her eyes," he warned quietly, aimed and shot. The arrow landed in a man's chest and felled him to the ground. "Does anyone else want me to share?"

Camelee stood staring at him, horrified after he killed one of the king's men for asking a question. Granted it was a vile question, but—

When she didn't move quickly enough for him, he snatched her wrist and pulled her away.

"Do as I wish in public, Camelee," he warned her.

"All right. In public, I will. But alone, I will fight you every step of the way! I mean, you just killed someone for asking a disgusting question, and right in front of Hild!"

"Good. Let her know, too, that I will not stand for any insult or threat against her or her m—friend. As for killing someone," he bit out at her, "if he thought about having his way with any of you, he would do it. He would always be a threat to you, to Genevra…and to little Hild. No. I could not allow it. And now the rest of the men know it."

"But I thought you didn't want anyone to know that you cared."

"Possession and caring are two separate things, Camelee."

She lowered her gaze and walked behind him. What could she say? For now, she was tired of fighting.

He stopped and turned to look at her with the slightest, most handsome smile. "What are you doing back there? Come, and walk with me."

CHAPTER TWELVE

THE NEXT FEW days went by with Camelee growing more miserable. She didn't have to tell Wolf how she felt. He could see it in her eyes, or the faraway look in them every so often when she was washing a dish or serving a meal. The bustle of the keep, with cooks and tanners, and seamstresses, and dozens more, all preparing for Christmas swiftly approaching only seemed to make her more unhappy. He did what he could to keep her, and Genevra as well, from serving. Hild needed them. No one questioned that a little girl should need her mother and grandmother.

They couldn't find Alric. It was as if he had disappeared.

"Maybe he found that dentist of his," he told her one afternoon while they watched Hild play in the inner yard with some of the Danes' children. Genevra stayed close to the girl, standing a few feet away. Wolf and Camelee stood off to the side.

Camelee gave him a hopeful look. "Oh, do you think so?

He didn't know, but the sting of her wanting to leave wasn't getting any easier. In fact, he hated that she couldn't wait to be away. What truly troubled him though was that he cared about what one of his captives thought. She was a servant, just as Genevra and Hild were servants now. If they didn't learn it from him, they would from some other chief, and life would not be as easy as it was now.

His side had won and took the throne. All Saxons held captive were the property of the warlord who took them. Like it or not, Wolf was master over them, over Camelee.

But he felt it was the other way around. He did whatever she asked, or he promised he would—as if *he* were *her* servant. He wanted to groan at the terrible truth—that he was allowing a woman—a Saxon woman to break through his impenetrable defenses and come to his heart. She circled it, studying it for a way to get in, the tip of her sword dragging along the ground behind her. But he suppressed his anguish and refused to think about the consequences another moment.

"You look upset."

He turned to her. "Upset?"

"Worried. Troubled," she supplied.

She was discerning. A good trait. "I think too much," he told her with a smirk as he kept his gaze on Hild.

"I know what you mean," she said, smiling at something Hild did. "What are you thinking about?"

He ground his teeth. What could he say without sounding like something she hated?

"The coming years…the *future.*"

"What about it?" she asked, and her voice stroked his eardrums and played like a song he wanted to hear for the rest of his life.

"Let us speak of something else."

"No," she protested softly, weakening his resolve. "Why?"

"There does not have to be a reason. When I say something, I do not like to be questioned."

Her head snapped to the right so she could look at him square in the face and let him see the fiery darts ready to shoot from her eyes.

"You want me to hate you, is that it?"

"No." He offered her a confused look. He didn't want that. "I want you to stop—"

"It doesn't matter what era you're in," she spoke over him and rose, ready to leave. "People don't change. You're just like everyone else. Pride and arrogance rule you."

He wanted to fire back, but he had nothing to say that would benefit him. He remained silent while she gathered the child in her arms, said something to Genevra to make her follow, and walked away. He should tell her to wait for him. Her storming off appeared rebellious and troublesome. But if he ordered her about and she disobeyed in the sight of many, he would have to punish her.

When they reached the door to the chambers, she stopped in front of it and turned to him. "Can I have—can Hild, Genevra, and I have a little while without you? Just to change clothes from the wardrobe the queen has provided us without you being in the same space?"

"I always turn my back to all of you—" he defended.

"Yes, but you're still there. You can stay here and guard the door."

He said nothing but stepped around her and entered. He looked around and checked every inch of the place. When he was satisfied that no intruder was waiting for them, he set his gaze on Camelee and left the chambers, closing the door behind him.

In the hall, he settled against the wall and guarded the door.

He gave in easily because he was not altogether prideful and arrogant *like everyone else*. And he would prove it to her.

He smiled at the memory of her surprised look when she realized why he went inside, and when he left. He did not want to make any of the three females feel unsafe because of him.

Was she truly from a thousand years from now? At least she wouldn't be a Saxon. She would be whatever she was. His brow creased at the little he knew about her. He would have to remedy that.

A thought occurred to him, and his belly sank. Did she hate him? Was that why she wanted to be free of him? He had to admit, there was no privacy in the chambers. One morning, Camelee had been slipping out of her clothes. Wolf could see her through a bronze bowl on the table. He remained hypnotized by the silken image of her. A siren, come to lure him away. When they slept in the dead of night, he remained awake, listening to her breathing, falling into the rhythm of it, afraid of what was happening to him.

"My lord," a passing soldier stopped. He then said, "I did not know you were here. I am on my way to speak to the king about your brother."

Wolf snapped to attention. "Fin. What about him?"

"I saw him back in Mercia while I was traveling. He was a prisoner of a Saxon regiment. I came back to tell the king."

"Where in Mercia did you see him?"

"Going toward Warwick."

Wolf's head pounded with every beat of his heart. He needed to know what this soldier would tell the king. But he couldn't leave Camelee and the others alone. There was no one else he trusted to guard them.

"Will you plead with the king to send his men to rescue my brother?"

"I will."

"What did Fin tell you?"

"I did not speak to him. I saw him only. He was with the Saxons. Why else would he be with them if he wasn't their prisoner?"

"Was he bound?"

"Yes. He was bound and tied to a horse. He could barely keep up with the pace and was dragged. He was their prisoner, Sir."

Wolf nodded, controlling the rage bubbling up inside him, twisting his insides. He was going to end those bastard Saxons once and for all. "You must be sure of all these things before you bring a request before the king to send an army out for one man."

"A Kristiansen," the soldier corrected.

"Yes," Wolf agreed. He knew how valuable he and Fin were to any regiment. His men trusted them to keep alive as many of the men as they could. Wolf would give his life for any warrior, and he would kill anyone for those he loved. He looked toward the chamber door. His heart pounded like a quick beating drum. "Go. I need to take care of something here, but be sure to tell the king that if he sends an army, I will lead them."

"Yes, my lord." The soldier hurried off to see the king.

Wolf remained at his post, aching to go rescue his brother. But he had just made a choice when he decided to remain here to go to her one more time instead of running off to save Fin.

When had this happened to him? How had he allowed it with a servant from God only knew where? Not many things in his life frightened him, but this did. This had the power to change him, to make him change his mind about many things before he could stop it. It was like a fever running hot through his veins, searing his nerve endings, and touching her was the only way to find relief.

He knocked softly and opened the door. If not for Camelee and her little family, he would leave now. What was she going to do with them while he was away? How could he keep them from the ravenous beasts around them?

"Camelee?" he called out when he found the small outer, or sitting room, empty.

"Yes?" she called back from the bedroom. "I told you we were changing our clothes."

"Yes, I only want to inform you that I must leave for a short while."

She appeared from around the doorway half-dressed in nothing but a kirtle. Her thick blonde tresses tumbled around her face. His knees hurt. He suddenly felt like a boy, awkward, unsure. Where should he look?

"For how long?"

"A few days."

She dipped her brow and pouted her enticing mouth, drawing his gaze there. "A few days isn't exactly a short time."

"My brother has been captured by the Saxons. I must go."

Her enchantingly blue-gray eyes opened wider. "Oh, no! Of course! Why are you here telling me and not already gone?"

"You are..." He wasn't ready to confess his weakness for her. "...under my protection, under the king's protection. I will go to him before I leave and request that you are all moved to the queen's quarters."

He hadn't asked the king yet, but Cnut owed him something. Wolf had helped him take England. He was still subduing the king's enemies while the king stayed home with his new wife. "I will do my best to be quick."

"I'm sure we'll be fine."

He nodded, feeling a little ill. Why had Fin foolishly gone off alone?

"Where are Genevra and Hild?" He looked over her shoulder, but the child hadn't come out looking for him.

"Resting. Genevra is trying to get Hid to take a nap."

He looked down into her eyes and thought of kissing her. He had the right to. She belonged to him. But he wasn't certain how she would react, so he did nothing.

"Christmas Eve is in three days," she reminded him softly.

Had she wanted to share the festivities with him? He wanted the same thing, and he wanted more.

"Uf." Hild appeared at Camelee's side, her pale blonde curls disheveled around her face. She held up her arms to him.

He truly had to stop picking her up and holding her. He would spoil her. And she was a Saxon after all.

"Uf!" she demanded, crinkling her nose.

He bent and scooped her up.

"Yes, my lady?"

"Me sweep. Aye, Uf?"

She meant to go to sleep in his arms. She'd been doing it since the second night here. The first, she'd spent crying for her mother.

If Fin was a prisoner of the Saxons, then every moment of his captivity brought him closer to death. But Wolf held Hild and did not leave her until she fell asleep. When she did, he handed her over to Camelee and watched while she laid the little girl in bed.

This…this is what he wanted. A family. A woman he came home to after a day of farming and fishing. A wife who took him, after a bath in the stream behind his longhouse, and grew with his child. It made him feel like a drunken fool—a drunken, happy, fool—thinking about it. He wanted to smile at her. Again. It seemed as if all he did now around her was smile. He controlled himself and fought back these useless notions.

His glance slipped to Genevra watching him. She was smiling as if he were as transparent as water. His resolve returned full force. He couldn't let her see his weakness.

"So…uhm…" Camelee straightened and turned to him to find him scowling. "We are to go to the king, you say?"

For a moment, he thought she was going to defy him. He hoped not. He needed to go, and he needed to know she would be safe.

"Yes. To the king. My man, Odger, will be outside the door as soon as I get him. He will be waiting to bring you to him."

"Okay."

Wolf waited. Was that it? She would go without quarrel? He wanted to growl with frustration. Why did she have to be so—he tried to find the correct word but only one reigned over them all. Perfect.

He shifted his gaze to Hild to keep from staring like a lovesick boy.

"I must go," he said softly.

"Wolf?" She stopped his departure with her fingertips along his wrist. Her touch was light, like being touched by rose petals. "Come back. I don't want to be here without you."

Her eyes were like the skies at twilight on these cold December days.

"I will," he replied, and before he knew what he was doing, he dipped his head and pressed his lips to hers. It was a soft peck. It lasted for an instant, for the usually fearless warrior was afraid of whatever was happening between them and of possibly ruining it. He left the room quickly.

CHAPTER THIRTEEN

FIN HAD COME upon the Saxons while they slept. He had thought them careless to leave the fire burning. It had given away their position. He'd looked around the camp hoping to find Camelee and the child. There had been about twenty men, but no sign of her. He'd stood over a man snoring while on his back and cut the man's throat. There hadn't been a sound. He killed six more before the others woke up and began to fight him. When they had, he'd killed four more. He could have killed even more but three of them had come from behind and smashed him in the head with something almost as hard as his skull. He awoke hours or days later. He'd lost track of time after being beaten unconscious so many times.

His wrists were bound behind his back. He was given nothing to eat and a few drops of water and then tied to a horse. If he didn't stay on his feet, he would be dragged. He stayed up. He was beaten almost senseless by the remaining ten men over and over again, until he could hardly walk. But he did. He didn't know how. But he did. Wolf would find a way to keep going. So would he. He would kill these men just as he killed their friends.

When they stopped for the night, he heard them speaking. He knew their language, thanks to Wolf. They considered him a savage, a mindless barbarian. But they feared him. He'd killed half their group by himself.

Then one of them mentioned that he was Wolf Kristiansen's

brother, Fin. Wolf's brother, his family, his weakness.

So they beat him again and then sliced him with the same knives and promised to deliver him over to their generals, Aethelwold and Leofric. Cuts, just deep enough to be painful, but nothing serious. They were saving him to give to their leaders. But first they would make him pay for all their comrades he and his brother had killed.

"I am not finished," Fin promised through swollen lips and a bloody mouth.

The leader, a man who had lived out of the twenty—for now, chuckled and kicked him in the face.

There went his nose again. Bastards. They were going to pay for this.

They left him alone to soak in his blood and plan their demise.

It began in the morning when he called out his need to relieve himself. One of the men was sent to take him inside the trees, away from the camp.

"You have to take it out of the fold in my pants, hold it, and aim," Fin advised the Saxon accompanying him.

"Take what out of where?" the soldier asked, dumb.

"My cock. You—"

"No! No! You can forget it!"

"Make haste!" Fin cried out. "Give me my hands and I will do it myself. Or take out my cock and hold it steady."

"What do I care if you piss your breeches?"

"I have to shyte, too," Fin let him know. "I do not think you want that stench around the camp. Your men will abandon you."

With a taut jaw and a strangled oath, the Saxon spun him around and untied the ropes securing his wrists.

On the other side of him, a merciless light shot through Fin eyes, and he smiled. He turned around, and fighting a wave of dizziness, he snatched one of the knives on the Saxon's belt. He flipped it in his hand before his enemy had time to swing his sword and plunged the blade into the soldier's guts, cutting him wide open. Nine men left. He reached down and took the Saxon's sword. Now he was armed.

He was going to have to move quickly. He wasn't sure he could. He was certain a few of his ribs were broken, for he knew the feeling well. It pained him to breathe. He was cut and bruised everywhere on his body. If he turned too quickly, it made him lightheaded and unbalanced. His belly felt a little ill, too. But he was fighting to save his life. He couldn't be slow. He was going to lose the element of surprise after he killed the first man.

Just inside the tree line, he watched the men move about. Three to the left, four on the right, two on the other side of the camp. He would have preferred the least number to be closest and the four men be farthest away, but it was better to get the most difficult over with first.

He went to the right and moved out of the trees like a breeze on the pine-scented air.

One hefty swing that snatched the breath right out of him removed the head of one. No time to refill his lungs, for the other three were beginning to react. He brought the blade around, angled his arms and wrists, and jammed the blade into another man's neck. It came out on the other side and flashed crimson in the sun. He didn't have time to pull it back before someone else swung his sword. Fin ducked low to avoid losing his head. He closed his eyes and swallowed, hoping for his balance when he opened his eyes again. He was thankful that Wolf had made him practice from a young age and hadn't shown him mercy. He came back up, closer to his opponent and punched him in the chin. He heard a crack and watched yet another man crumble to the ground.

Someone hit him from behind. He shook his head to keep from passing out.

But he felt himself going. He was too weak to stand.

Someone screamed behind him. He turned and fell to his knees. He saw his brother yank his heavy blade out of a Saxon's skull. Fin fought to stay awake to watch Wolf kill the remaining

Saxons like a beast with no soul.

When he was finished, it took him a few moments to stop chopping and gather his wits.

When he did, he hurried to Fin's side. "Brother! Bring me water!" he shouted to someone. The men. The other half of their regiment was there, looking concerned over Fin since there was nothing else to do and no one left to fight.

"Wolf," he managed. "The Saxons have…Camelee."

"No. I have her," his brother corrected.

Fin opened his eyes and tried to see without everything being blurry. "You?" Was this truly Wolf. Yes. No one fought like his brother. Not even him. "That is good news."

"It is." Wolf smiled. "You look as happy as if I just told you there were three more wars to fight."

Fin chuckled softly and closed his eyes. "I am happy you are reunited with her. My neck is saved."

"Well," his brother said while Fin drank from the skin Wolf offered him. "We shall see about that. We will speak about where you were when the Saxons came. Can you rise?"

Fin tried and almost went down gain, but Wolf held him up and helped him to his horse. "You will ride back with me. You are too weak to sit in the saddle alone."

Fin didn't argue with him on any of it. He had been about to die at the hands of the Saxons. His brother saved his life, just as he had many other times before. What would become of Fin when Wolf returned to Denmark?

"Get him a blanket!" his brother called out. "What happened to the buttons on your jacket?"

"The Saxons cut them off." Fin looked down at the jacket. The one Genevra had given him. He thought of her. True to his nature, when he'd first considered her, he thought of her countenance, but, in truth, he liked her motherly nature. He'd never had a mother.

"And Genevra?" he asked Wolf. "Is she with you, as well?"

"Yes. She gave me the message you left with her."

"I see." Fin wondered what she'd told his brother, anyway. But he wouldn't ask. He didn't have enough breath in him.

After a moment of rest, he turned slightly to his brother. "Once they realized who I was, they wanted to bring me to two chiefs, Aethelwold and Leofric."

"The first is already dead," Wolf informed him. "He had Camelee. I killed him. Leofric will come to me I am told."

"I will be at your side."

"I know, Brother."

"Do you?" Fin put to him. "Did you doubt me when you discovered I was gone but not dead?"

"Yes," Wolf told him candidly. "We have grown apart."

"That does not mean I would betray you," Fin replied, insulted and brooding.

"You are correct, Fin. Forgive me, Brother. You see? I am not this superior being you have created in your thoughts."

"You saved me today."

"God's intervention. I had no way of knowing where you were."

"Which god, Brother?"

"The One." He pointed up and smiled at Fin.

"Thank Him for me, will you, Wolf."

"You just did, Fin."

CAMELEE KNELT OVER a patch of brown grass in the snow-dusted field. Her belly ached and her heart, as well, as memories of Wolf rocking Hild to sleep filled her head and drove her mad. Was this why she'd never met anyone in the future? Because she wouldn't be staying there in the twenty-first century, and it would have been worse to lose a man like Wolf than to never have him at all? Did that mean she was stuck here for the rest of her life? Would Wolf take her home and get her pregnant and then dump her the first chance he got? She'd said he was like the others. But he wasn't. Did she want a future with him?

She couldn't give up the hope of returning to her own future. But she was and that was why she was in the position she found herself in right now.

But she would never ever forget the fierce Viking warrior putting the need of a little orphan girl before his own brother. While many at home might think him ruthless and disloyal to his family, she found him admirable and honorable to the innocent.

And it was so very attractive.

But there couldn't be anything romantic between them because if she were given a chance to go home, she would take it.

Home to what?

Um…prime-time dramas, pain killers, coffee, cell phones, electricity, down comforters, a solid roof over her head? She'd refuse all that for some guy. Right.

She stood up and thought of Karen, her "assistant". Camelee treated her more like a servant. In fact, most of the people around her behaved like her servants. Had she ever told them to stop waiting on her hand and foot?

No.

She bent over again.

"Woman," Ivar, one of Wolf's men, called out. He'd escorted her when she left the king's guest chamber. "What is your trouble?"

"Self-loathing, Ivar…and where did you say Odger was?"

"Seeing to his wife."

"Well," she smiled reassuringly. "Don't be afraid. I'm well."

"Return to your chambers then."

Yes. It was too cold for her down jacket. "Sorry. I wasn't thinking when I came out into the cold." She went toward him but instead of letting her pass, he hooked his arm around her waist and pulled her in with her back against his chest and her backside against his groin.

For a moment, Camelee was too stunned to move. She

should have been prepared for this! She tried to fight back, but it seemed to excite him further when she did. He tore her jacket and the sweater she'd had from home, washed by her own hands, and dried in the sun this morning. She thought it strange that she would think about her stupid sweater or the jacket her mother picked out at Macy's last month while on one of mother's rare trips back home to NYC. They'd gotten together the day after Thanksgiving for lunch and a bit of shopping. Then Claire Pendrey was gone again.

It wasn't that she had some important job to save the world that made her miss Camelee's life. It was parties and playtime with the rich. Her mother was a socialite and nothing more.

Genevra liked the jacket. She said it brought Wolf's eyes down to Camelee's butt often. She and Genevra had shared more than a few furtive giggles about it when Wolf was here.

Wolf. She wished he was here now. "Wolllllllffffff!" she screamed because she needed to. She was going out of her mind thinking about sweaters and her mother now.

Ivar reeled back and smacked her in the temple. She swayed in his arm, locked around her waist. She prayed that she wouldn't pass out. She felt him shove his hand under her torn sweater. When he felt her bra, he groaned behind her as if she'd worn the thing just to keep him from her. She wished it could have done such a thing. He grabbed hold of it between her breasts and pulled as hard as he could. It snapped and tore away.

She screamed and sank her heel into his foot. He loosened his hold a bit and then completely. She spun around to find Alric staring and the soldier's body falling to the ground, Alric's short-sword in his back. He pulled his weapon free and they both watched Ivar sink to the snowy ground.

Alric dropped the sword, and Camelee dropped her defenses and hurried to him. "Oh, Alric! Alric, I'm so happy to see you! He was going to rape me," she cried and pulled away, then covered her body with the cloak Alric offered off his back.

"Where is Wolf? Why are you alone?"

"He left to find his brother, Fin. He put Odger in charge of us, but Odger's wife delivered his baby, so he left for an hour. I thought it would be okay."

Alric brooded. Neither of them should have left.

"Come on." She took his hand and led him forward. "We need to find Odger. I'm afraid what the other men will do to us if they find this out."

He paused. She stared at him. "You're not going to leave me again, are you, Alric?"

"I do not want to travel with the Danes or be their slave."

"Wolf will keep you safe."

"When he is here. And when he is not?"

"You will keep yourself safe." She smiled. "And, of course, you have me."

They smiled at each other and even laughed a little. Despite it feeling good after what had just happened, a part of her feared she was growing hard, like them.

"Where have you been?" she asked Alric. "Wolf searched and searched."

He gave her a surprised look. "Wolf did?" Then his grin softened. "He did it for you."

"No. He—"

"He did it for you, Camelee. He is in love with you."

She wanted to scoff but her hands were still shaking. She wasn't in any mood to play games. She didn't think Alric was either. After all, he'd just killed a man.

"I think I may love him, too," she told him the truth instead. "But how can I? I don't belong here."

"Our hearts do not listen to good sense."

She smiled. "Where have you been, Alric? We looked everywhere for you."

"I was walking to my home in Sheffield."

"What happened? Why did you come back?"

"It is a long walk. I decided to return."

"Well, I'm glad you did. But what should we tell Odger?"

He eyed her. "The truth."

"Will he care that Ivar tried to rape me?"

"I imagined Wolf would not have chosen Odger if he thought the soldier would not care."

"Yes. I think you're right about that." She couldn't help but hug him again. "I really do hope you'll stay with us, Alric."

She would swear she felt his breath stall. And then he spoke into her shoulder. "And what, Camelee? We will be a family—until you leave?"

"Oh." She had no idea what to say to him. He was right. She was only thinking of herself when she asked him to stay. She withdrew and looked at him. "Maybe you can come with me?"

Sure! She could see Alric in designer jeans and a nice cashmere sweater. He'd fit right in!

"Is Hild coming, too?" he asked.

She looked away, disgusted at herself for caring what he thought of her when he realized she hadn't thought about bringing Hild. Of course, it seemed Hild loved Genevra and Wolf and no one else. Perhaps they all would be happier here. What about Wolf? Would he come with her? Did she want him to? Yes. She missed him. She missed seeing his face everywhere she looked. She was never out of his sight. And now, thinking of Ivar, she understood why.

They entered the keep and met Odger, with Genevra close behind him, with Hild crying in her arms. Genevra rushed to her, ignoring Odger's command to stay close. She hugged Camelee and doted over her bruised temple.

"You see, Hild, dear, I told you she would return."

Camelee's heart skipped like a stone across the water. Hild wasn't crying anymore.

"Woman!" Odger shouted to be heard. His cool gray gaze was fixed on her. He was daunting with his bald head and thick handlebar mustache. But he paled, seeing her swelling face, and then turned red with anger. "Where did you wonder off to? And who is this?" he demanded, staring down at Alric.

"How is your wife and baby?" she asked him, breaking his gaze on Alric.

He set it on hers, surprised, confused. "They are well. I have a son." He almost smiled.

"Congratulations!" What did one say in the eleventh century? "Huzzah? Anyway," she said when he didn't react. "I felt really sick." She gave Genevra, who was, by now, doting over Alric, a repentant look for causing her any concern fixed on his young face.

"Ivar said he would take me out and stationed another man at the door. But he grabbed me and struck me when I screamed out for Wolf. He tore my clothes and was trying to rape me, but I smashed my heel into his foot. He fell back into young's Alric's blade."

Odger hovered over Alric with an amused look on his face. "He fell onto your sword, eh?"

"Aye," Alric answered, sounding unmoved and unafraid. "After I stabbed him in the back when he was humping the chief's woman."

Odger narrowed his eyes on him. He knew Wolf was going to ask what happened. He wouldn't be angry with Alric. "Hmm, you may go then. Do not let me see your—"

"He saved my life, Odger," Camelee interrupted softly. "Or do you think Ivar would have left me alive to tell Wolf what he'd done?"

"You know Wolf cares for her," Genevra added with a bit more boldness. "He will thank this young man."

Odger shrugged his wide shoulders and chuckled. "Unless he is angry with the boy for taking his kill."

"Taking his kill?" Camelee asked, filled with indignation and disgust. She shook her head and held up her hands. "First of all, what was he supposed to do? Worry about Wolf or save me? Ridiculous. Second, you men really are barbarians."

"Yes," he told her as she stormed past him and headed for the keep. "I know."

Chapter Fourteen

W OLF LOOKED DOWN at the body abandoned in the field. He recognized one of his soldiers. Ivar. Stabbed in the back with a blade discarded beside him. The body was a day old. What about the rest of the keep? Had they been attacked again? His horse was too slow with him and his brother on it so he ran back. Camelee!

He almost collapsed in relief when he reached the keep and the Danes were still holding it.

"Where is your horse, m' lord?"

"He will be along. When my brother and the rest of the men get here, tell them to eat and drink. I will see them after."

He didn't wait around for the stable hand to reply but hurried toward the queen's side of the castle where Camelee was. He saw Odger at his post and reached him with a nod.

"Chief," Odger stopped him when he put his hand to the door. "I would have a word with you."

"What? Has she been harmed?"

When Odger didn't answer fast enough, Wolf pushed him out of the way and burst into the room. It took him a moment to find her in the four-room chamber. She was standing by the window. When she heard him enter, she ran to him and stopped short just when she reached him.

He bent over her to run the backs of his knuckles over her temple. "What is this from?"

"Ivar struck me," she told him quietly. He exhaled like some dragon getting ready to breathe fire. "Wolf—" she grabbed his cloak. "Odger has a son. He left me in Ivar's care for one hour to see to his wife. Don't you dare punish him."

He didn't promise anything but knelt in front of her. "I will not leave you again."

"Did you find your brother?"

"Yes. He is alive. The Saxons were not far from the border. That is why I have returned so quickly."

She smiled and reached up to the side of her face.

"I saw Ivar's body," he ground out, wanting to touch her again. "Who killed him?"

She motioned over his shoulder. He turned and saw young Alric. "You?"

A thread of fear passed over Alric's features but he stood strong against Wolf's scrutiny. "Aye. He had torn her clothes and struck her and—"

Wolf, stood to his feet and held up his palm to stop him from speaking further "I am in your debt, Alric."

The boy's eyes opened wider. He finally smiled and looked at his feet.

They heard Hild running before they saw her. She ran from another room and when she spotted Wolf, she squealed with happiness.

"Uf!" she exclaimed and held up her arms for him to pick her up.

Like an obedient servant, he did as he was told.

"Lee came back!"

He gave Camelee a surprised look, but her gaze was on Hild, along with a tender smile. Were things better between them? It seemed so. He was glad.

"I must go see the king and tell him I have returned, and my journey was successful. Will you wait for me?"

When both Camelee and Hild said yes, he thought about who he'd been asking. He thought Hild, but now he wasn't sure.

"I will keep Odger outside and Alric with you inside for one more hour and then I will return."

Alric straightened his shoulders and nodded.

Wolf handed Hild over to Camelee and stared in the latter's eyes. He wanted to kiss her, to take hold of her and kiss…no, she was hurt. He would kiss her softly and…no, he was too afraid of hurting her, or maybe she would reject him. What if she was angry with all men for what happened? He knew he would be, were he a woman.

But her smile heated on him. She did not seem angry. Did she want to kiss him?

He had to leave. He grinned at her. "It is good to be back."

She veiled her gaze beneath her lush lashes, making him want to—he had to leave.

He raced out and after asking half a dozen people where the king was, ran to the small chapel to meet with him.

He slipped onto the wood bench near Cnut and waited respectfully, silently praying words of his own with the Lord.

"It is good to have you back, Ulf," the king finally said. "Did you find Fin?"

"Yes. He has likely gone to clean up before seeing you."

"Oh? Did you leave him?"

Wolf wanted to close his eyes and groan. "Yes."

"To come to me?"

"Yes…and—" he cleared his throat and explained about seeing Ivar dead just beyond the wall and how he got that way. "I wanted to see that my servants were well. One of them was attacked."

"Yes, I know." Cnut leaned in and whispered close to his ear. "The queen would skin me alive if she heard me say anything other than, yes, I understand your haste to see to her."

Wolf didn't know whether to laugh or pity the king for giving her so much power.

"Especially when it comes to your Camelee," the king continued. "Emma is quite fond of her."

"That is good news, Sire," Wolf said with a slight smile.

"Do you believe in Him, Ulf? The One?"

Wolf looked at the crucifix on the altar. "I do, Sire."

"I have much to answer for."

"As do I, my lord."

They were quiet for a few moments and then the king dismissed him.

"Go. Go to her."

Wolf did not have to be told twice. He rose, turned, and left. Eventually, he would have to tell Cnut that he wanted to leave. He was allowed to if he chose. But not today. Today, he wanted to be with Camelee.

He found his brother on the way to Camelee's new chambers. When he reached her door, he dismissed Odger and told him to go to his family.

Wolf stepped inside with his brother and found Camelee and the others in the front room. Alric had not left them and sat with her, with her and Hild in the small chairs across from them, before the hearth. When she saw him, Camelee stood. A flash of blue lit his eyes.

"Chief, Fin, you've looked better, but it's good to see you alive."

Wolf gave her a slight smile and Fin thanked her and looked around. "I would not be if my brother had not arrived in time to save me."

She turned her smile on Wolf.

"Where did you get the dress?" Wolf asked, delighting in the sight of her.

"The queen gave it to me. Do you like it, or do I look ridiculous?"

The pale vivid blue against her skin and hair made her radiate light. The gold braided cloth hanging low around her waist accentuated just about every sensuous curve she possessed. She no longer looked like she didn't belong here. "The sight of you thrills my weary heart."

Alric gave him an incredulous look. But it was Fin's reaction that made him cringe and close his eyes.

"Well Miss Pendrey," Fin drawled, scanning her face and her bruised temple. "What trouble have you stirred up this time?"

Wolf expected her to bite his brother's head off. Why did Fin have to be such an arse?

She stared at Fin for a moment and then folded her hands in her skirt and softened her gaze. "We had to kill one of the soldiers here. Ivar was his name."

Fin's face grew dark beneath his furrowed brow. "We saw his dead body. Why?"

"He tried to rape me, tore my clothes, and struck me." She pointed to her bruise.

He ground his jaw and looked at her temple more thoroughly, all humor gone from him. "Who killed him? Brother, he must be raised in rank."

"Young Alric here killed him when he came upon Ivar forcing himself on her."

Fin turned to Alric. "It is good to see you returned to us." He turned to Camelee again. His gaze burned on her. "This is my fault. If I had not left—"

"You left to find me, didn't you?" she stopped him.

"Yes."

"This is not your fault. I don't blame you."

"Nor do I, Brother," Wolf said, stepping forward.

Fin nodded and looked relieved, but when he saw Genevra entering from the next room, he smiled the widest.

"Fin! Look at you!" she sounded horrified and hurried to him. "Oh, my dear, what did they do to you? Do you have a room? Come. Let us go to it and I will tend to you. Come!"

Fin offered his brother a helpless smile that Wolf had never seen in his life and watched Fin leave the chambers. Alric and Hild went with them.

Alone, Wolf offered Camelee a seat and then sat beside her. He couldn't breathe. Could she tell? He wished she saw him on the battlefield so she could know that he was strong and courageous and cunning. He was not ruled by concerns.

But here with her, he was a heap of nerves. "Camelee, I—ehm—"

She stretched across her chair and stroked her hand down his cheek. "It's good to have you back."

Staring into her eyes, he took hold of her hand on his cheek and covered it with his.

"I was not pleased about being away." His lips roved over her palm and then her wrist while he spoke. "And now you see why. I will not leave you again."

She leaned in. He let her. When she pressed her lips to his, he breathed. It took no time for him to respond. He curled his fingers around her nape and cupped her face with his other hand.

He consumed her in his arms, feeling as if she had been born to be there. He wanted more of her, but he wouldn't force her. He would do the good thing and make her his wife, but until then, he had to find a way to resist her.

"I cannot mislead you," he told her, withdrawing a little. "I must admit that I do not want you to leave. I cannot imagine how difficult being here must be for you, but I will do everything I can to make the change easier if you will stay."

She shook her head, breaking his heart, smashing his hopes. "I don't belong here, Wolf."

"Very well," he said after a short pause and held up his hands in surrender. "I will trouble you no more."

"What's that supposed to mean?" she asked him.

"It means I accept the life you choose."

"I'm not sure when you thought there was any other choice, but okay. Good."

"Yes. It is good," he agreed sourly and began to rise. "Now I can get on with my day."

Her hand landing softy on his stopped him. "You couldn't before?"

He scoffed, but not at her. He disgusted himself for how he

felt when she told him every chance she got that she did not belong here and wanted to go home. He hated himself for letting it hurt him.

"Though I sleep, my thoughts do not," he confessed, angling his head to look at her. "I am weary. I, too, want to go home."

He moved away, taking his hand with him. "I am going to sleep for a bit in a warm bed. The ground is hard and cold beneath a body."

She nodded but said nothing as he went to the bedchamber, much bigger than the one in the room near the kitchen.

Finally, he was behaving wisely and not allowing her any further entry. Why would she touch his hand again? To beguile him, of course. But to what end?

He went to a door that adjoined a second bedroom. He knew these chambers, since Cnut entered this keep, Wolf and Fin and the men helped build these extra quarters in the queen's section.

This bedroom was smaller than the one where Camelee and Genevra slept with Hild. But the bed was just as soft. He shut the door behind him and lay down on the feather mattress, especially made for all the beds in the royal guest quarters. He groaned sinking into the softness, and then swore an oath when he smelled her on the bed. She had to have known that when he returned he would sleep here. Why had she slept in this bed? The one she shared with Hild and Genevra wasn't big enough?

He heard her enter the room and ground his jaw. He needed to be away from her.

"Did you think of me when you slept in my bed?" he asked to rile her up and get her to storm out.

"No," she answered, closing the door behind her. "I slept in it because I was thinking of you."

He opened his eyes and watched her come toward him like a dream coming to life. She sat on the edge of the bed.

"I'm sorry for adding to all those thoughts in your head, Wolf. I don't want to be apart from you either. I want...I want you to come with me if I get the chance to return."

"To your future?" he asked, eyeing her mouth and the beguiling shape of her lips.

"Yes. Would you? Would you come with me?"

He suspected there would be times like this when he would agree to anything she wanted. But going so far ahead would be as foreign to him as being here was to her. "I do not know, Camelee." He would not lie to her. "I know only that everything I thought was so important is being changed into the silhouette of a woman and a child. I understand your desire to go home. I want to hold you, and comfort you…because I believe your fantastical story. Or at least, that you believe it. I do not know how to find a way to the future, and I imagine that must be heart-shattering for you. I—" He stopped talking and closed his eyes as she leaned down to kiss him.

She tasted like desire, pleasure, apprehension.

He caressed her glorious face, where she bared her heart to him if he looked hard enough.

Wanting her closer, he slid his hands down her back and dragged her in and down onto the bed with him.

"Wolf?" she whispered, withdrawing from their kiss and facing him inches away. "I'm afraid."

"I will do everything in my power to keep you safe—and if it is not enough, I will myself hurl you through time if it will save you."

She smiled. "I would prefer you not to hurl me anywhere."

"Whatever you wish," he promised, then grimaced at what he was helpless to stop.

She pushed forward and kissed him again, sweeping her tongue inside his mouth with curious, sensuous strokes.

He fought hard to control his desire to lay her down and set himself atop her. He thought of the king and his own vows to God. Unless she agreed to be his wife, *becoming one flesh* was not permitted.

"What are you doing to me, Woman?" he moaned and raked his teeth over her chin.

"I didn't know I was doing anything to you at all," she leaned up on one elbow and rested on his chest. "Describe it and I'll tell you if it's love or a disease."

He stared at her for a moment and then laughed. "You are doing it this moment."

She kissed his chin. "What?"

"Rendering me weak, like Samson after Delilah cut off his hair."

"Do your braids give you power?" she teased, pulling on one.

"My power cannot stand against you alone, Camelee. I need God to help me, but I cannot bring myself to ask Him."

She ran her fingertips over his lips. "Your words are like beautiful music to my tired ears. I'll continue to entice you to follow me into the future."

He kissed her fingers and smiled against them. "I will enjoy the temptation."

"Yes," she agreed, and it sounded like a purr. "You will."

The door burst open and Hild hurried to the bed. Genevra followed close on her heels, flustered and repentant.

"Uf!" the child cried out and stood at the edge of the bed.

"Greetings, Hild," said Wolf cheerfully.

"Lee sweep with me, not you," Hild claimed as possessively as any Viking.

"Lee is not going to sleep," Wolf explained. "We were playing." He tickled Camelee's side. She reacted at once, laughing and slapping his hand away.

Hild leaped into the bed and shoved her fingers into his belly like five little blades. He laughed nonetheless, sat up, and showed the four-year-old girl how it was done.

But it was Camelee's touch that caused Hild to break out in laughter and ticklish giggles.

"It surprises me," he told Camelee while she sat on the bed with Hild close by.

"What does?"

"How you deny wanting to be a mother, and yet you are

winning over an honest little girl."

"Just because I win her over doesn't mean I want that title," she let him know. "It seems very important to you and is therefore yet another obstacle between us."

"Obstacles do not frighten me, Camelee," he assured her.

From where they were about leave the room, Genevra tossed Alric a knowing smile.

Wolf saw the exchange. He knew it exposed his weakness. Her. He could not stop it. He didn't care who saw it.

"Where is my brother?" he called out to them.

"He insisted he was well enough to see the king," Genevra told him, smiling. "He also insisted on bathing in the stream outside. He was shivering!"

"It is good for a man to shiver occasionally," Wolf said, leaving the bed. "It keeps him humble."

Genevra stopped and smiled at him. "I like your notions, my lord. A humble man is difficult to find. If that trait is important to you, then you are a good man."

He smiled, finding himself doing it more and more. He scowled. Alric must have thought Wolf was scowling at him, for he looked anxious.

"I am pleased to have you back with us, Alric," Wolf told him as the boy passed him.

"For her sake," he heard the boy mutter under his breath.

"And yours," Wolf called back. "You are brave. She needs brave people in her life to protect her from men like Ivar."

"She needed no protection from me," Alric let him know. "She almost had him down on his knees. She might have been able to outrun him."

"Or she might not have been able to. You saved her," Wolf said sternly. He hoped the boy listened to him. "No one will come against you. Yes?"

Alric nodded. "Aye."

"I want you to be her protector. But if you want to cook," Wolf continued, "that can be arranged, too."

Alric smiled and nodded again.

When everyone left but Camelee and Hild, he turned to them and smiled. He didn't realize how hard he was smiling until Camelee asked him if he was ill.

Yes. He was ill, and it was too late to be saved.

CHAPTER FIFTEEN

Tomorrow night was Christmas Eve of twenty nineteen in NYC. How many parties would she miss? How many men's meaningless advances would she have had to fight off? Only to go home drunk and alone with no messages on her phone?

"After we sweep the great hall and straighten the holly and the ivy, we will help in the kitchen." After a moment, Genevra stared at Camelee curiously. "I was not expecting to see you smiling at the day's activities."

"Oh, it's not that—believe me. You said the holly and the ivy. It is the name of a beloved Christmas carol in my time, well, before my time as a matter of fact."

"Who will you miss tomorrow eve, Child?" Genevra asked her lovingly.

"I—okay, well, there's—" She thought about it another second. There was no one. She looked down at the nearest chair and sat down in it. The sad realization hit her. There was no one she would miss. No one who missed her right now. Maybe Karen.

"What is it, Camelee?"

"Oh, Genevra, my life has been so empty. I haven't had a genuine friend…or anyone in my life for so long I've forgotten what it's like. I've pretended my way around relationships, faked contentment, happiness, and I did it well—or no one really cared if I was faking it. That might be even worse."

"Surely the parents who adopted you—"

"No. They don't. Didn't."

"Poor darling," Genevra soothed and wiped her eyes. "I wish I could have been there for you."

Camelee believed her and let the older woman comfort her. No one ever had before. Wolf had offered, too.

"Have you always wanted to be a mother, Genevra?"

"Of course," she said as if there were no other way to feel.

Camelee thought in this time there might not be.

"And yet you never married so that you could have children."

Genevra shook her head and looked off into the distance. "They would not be the *correct* children."

Camelee stared at her. She said nothing though. Maybe Genevra was right.

"Besides," Genevra said as she shook her head again. "As I told you, my heart has never felt as if it were mine to give away. I believe my true love will come find me and when he does, I will know he is the right one. If waiting has cost me children, so be it."

Camelee thought she should feel sorry for Genevra, but the woman was too happy and comfortable in her skin to pity. Genevra knew what she wanted and even if Camelee didn't understand it, she admired Genevra for following her heart and not marrying a man she didn't love. Women of this era didn't have the luxury to denounce marriage.

Fin, shockingly, was no exception to Genevra's motherly attention. In response, he made certain at all times that she had enough food and that she was protected. In fact, he smiled almost as much as Wolf did.

Wolf. What could she say about him? Was there enough time in the day?

"The women whisper that Chief Kristiansen is in love with you," Genevra told her, smiling secretively.

Camelee waved her hand, casting off the gossip. But in her heart, she believed it. He kissed her like she meant something to him. And it wasn't just a feeling. He gave in to her when it came to just about anything. She wouldn't use it to her advantage for just anything though. It sometimes sent him off angry with himself and some poor unsuspecting fool, namely Fin or Alric. Both almost had their hands bitten off when they offered them to him. If, in mid-bite, she called out to him, he stopped and warmed instantly. It made her feel important to him. She liked it.

When she wasn't thinking about how love felt like a foreign germ she needed to expel, she was letting it touch her when he looked at her, smiled at her, kissed her.

He was falling in love. The same as she was.

So, she cooked, or she tried to. She guessed she should learn how. It was a basic survival issue, wasn't it? Sadly, she didn't know how to do anything. It hadn't been something she was ashamed of before she came here and met Genevra, and many other women here. Now it was.

Genevra assured her that she had nothing to be ashamed of, but the more Genevra and the others knew how to do and the less she knew how to do, the worse she felt about her life so far.

Genevra smiled when she saw Alric entering the kitchen. He appeared a bit overcome with happiness at such a place, for here were loaves of bread hanging from the rafters, bushels of apples, whole lambs and pigs, and fish roasting over long spits. People were chopping, kneading, rolling, slicing and more everywhere he looked.

He made his way to her table where she stood chopping an endless supply of carrots. It was the only thing anyone trusted her to do.

"The chief sends for you. He is with Hild in your chambers. Tell him, please, that I will be here for the remainder of the day."

Camelee smiled at him and then motioned for Genevra to follow her. But her friend refused to go. She wanted to be a part of the celebration from the other side of the great hall, where she felt comfortable.

So, Camelee left on her own. She should have known Wolf would be close by when Alric let her leave the kitchen alone.

"Hild and I thought you might want to come with us for a

walk."

"Outside?" she asked, seeing their furs. Queen Emma had a fur-lined coat made for Hild with a matching hood. Of course, the queen had also had a fur cloak made for Camelee. The two were fast becoming friends.

Wolf carried Hild in one arm and her cloak in the other. "Would you prefer to remain in?" he asked at her seeming reluctance.

"Are you kidding? It snowed last night. Of course, I want to go out!" She took her cloak and didn't wait for him to help her put it on, then led the way to the front doors. "Hild, I'm going to teach you how to make snow angels."

"Okay," Hild replied merrily to which Wolf laughed.

Camelee wasn't sure he made the sound more than a few times since she'd been here.

"Will you teach me as well?" he asked, melting her bones with the deep cadence of his voice.

"If you like, but your men will see you having fun with a couple of servants."

"And if they dare look at us askance, I will cut them limb from limb."

"Limb from limb!" Hild growled in agreement.

"Wolf!" Camelee admonished. "Please don't speak like that around her."

He promised not to in the future, but it was clear by the grins he offered Hild that he was proud of her.

"So, what do Vikings do for Christmas?" Camelee asked, wishing she had paid more attention to her history lessons.

"Because we are Christian, and belong to the Catholic Church, we celebrate the birth of our Lord. Many others practice the traditions of their Norsemen fathers, sacrificing to their gods for twelve days, burning wreathes and praying to trees. But some traditions they both share are drinking and singing, feasting and celebrating. Which we will be doing." His smile widened into a salacious grin that made her feel drunk looking at it. "But you must stay close to me. Many will be deep into their cups, so stay close to me."

She nodded and smiled like a love-struck imbecile. He wanted to keep her safe. This was his world, not hers. She intended on looking nice. She didn't want to look like a poor slave, for her sake, and for Wolf's. But some of the men here…Ivar's furious growls when he struck her and grabbed her by the bra…some of the men were dangerous. She would stay close to Wolf. She didn't have to be told twice.

She could try to learn the skill of defense many of the Norse women practiced. They kept themselves safe with techniques on how to bring a man down with or without a weapon. But this was a time of violence, not talking it out. There was danger around every corner, at least until you earned the men's respect. She didn't have the energy for that. She'd rather Wolf do it for her.

"What about—" Camelee eyed him and then Hild, hoping he understood.

He creased his brow and looked where she looked. "What about her?"

"She must have gifts in the morning. What shall we get her?"

"Get her? From where?"

Oh, right. There weren't any toy shops around here.

"Maybe I'll bake her a treat or two," she murmured.

They came to one of the keep's exits and stepped outside to the snow-covered inner yard. The few trees in view were gnarled and white. Wolf put Hild down in the snow, where she proceeded to purposely fall face down.

Camelee and Wolf both rushed to her and pulled up. Camelee realized as they doted over her that they were acting like a little family, and it felt more real than anything she'd had in her life.

Fearless of the cold, Hild loved making snow angels, but she loved building a snowman even more. After it became clear what they were doing, others joined in and built their own, until it looked like a village of various sized and shaped snowmen.

There was a great snowball fight with about thirty-five participants. Camelee and Wolf paired up and fought a good fight—until one of their opponents ran to get away from Wolf's steady arm and passed the king, who happened to turn in Wolf's direction at the very moment and was pelted in the face with a snowball.

Everyone stopped. Camelee thought for a moment that time had stopped. And then Hild's laughter shattered the stillness. The Danish king's laughter rose with hers.

Camelee could read the relief in Wolf's face. Why? How much power did he have over Wolf? And if any at all, then wasn't Wolf a servant, just like her? She would ask him later.

"Papa kiwt him," Hild whispered.

Camelee heard her. So did Wolf. It was treason. But he appeared more shaken by emotion than fear. She'd called him Papa.

Camelee wasn't about to correct her. Hild had been distant toward her once because Camelee told her that her mother wasn't coming back. She wouldn't make the same mistake twice. Although she didn't like how Hild's opinion of her mattered so much. She wasn't the child's mother. No matter how much Wolf wanted it to be so.

She needed to get warm.

The king called out to Wolf and began walking over. Wolf bent and pulled Hild up into his arms then handed her over to Camelee.

"Who is this perfectly divine child?" King Cnut asked while snow melted off his long beard.

"She is Hild, a Saxon orphan," Wolf told him.

The king's clear blue gaze shifted to Camelee. "And this must be Camelee of Pendrey."

"Yes," Wolf answered.

Camelee smiled and curtsied with Hild on her hip. She stayed quiet, hoping to lead Hild by example.

"Let it be known here and now!" the king shouted his command. It echoed throughout the inner yard, and possibly the outer yard, as well. "Camelee of Pendrey and Hild, the Saxon orphan, belong to Chief Ulf Kristiansen and shall not be touched upon pain of death!"

"And Genevra." The words burst from Camelee's mouth as if they had a mind of their own. Though with a second to think about it, she would blurt it out again. "Please, Your Majesty. She is…" She shook her head slightly and swallowed her insides. Then began again. "She is my mother."

"Of course!" the king said and proclaimed her "mother's" protection to all.

She pulled a scene from a play she did in college. "Your gracious king, if I may humble myself before you one more time?"

"Your brother in my kitchen, who is preparing a feast that will be talked about for years to come."

Camelee smiled. "Yes. That's him."

The king shouted his command again, this time to include Alric.

Wolf turned to her and grinned. "You have power over many."

"And," the king added, reaching them and hearing Wolf's words. "She has the affection of the queen."

"I'm honored to have it."

He narrowed his eyes on her. "See that you do not take it lightly."

"Never, Sire."

Satisfied with her answers, the king promised to see them tonight and left them.

"Whatever you want to say," Camelee said to Wolf, "can we do it inside? We're freezing to death out here."

"Truly?" Wolf asked. "I feel a little warm."

They laughed as a horse and wagon passed through the yard, heading for the outer court. The wagon was really a large cage filled with people, much to Camelee's horror. They were filthy and freezing in their tattered rags.

"Mumma!" Hild shouted and then screamed. "Mumma!"

A woman from inside the cage reached her arms through the cage. "Hild! Give me back my baby, you Danish bastards! Hild!" she wailed.

"Wolf," Camelee cried out. "Is that Hild's mother? I thought she was mauled by a bear."

"It must not have been her," he said. "The body was unrecognizable. Come. Let us stop that cart and speak to her."

They hurried forward while Hild shouted for her mother. Wolf was able to stop the slave cart. After telling the driver who he was, the man dropped off the driving bench and went with Wolf to the back of the cage to unlock it.

"Good King Cnut said we can sell or trade any slaves we catch," the driver said.

"Mumma!" Hild shouted again when Camelee passed her mother.

"Give me back my baby!" the woman screamed at her.

Hild's mother! Hild's mother was back from the dead. Only, she hadn't been dead. They had assumed...she had blamed Fin and she was wrong. She had also been wrong to tell a little girl that her mother wasn't coming back. Hild's mother. Camelee was losing the child she denied from the day she met her, and now, would have given anything not to lose. "We thought you were killed by a bear," Camelee told her, shaken to her bones.

"You thought? Did no one bother to be certain, Dane?"

"I'm not a Dane."

Hild's mother spat. "Saxon traitor. Even worse."

"Mumma!" Hild reached for her mother, and Camelee's heart broke.

Why should it? This kid was no one to her. She'd told Wolf over and over, but he wouldn't listen. He wanted her to pretend to be Hild's mother while he pretended to be her father and they would be a nice little pretend family.

She wouldn't let Hild go into the cart to her mother. "Just a moment. We're getting you out of there first." She walked away with Hild kicking and crying over her shoulder. She reached Wolf as he opened the cage door.

"You," he called and pointed to Hild's mother. "Come out."

"Wolf." Camelee stared up at him. "Why didn't you or Fin make certain the person mauled by that bear was her mother?" She handed the little girl to him. "Give her back and let them all go free."

She left him without waiting for his reply. She wanted to go to the kitchen, to Genevra and Alric and tell them what was happening so that they could say goodbye to Hild.

She fought not to cry on the way. She was done crying. This was all her fault for letting herself get attached. She knew better. She'd let herself feel something for Hild…for Wolf. Idiot! Love always hurt. Nothing had changed. Nothing ever would.

She burst into the kitchen and hurried to Genevra and Alric and told them what had happened. When they rushed out of the castle, Camelee ran to her room, pale and already forever haunted by a little girl's laughter. She preferred not to go out there and see Hild leaving them all. She didn't want to see Wolf or speak to him. He could have saved them all the trouble by checking the body.

All the trouble of trusting in what she hated most in her life. Motherhood.

She entered her room, holding back her anguish until she nearly choked, and looked at the beautiful gown laid out on the bed. It was olive-green, embroidered around the hem and neck in gold thread.

She went to it and picked it up, ignoring the small yellow gown beside it.

It was getting late, and she hadn't even started getting ready for the party.

CHAPTER SIXTEEN

"I INVITED FRIDA to stay here in the keep with Hild," Wolf told her when he returned to the chambers. "If she decides to stay, she will come back tonight."

Camelee didn't answer him. She thought it would probably be more difficult to have Hild so close. She knew she was being selfish. But she'd never almost became a mother…and didn't hate it. She was raw. She didn't want to talk or hear anything more about Hild.

"I guess she will decide what's best," she remarked and pushed the last pin into her hair.

"You are taking this well, Camelee."

"Would you rather me weep into my pillow?"

"If that is what you felt like doing," he told her. "But I fear you do not feel much."

"You're right, I don't," she muttered. "Remember that next time instead of insisting that I become something I didn't want to be!"

She stormed out of the bedroom and then out of the chamber. She was surprised but thankful when she didn't hear the door open behind her. She had to get away, be alone. She guessed Wolf did, too.

She took one of the woolen cloaks by the doors and left the keep. She saw a woman's tattered skirts leaving the gate with a group of people. Was that Hild? She hurried after them, but they disappeared in the crowd leaving the inner yard.

She followed the crowd out of the next gate and watched it disperse into the snow-covered hills in many directions. Had it been Hild? Had her mother come back and then changed her mind?

She went south, following a band of villagers. Maybe Frida lived among them? So what if she did? Hadn't she just decided that she'd rather not see Hild? Of course, it wasn't true. She missed the little girl so much it hurt.

That was why she'd gone too far away from the keep—because every part of her hurt.

She was thinking about Hild calling Wolf Papa when something tangled around her ankles and knocked her to the ground.

She screamed out and was kicked in the side.

"Shut up!" a man yelled above her and then spat. "Do not make this more difficult for yourself than 'tis already going to be."

"No! The king decreed that I am not to be—"

He pulled her up by her hair and set her on her feet. "I can cut your throat now. He will not know you are already dead when I let him know I have you. Do not tempt me, Whore."

She opened her eyes and looked at him. She knew him and his log red braids. Leofric. The man who killed Akkar. Did he just stumble upon her on the single time Wolf hadn't come with her? "I don't know who you are talking about."

"The Dane you have been sucking at night."

"You have the wrong person."

He yanked her hair and pulled her to his horse.

"I know who you are." His voice was gravelly and rough against her ears—like nettles to her nerve endings. "You are the one that cursed Dane chief Wolf Kristiansen loves. Deny it again and see what I do to you."

She deserved this for leaving the keep. She was a fool enough for ten people. She kept her mouth shut while he forced her into his saddle at knifepoint.

"You saw him kill my brother," he said ominously and then

leaped into the saddle behind her. "Would you like to know how I will exact my revenge?"

"No. I don't think I would." Camelee stiffened and her skin crawled at his closeness. She wished she were a man. A man as big as Wolf. A man who knew how to fight and kill.

Leofric blew out a piercing whistle and another group of riders appeared.

Camelee felt a scream bubbling up in her as she laid eyes on tiny Hild and her mother tethered to a rider. Alric was tied to another.

"Let them go!" Camelee demanded on a shaky voice. "I'll do whatever you want."

"You will do that anyway," Leofric promised as more than fifty of Leofric's men rode toward them. "Now, be silent or lose an eye." He rested the tip of small blade below her eye socket.

"Cook," he shouted to Alric next. "You not only betrayed me, but all your people by friending these savages. I saw you in the courtyard with them today. You were not the Northmen's captive."

"I will befriend who I must in order to stay alive, Leofric," Alric told him.

"Your own life comes before the lives of your countrymen. For that—"

Camelee's cries distracted him, and he applied more pressure to the blade until he drew a drop of blood.

"Leofric," Alric called out. "They say the chief is a *berserker*. He has King Cnut's army to back him. There will be nothing left of us. Let the women go and let us flee with our lives."

He sounded so convincing that Leofric hesitated for a moment before nodding to the rider at the other end of Alric's rope. "Take him somewhere and kill him. He was once my friend and I do not want to see his end. When you are done, send his head to Kristiansen."

No! No! Camelee didn't care about her eye! She was about to scream when she noticed the rope tied around Alric's wrists was no longer tied. He saw her looking and let the rope dangle to show her he was free.

The wily teen was free. He would get away. He would get Wolf.

Leofric flicked his reins, and everyone followed him. The rider yanked on the rope. Alric held it securely and let it pull him behind the horse. They separated from the rest and blended into the skeletal, snow-covered trees.

Camelee prayed for the boy. She had to keep her cool and protect Hild and Frida. She looked at them, Frida walking and carrying Hild in her arms.

"They are Saxon." She pointed to them and fought not to tremble while she waited to find out if he would stab her in the eye. "The mother hates the Danes."

"So?" he growled.

"So, I'm surprised you treat them the same way the Danes did."

An eternal moment or two passed and she still had both eyes.

"Give them a horse," Leofric ordered.

"Where are we to get a horse?" someone called out.

His answer arrived out of the trees. Its saddle was empty, the rope, trailing in the ground behind it.

Everyone looked at it as if they had never seen anything like it. And then Leofric shouted. "Find that boy and kill him! Bedric, take fifteen men! Do not return without his dead body. I will cut off his head myself!"

Camelee closed her eyes. *Run, Alric. Run and hide.*

"I am going to kill the child next, but she will not die as a slave."

"Please, don't," Camelee begged him.

"What is her importance to him?"

She shook her head and prepared to lie through her teeth. "She has no importance to him, but to me. He kept her alive because of me. I am the one who is important to him. Otherwise, he is a beast with no heart. The boy was right. The chief is a berserker." She knew what a berserker was, thanks to the few Viking series she'd seen on television. "I've seen him fight. He killed all your brother's men by himself. He howled while he killed them and foamed at the mouth. He even gnawed on his sword. It was like he was possessed by the devil."

Leofric looked worried. So did the nearest ten men who heard her.

"We go on!" Leofric shouted to them. "Find your courage, men, and move on!"

Camelee was happy to have planted the seed of fear in them all, even Leofric. She wished she knew if Alric had gotten away. She would have to wait and find out.

"My second act of revenge," Leofric whispered against her hear, "will be to get you good and fat with my babe tonight. We will not stop until I am empty."

She was going to throw up. Oh, she had to get those images out of her mind before she exploded.

She traded his images with Wolf's and immediately her thoughts of violence became tender. Wolf kissed her slowly, exploring her mouth, her neck. She wanted him to kiss everything, every part of her. If she lived through this, she would offer him all.

Leofric remained quiet when he realized she wasn't listening to him. She didn't care if he killed her, if he tried to rape her, she would kill him first.

"What language is it that you are speaking," Leofric asked. "'Tis close to ours, but there are differences."

"I come from the east, from a large village called Manhattan."

"Manhattan," he echoed. "I like the sound of it."

"Shocking," she mocked under her breath.

"He could not tame you," he remarked silkily and moved closer. "I will."

"He doesn't try to tame me. He's man enough to take me on the way I am. You should try it."

"You will find that Kristiansen's way of taming you is different than mine." He dragged her in closer and groped her breasts while licking and kissing her neck. "I will break you."

What a sick s.o.b. he was.

She decided to keep her eyes on the path behind them to forget the monster touching her.

"What are you looking at?" he demanded.

"I'm watching for him. He'll come. You took something of his. He'll come."

"Let him," the monster said behind her. "I have men every-where. We will finally be rid of him."

Camelee hoped he couldn't feel her heart beating. Would his men ambush Wolf? Were they hiding in the trees? Oh, how could she warn him? Would Alric make it back to tell him? She fought not to tremble. If Wolf died…she couldn't finish the thought. Did she feel like screaming because he was the only person she had ever truly cared about? Or because she was terrified of living here for the rest of her hopefully short life with Leofric?

She fought to keep from trembling in Leofric arms. If Wolf didn't come and anyone hurt Hild, Camelee was going to push Leofric to kill her.

She prayed Wolf lived through this and came for her and the little girl.

CHARLES LANCASTER, AKA King Arthur Pendragon, smiled at Viviane, one of the Sisters of Avalon as they prepared to leave his apartment in NYC. Now that the enchantment was lifted and everyone's memories were returning, he could return home to the magical realm, not to live there permanently, but to remember and rest. The earthly realm was his home. His children were all here. The love of his life was here.

"How can we find Guin?"

Viviane looked up at him and smiled. "Leave that to me."

She held up her hands and said a few words and a rift appeared in the air.

"We will bring Morgan to where Merlin tells us." Viviane stepped through the rift.

Arthur could smell the apples. *The Isle of Apples.* He turned back for an instant to smile at Mordred, his oldest son with Morgan. He thought of Micajah and Camelee, born of his beloved Guinevere, and his baby, Kestral, born of his second wife, Cynthia, who died long ago. He would find his children.

He stepped through the rift. First, he would go home and use magic to find his Guin.

The sight before his eyes changed in an instant. He stared at rolling hills of emerald green as far as the eye could see. Apple orchards lined the valleys, filling his vision with small red dots, and his nostrils with the comforting scent of apples. The sounds of waterfalls and birds singing were like music to his ears. He dragged in a deep breath. Home for many years.

"Where are your sisters?" he asked. "I wish to thank whoever was dear *Aunt Eleanor* for hiding my children through time with the brooch."

"I don't know who she was but I do know that they will be happy to see you. You are like a brother to us. Well," she corrected, "to almost all of us."

"Then please tell me, Viv, how will Guin receive her memories? Will it be instant as it is for some of us or slow, over time? I wish to know when it will be safe to reveal myself to her."

"We must find her first, Arthur."

"Yes," he chuckled. "Of course, you are right. Patience is a virtue I have trouble with."

"We will find her," she assured him.

"We will find her," he echoed at her side. When he saw his horse, he knew everything was going to be all right Now that Morgan was being locked away again, they were safe.

It seemed as if they rode a short distance when the City of Glass came into view, the multi-faceted glass turrets of the palace puncturing the clouds.

Avalon. His heart longed to go to it.

"Arthur!"

He turned and pulled his horse around. It was Merlin. He'd been leading Morgan bound in golden vapers. They were bringing her to justice, to a prison from which she could not escape.

"She broke the spell and got away. I think—"

She got away? No! Oh, no! He'd hidden himself for almost half a century from her. He'd given up everything, his wife, his children, his best friends, to keep them safe from her.

She got away?

Almost instantly, his expression went dark. He had to find them all. Today! "Rally the men and lead us to her, Merlin!"

His oldest friend, whose memories of his past were as freshly restored as everyone else's, hit the bottom end of his new walking stick.

Gawaine and the others who were here rode through the mists and stopped when they came to him.

"We are at your service, our king," Sir Gawaine bowed.

"Morgan is free. My family is in danger. All of you are in danger."

Gawaine looked at Lucan and Kay and the others and nodded. "On our lives, we will find her," the burly knight declared.

"She might go after one of my children. You know where Michael and Kestrel are. Find Camelee."

"Aye, Sire."

Alone with Viviane again, Arthur looked at the glass city. "Help me find Guin now, Viv. It must be now before Morgan finds her."

◆┈• •┈◆

CHAPTER SEVENTEEN

I T WAS CHRISTMAS day. Everyone hurried to and fro, from the kitchen to the hall with various platters of food, but Genevra had to sit. The laces of her dyed gown were too tight. She felt faint as memories came rushing back to her. It had been happening since last night. Scattered though they were, she had no idea where these memories came from but could only guess they were from her lost years. But they made no sense.

Had Camelee and Hild's disappearance pushed her memories to the surface? Oh, where was Camelee? Had she run off with the child? What about Frida? Had someone taken them? Who? Where was Alric? He was also missing. Why take those people in particular? Was this a message to the chief?

He—

Her thoughts wandered as if having a will of their own, to the memory of another child. Younger. Wrapped in a blanket and set in a basket. Genevra had wept so much she was sure she would wither and die as she gave up her children…her babies! She never saw them again. She hadn't remembered them.

She shook her head. What was she thinking? Was she possessed by some kind of devil?

Camelee. They had named her Camelee hoping that should one of them meet her, her name might pull up a memory of Camelot. It hadn't. She had no idea who Camelot was. She remembered the name though. These tattered memories invaded her mind, and she was completely powerless to stop them.

Camelee. Her daughter. Her baby. She had left her. It had been raining. Cars' tires crunched over wet blacktop—cars? She, and a faceless man had dropped the baby off at an orphanage in a basket with a blanket and a piece of paper with her name on it. Camelee Pendrey.

Genevra stood from her chair. She couldn't sit. Where was her daughter? Who was Camelee's father? Was she mad?

She saw Odger and pulled him close by his sleeve. "Where is the chief?"

"He has gone off to find his servant."

"She is more than a slave," she told him. *She is a princess.*

Genevra shook. Her blood felt frozen. How could her daughter be a princess? That would make her a queen. She would have laughed, but she felt this was real…somehow. "We have to find them."

"That is what the chief is trying to do."

She spotted Fin returning with some of the men. What was he doing back here? She ran to him. He would help. They were good friends. "Fin why have your returned already? What have you found?"

"Him," Fin stated and tilted his head to a body draped over a horse. It was Alric.

"Oh, Alric!" she cried and turned back to Fin. "Is he dead?" She didn't want to know the answer. Had he been with Camelee and Hild?

"No," he told her, relieving her. "But he's close. He needs attention. Where should I bring him?"

"To my room!" She clapped her hands together to hurry the men lifting him. "Softly! Gently!" she demanded at the same time.

"Is there no sign of Camelee or Hild?" she asked Fin as they hurried to her chambers.

"Not yet," Fin answered. He echoed the words, this time more somberly. "Not yet. Wolf rode north toward Mercia, but my men found Alric in a forest three leagues south of here."

"So, he is likely going the wrong way," she surmised with a sinking heart.

"Likely," Fin agreed. "We must get Alric to talk to me. Tell me what he knows, so I know which way to go to get word to my brother."

"Aye. You are correct,' she told him. There was no time to worry about her sanity now. She had to save Alric. She cared for the boy. She knew Camelee did, too.

Camelee.

She didn't want a mother. She had made that very clear from the beginning. She'd been adopted—Genevra had set the babe down in her basket and left her at the orphanage. Left her to be raised by people who did not show their love for her, people who had abandoned her to her nannies. Genevra's decision that day ruined Camelee's life and crushed her heart under the weight of mistrust.

What about Michael?

How could Genevra tell her—tell her what? That she was having dreams while she was awake? That those dreams were about her being Camelee's mother? But how could she be her mother when they were born a thousand years apart? But…the basket, the orphanage, the memory of *cars* that moved around her on four wheels and with no horses were not a part of this eleventh-century world.

"Gen, are you ill?"

She blinked up at Fin—no, it was another man. He was hand-some, with dark lush waves falling around his beautiful blue eyes. But he was faceless. He called her Guin.

"Genevra?" Fin reached out and gave her a little shake. "Are you ill? Hurt?"

"No. No, forgive me," she reassured him and hurried forward to catch up with the men carrying Alric to her room. She forbade herself to think on anything but what Alric needed. She hovered over him while they lay him in Wolf's bed.

She was no doctor but—*doctor*? What a strange word to come

into her head.

Upon careful examination, she discovered that Alric had been shot with an arrow in his side and had, at some point, pulled the arrow out. He had also been stabbed twice. Both times in his legs.

She didn't think any of the wounds were serious enough right now to kill him. But the wounds needed the right care.

She wasn't surprised to find the queen at her side, calling for more help from the other women. Thankfully, they all knew how to clean and sew.

"I will need fresh, bleached cloth and alcohol. Touch the cloth as little as possible. Germs," she added for the women's curious looks.

"Germs?" the queen asked.

Genevra smiled and waved her hand. "A Welsh word."

Fin remained in the room, keeping off to the side while they worked. Within a quarter of an hour, the boy opened his eyes.

"Keep it short, Commander. He's exhausted."

He nodded and kept his eyes on her when he came to the bed. "You seem and sound different. Are you certain you are well?"

Without answering, for she didn't want to lie to him again, she stepped aside and away from the bed.

Alric came to long enough to tell Fin that Leofric had Camelee and Hild, and her mother and he had men guarding a small part of the forest, beyond the two crisscrossed trees.

Before Alric finished, Fin dispatched men to find his brother and give him this information. He left the keep soon after that.

"Come, rest in my chamber, Genevra," Queen Emma urged. "Sleep for a bit. You look weary, dear friend."

"I will remain here with him," she said and fell into the nearest chair. She couldn't tell the queen she'd gone mad. She couldn't tell anyone any of it.

She sat by the bed for a long time after everyone left. The room was quiet, haunted by Hild's laughter and Camelee's voice.

Who was the man who she'd seen in her vision? The man

who called her Guin? Whoever he was, he made her heart almost come to a full stop when she looked upon his face. Was she sharing someone else's thoughts? How could it be? But Camelee claimed to be from the future. Did her future have the man Genevra had been waiting for her whole life?

She shook her head at herself and thought about how Camelee didn't want parents, nor did she want to be one. It was because of her. She was the one who had given Camelee up. She wasn't sharing someone's else's thoughts. These were *her* memories. This was her pain she was feeling having her babies…both of her babies taken from her because of—what? She didn't know. She didn't remember. Was the man Camelee's father? Had they come from the future? Is this what she couldn't remember?

Feeling more insane than before, she left her chair and paced before the bed. She wondered if Viviane had something to help her splitting headache.

She stopped pacing. Who in the blazes was Viviane? Oh, she wanted to just…fall apart. For the first time in her life, the part she was aware of anyway, she wanted to let go and fall apart. She wanted to scream and shout for the years she'd spent alone, making up excuses to others because she lived alone and did not marry. It wasn't that she didn't want to marry and have children. Her heart wouldn't let her. She pined for another. A man she did not know.

Now she knew what he looked like. Who was he? She would go mad if she didn't find out. She couldn't live this way!

Panic overwhelmed her. She threw her hands to her head and began to cry.

Guin. Guin. Who was she? Fin had called her Gen. She shook her head. What had she forgotten all these years?

She stopped crying for a moment and remembered Camelee telling her that she was named after King Arthur Pendragon's castle, Camelot.

Camelot wasn't a person, but a place. Camelee's name was a symbol of who she was and where she came from.

They had given her the name to carry that night at the orphanage. She and Camelee's father. Who was he?

"MOVE YOUR ARSE when I tell you, Whore!"

Leofric the Merciless, as he was called and loved reminding Camelee, took a handful of her hair and yanked her to her feet. Hild, who had been sitting beside her with her mother, began to scream. Leofric glared hatefully at the child and pulled back his fist to strike her.

Camelee hauled back her foot first and kicked him in the groin as hard as she could. He went down in a writhing ball.

Without haste, she picked up Hild and took Frida by the hand. "Run!"

They ran for about ten meters when Leofric's men took off after them. They weren't going to get away. Dear God, don't let this be real!

Frida fell and broke away. Camelee stopped and tried to pull her up but she cried out. Her ankle had snapped.

"Go!" Frida screamed, pushing her and Hild away. "Take her and run!"

Camelee did just that. She turned, took a step, and entered a hall, cut from faceted glass…maybe diamonds. Hild was screaming in her arms, but not because they had entered *someplace else*.

"Mumma! Mumma!"

Camelee's heart broke for her.

"Let us take her," said a beautiful woman who appeared by her side. "We will comfort her."

"No!" Camelee pulled back. "I will. She's mine."

The woman smiled at a handsome man sitting in a large, glass chair at the front of the grand hall. "She has picked up much from them already."

"Mumma!" Hild wailed.

Camelee looked around. "Where are we? How did we get here? There were men about to…her mother…"

"They are gone," said the woman.

"Gone where?" Was everyone from back there gone? What about Wolf and Genevra? "Where are they!" she shouted. Her voice blended with Hild's, echoing in the cavernous hall.

The woman placed her hand on Camelee's arm and patted it. "There now, little one. All will be well."

Camelee and Hild stopped crying.

"What did you do?" Camelee asked her.

The woman looked familiar. She had jet black hair, striped with gray, that draped her shoulders and fell to her waist. It was held away from her fathomless, violet eyes by a bronze circlet around her brow.

"I comforted you," the woman replied.

"Who are you?"

"I am called Viviane. That man is Arthur, King of Camelot, and your father."

Her what? Camelee blinked and felt laughter bubbling up inside. "I don't know what you did to me, Lady, but this is serious stuff." She looked down at Hild, calm and quiet in her arms. "How do you know you didn't give her too much?"

Viviane smiled and for a minute Camelee thought light came from her and bounced off the glass.

"Daughter."

Camelee turned and looked at the man from the chair. Now, he was standing in front of her. King Arthur. He was tall and very handsome with gray hair at his temples and dark everywhere else.

"Hiding is over," he said quietly, his eyes warm with tenderness mixed with warning. "She is loose. We must band together."

"What are you talking about? Where are my friends?"

"They are in their time. Nothing has changed for them, save that you are no longer there."

She thought of Wolf. He loved her. "Then everything has

changed for one of them. What is happening? Will they remember me?"

"Yes. I cannot tamper with memories again."

"Right," Camelee scoffed. "King Arthur is fictional. Am I dreaming you?"

He shook his head slowly. "I am real, so is Morgan, an evil sorceress bent on destroying me and taking away everyone I love."

"Morgan Le Fey?" Camelee asked, recalling the tales.

"She is known by many names."

First the Vikings, now King Arthur? How much crazier could this get? "All right, well, I've heard enough. I want to go back now."

The man in front of her gave her a solemn look. "You cannot go back. Neither to the eleventh century nor to the twenty-first. I'm sorry, Daughter."

"Stop calling me that!" she hissed at him in an effort not to scream and frighten Hild. "I don't know what's going on. But I'm no longer participating. I'm not your daughter, and if I thought for one moment that you were my biological father, I'd slap you in your face."

"Child, he is the king," Viviane reminded her softly.

"I'm not a child. Please. Enough is enough. It's cruel to pretend to be my father."

"I'm not pretending," he told her. "Your mother, who I intend to find, is Queen Guinevere. You have a brother named—"

"Stop!" Camelee cried out. She felt someone taking Hild out of her arms. She couldn't do anything to stop it. She felt lightheaded. She swooned forward and fainted in the king's strong arms.

SHE DIDN'T WAKE up again until the next morning. When she did, she was in a bed in a private room. There was another woman with her, smiling like a painting of some beautiful enchantress come to life.

"I am Nimue."

"Where am I?"

"Avalon."

Camelee's heart pounded. Avalon wasn't real. That meant none of this was real. She couldn't help it that her first concern was Wolf. Was he real? Would she ever see him again?

"He is real," Nimue told her, leaning in. "He is rather wild though. He might change a bit of history with all the Saxons he is killing.

"I want to go back to him. Please."

Nimue stared at her with wide leaf-green eyes. She appeared to be genuinely surprised. "Truly? You wish to go back to him?"

Camelee opened her mouth but then paused.

"You hesitate," Nimue pointed out.

"No."

"You did. You hesitated. But even if you didn't, we cannot send you back. Too much has already changed."

"Then bring him to me!"

"It does not operate that way."

"Then how does it operate?" Camelee demanded. "And where is Hild?"

"She is with the other children in the apple grove. She is a wondrous child!" Nimue's lips curled into a smile.

"I want her with me. I don't know you people. You took her without my consent."

Nimue's smile faded. "We would never harm her."

"That's nice to hear but like I said, I don't know any of you."

Nimue tilted her head at her as if she were trying to read Camelee. "She is not your own child, yet you protect her as if she is."

"She's an orphan…again. I feel sorry for her."

Nimue quirked her blue-black brow at her and rose from where she was sitting on the bed. "Is that all?"

"Yes! What are you, a psychiatrist?"

Nimue laughed and Camelee thought she saw a misty vapor leaving her mouth, sparkling air. Just like the air around the brooch that brought her to Wolf.

"You know," the enchantress said in a hushed voice. "Your father did what he did to keep you all alive."

"And what is it he did?" Camelee indulged with a smirk.

"He made us all forget. Well, maybe not you or your brother, Micajah. You were both babies when he and your mother had to give you up, so there was not much for you to forget."

"Oh, my goodness, please stop," Camelee begged as tears poured from her eyes. "This is cruel. I will die if you don't stop."

Nimue reeled back horrified. "Oh, dear, we do not mean to make you suffer more. I will return in a short while. Rest." Nimue began to dissolve and disappeared into a sparkling puff of air. Were she and Viviane responsible for the brooch?

Camelee hopped out of bed. She was still dressed. Who had moved her to this bedroom? Odd that though the walls and ceiling were made of glass, she couldn't see what was on the other side. The glass was not see-though. Every piece of furniture was made of different colored glass. The mattress was not glass. Many things weren't, but the room was the most beautiful room she'd ever been in.

Someone knocked.

"Come in." The door opened and the man who claimed to be King Arthur and, more importantly, her father entered the room.

"Nimue tells me you wish to return to the Vikings."

"I would like him to be brought here," she answered, not allowing herself to cower to him, king or not. "As I was."

"That is impossible. He does not share my blood, nor does he possess any magic in his veins. The only reason we were able to bring Hild through is because she is small and clung to you. He must stay where he belongs."

She scoffed in his face. "Since when does staying where you belong matter to you people? I want him brought here. Please!"

"I cannot, Camelee. I am sorry. I don't have the power to

bring him here."

The thought of never seeing Wolf again made it difficult to breathe. She loved him. She did. "Why was I sent to him?" she cried.

"Morgan used Mordred to try to kill me. My own son. I could not allow her to come near you and your brother. I foolishly enchanted the brooch to help you all find your true love. I didn't know it would hurl you through time until I heard from Kestrel from the fifteenth century. But she was happy. It was the only gift I could ever give you."

"And now you're snatching it from my hands?"

"I will not send you back while Morgan is free. She is devious, Camelee. I thought one of the sisters sent out the brooch to you all, but it wasn't anyone here. It was her."

"Wolf is a berserker," she told him hopefully, not really hearing his words. "He will protect me from her."

The king shook his head. "He has no magic. She would destroy him and then you."

Camelee felt her anger boil up in her. She didn't care who he was, or why he did it. He'd left her and she had grown up feeling abandoned. She realized now that it was mostly her adoptive parents who made her feel this way. But that hurt was born in the orphanage. "You don't get to be worried about me, *Dad!*"

"It nearly killed us to give you up, my daughter. Your poor mother wept until the day Merlin and I cast the spell. I didn't know who you were, Camelee. I didn't even know who your mother was," he told her gently coming to her. "It was the only way to be safe."

"Do you realize that I know these characters? Morgan, Mordred, all of you! You are all from books. My mind is somehow playing—"

"Camelee!" his otherwise gentle baritone voice boomed off the walls. He stood over her, angry and foreboding. "Enough of this. You are my daughter, behave like it! If I tell you something, you must believe me, for I would not be dishonest with you. Morgan's heart is twisted against good. She is dangerous in her madness. I separated us and made us forget who we were to protect us all."

"What changed?"

"Believing that we had captured her, and we were now safe, I lifted the spell. She escaped and is now free among us again. Now that memories are being restored, it will be easier for her to find you."

Was she supposed to believe this? Why not? Hadn't she traveled back in time to Viking England? Wasn't the name Pendragon responsible for setting her world upside-down?

"Okay, well you know what?" If he wanted to be her father so bad, then he was going to be the one to hear what she'd always wanted to tell him. She had issues and there weren't any psychiatrists here. "If you are my father—you ruined my life. In all my success, my heart was always broken because you abandoned me. The Pendreys forgot about me. But you were first."

His pretty blue eyes glistened with tears. He said nothing for an eternal moment. "I had to keep her away from you. If she hurt you, I would have done regretful things."

She listened to the rest of his defense and, deep in her heart, she wanted to believe him, trust him. But she'd never learned how to do those things, and everything was simply too unbelievable. It was easier to tell herself none of it was real than to believe it.

What better man to fantasize about being her long-lost father than King Arthur Pendragon, a hero from her childhood?

That more than likely meant that her dream man, Wolf Kristiansen, eleventh-century Viking was not real either. None of this was.

"I would like to be alone."

"Camelee," the king tried.

"Please."

He swallowed and nodded, reluctantly giving in. "Of course. I will make sure you are not disturbed."

"Thank you."

<hr>

CHAPTER EIGHTEEN

WOLF CIRCLED TWO of Leofric's men after Fin and the other men tied the two Saxons to the trees. Somehow, Leofric evaded him. But Wolf would find him and kill him. He wouldn't stop until he did. The Saxon had taken her. His Camelee.

Alric had recovered enough to tell him that Leofric had her and Hild and her mother. He'd had Alric, too, and ordered his death, but the young cook was wily and fast. He killed the Saxon solider and escaped, but he hadn't gone far when men hiding behind the trees shot at him. They aimed for his legs to stop him, not kill him. They liked to bring their prey to their leaders alive.

The first thing Wolf had done was bring forty of the Danes' best men in the forest to eliminate the threat. Three hundred more men from the king's army followed an hour behind.

It took a few hours to find Leofric's men. Wolf went mad looking for him. He'd killed more than he could count. Blood covered his hands, streaked his face. He bellowed Leofric's name as he hacked the Saxon men to pieces. But Leofric wasn't there.

Fin found the two who claimed to know about the "woman he was after".

"Leofric knows you love her," one of the men told him.

"Where is she?" That was all Wolf wanted to know. "I do not care about that coward you follow. Where is the woman?"

"We were…we were chasing her. Her and that little one and her mother. The mother fell and the men overtook her."

Wolf closed his eyes and fought to control the desire to shove his blade into this man.

"And then the woman and the child disappeared, my lord."

"They were there and then they were gone, and the air was all silver and Christmasy, or as you heathen would say, yule-ish."

Wolf glared at the second man who spoke. "Do you find humor in this?" He lifted the blade of his dagger to the man's throat.

"No, my lord, not humorous, magical."

Wolf felt his belly drop to the ground. Had she been taken back to her future?

He didn't want to believe it, but the timing could not be better. Whoever snatched her back had saved her life. Wolf knew Camelee had nothing to do with it or she would have sent herself back before this. It didn't soothe the beast inside that wanted to howl his sorrow until the sun rose.

The two men didn't change their stories even after Fin tortured them. Wolf didn't let it go on for too long.

Was it true? Had she been saved by going back to her future? He was thankful and happy she was saved but his world crashed into thousands of pieces at his feet. He'd lost her, just as if Leofric had killed her. She was gone. Everything stopped for him. He didn't want to go back to the way his life was before her, without her. He didn't want to give up. He wouldn't. He never gave up on anything. He wouldn't start now with the most important person in his life. Every idle moment was spent thinking of her. How could he ever find her?

They camped in the woods that night. He didn't sleep. He didn't want to dream of her. But even awake she haunted him. Twice he thought he heard her weeping and rose to his feet to check around the trees. "Camelee?" he called out. He waited but only silence met his waiting ears. He prayed that if he could hear her to please let him go to her.

Would he leave his brother, the king, Denmark? All of it for her? Yes. If there was even a chance of finding her, he would.

"Brother?" he turned to Fin and held back his anxious thoughts.

"I thought I heard her," Wolf explained quietly.

"I will wake the—"

Wolf grabbed his wrist, stopping him. "She haunts me, Fin."

His younger brother stared at him, looking deeper than most, save for Camelee. "I know, Ulf. It is clear that you love her. But do you truly believe her story about coming from the future? Because, Brother, I must tell you, it is beyond good reason."

"I cannot explain why, but I do. Just as I cannot explain why when I returned to the keep, Genevra had seemed afraid to speak to me. Does she know something and why would she not tell me?"

There had been no time to question her further before he'd left the keep. Maybe it was time to return and find out. Leofric would wait.

"She is loyal to Camelee, Wolf. I can assure you."

Wolf nodded, staring at his brother defending Genevra. "I do not doubt that and as long as what she is keeping from me does not harm Camelee, I will hold nothing against her."

"Very well," Fin said, believing Wolf's word. "What about our two prisoners."

"Let them go in the morning," Wolf answered. "Then gather the men. We are returning to the keep."

"Why are we going back? Leofric will be long gone if we go back now."

"I do not believe he has Camelee or Hild. I think they were brought back. I think they have gone into the future. I must figure out a way to get her back." Wolf stopped and thought about it for a moment. "You go, Fin. Find him and bring me back his head."

Fin grinned from ear to ear. It meant much when the chief sent you out to kill his enemy. It spoke of trust and that the chief thought you good enough to take his place. And this was an especially important enemy. "Yes, my brother. You will have it."

"And…" Fin added reluctantly. "If he has her and the child?"

Wolf narrowed his eyes on him. "Whatever condition they are in, bring them back to me, Fin. Forget his head. Just bring them back."

"Yes, Brother."

Wolf didn't wait for the morning to come but rode out with ten men. They headed west, toward Wessex.

Genevra was there, waiting for him at the gate when he returned. When she saw that he was alone, her expression faltered and did not recover.

"You did not find her."

"Genevra." He dismounted and went to her. "Two men saw her disappear into thin air. Her and Hild. I believe she went back to the twenty-first century."

"The future," she whispered as her eyes took on a glassy haze.

"Genevra!" He took her by the elbows. "Please tell me what you know of it. You must tell me. I intend to find her."

"A few days ago, I knew nothing," she said, going off into the distance again. "But now—we came from the past."

"What? We?" Wolf balked. "What are you saying? Were you a part of this? What do you mean you came from the past?"

"From ancient times. Fifty-two AD." She paused when he fell into the nearest chair. "We went to Ah—Ah—I cannot remember what 'twas called, but it smelled like apples, and we did not age."

"Genevra," he said, frustrated and impatient. "This is—do you know where Camelee is?"

"Aye, Chief. She is with him. The man my soul aches for. Her father."

"You need sleep, Woman." He began to rise from the chair, looking more defeated than ever.

"Wolf Kristiansen!" she shouted, stopping him.

He pivoted on his heel. No one shouted for him that way and lived.

"Camelee is my daughter. I am…or was a queen. I was wed

to the King of Camelot, but I do not know who that is."

"That is simple," Wolf told her, sounding less convinced than before. "If you were married to the King of Camelot, that would make you Queen Guinevere and your husband would be King Arthur. Do you not remember Camelee told us about her namesake, Camelot? So, you are telling me Camelee is your daughter and the daughter of a king from a book?"

"Oh, aye. King Arthur Pendragon," she whispered, saying each word slowly. As if she were hearing it for the first time and tasting each one. "Arthur."

Pendrey. Wolf remembered Camelee's surname. It was similar to Pendragon.

"How do I find her?"

"It feels good to tell this to someone. But," she shook her head. "I do not know. I can tell you this though, if the king knows where I am, he will come for me. I will see to it that you have time with our daughter."

"Time? How much time?" Let them try to separate him from her a second time.

"That is all I can promise now, Wolf. Please be patient."

He didn't want to be patient, but he would do it. For a little while longer. Mostly, he wanted to believe this madness Genevra was telling him.

"Very well. How do you know she is with him?"

"Last night, I started dreaming of them together in a resplendent glass castle. She was quite miserable. Oh, but not because she is being mistreated. She appeared very sad."

"Yes. I heard her weeping in the forest where she disappeared," Wolf agreed more enthusiastically. "I do not know much about magic, but if there is a kind of veil that separates us, I want to find a way through it."

"We need magic, my lord."

The fire in his eyes wasn't quenched by the impossible. "Where do we find it?

"YOU LOOK BEAUTIFUL."

Camelee didn't smile back at her father when she reached the grand banqueting table, made of frosted glass. Crystal chandeliers hung in a row of five across the length of the hall, illuminating the banqueting hall in a soft golden glow.

Her father. How insane was this? She was still expecting to open her eyes and come out of her coma. King Arthur was her father. Really?

But it made sense. Even down to her name. They'd named her after Camelot and kept her with people who were descendants. The Pendreys.

According to the king, he, his wife, Guinevere, his knights, and his illegitimate son, Mordred, lived here in the first century! There was a war, during which time Viviane and Nimue's sister Morgan, known as *Le Fey*, or *the Faery*, cast a spell on Mordred. Is that what the sisters were? Faeries?

Mordred tried to kill his father and almost succeeded, if not for Viviane who brought him to Avalon and there he stayed for many centuries, never growing old.

The sisters captured Morgan and made certain she would not escape her confines of her island prison.

But twenty-six years ago, she did.

Arthur escaped to this realm again because he was familiar with it. His family would remain here, growing old without each other. Everyone old enough to remember was enchanted to forget the king and who they were. The adults were sent away. The children given up for adoption.

All to keep them safe.

Camelee was tired of being safe. She wanted to face this Morgan and give her a good punch in mouth. She'd ruined all their lives. Arthur and his beloved queen Guinevere had grown older apart. Their children's paths had changed. At least hers had.

Camelee was certain Arthur would have been a devoted, loving father. She would have grown up here and stopped getting older at twenty-five to thirty. Morgan took it all from her.

"Please sit next to me, Daughter," the king invited, pulling out her chair. "I hope Avalon pleases you."

It was certainly majestic and beautiful. Everywhere she looked there were apple trees and waterfalls and children playing in the sunshine. It was perfect. But not for her. Wolf wasn't here.

How could she miss him so much? She barely knew him and yet she was falling in love with him. She didn't want to think about a life with him or without him, or that he wasn't real.

She thought she had never cried so much in her life as she had in these few days. She should he happy…like Hild. She had her father back. Soon, she might even get her mother back, that is, if the king could find her. She was out of the violent eleventh century. She was no longer a servant—a fact which caused the king to slam his fist down on the table and shout, "You are a princess!"

He didn't seem like a bad guy. He did what he said he would, like take care of Hild. And her. He treated her with respect, as though she were higher in station than he. She found him in the magnificent crystal chapel every few hours, praying to God.

So, he was nice. But, number one, she didn't want a father in her life anymore. She wasn't a foolish child fantasizing what it would be like to have a daddy who loved her. Those days were over. Number two, she certainly didn't want this legendary king—Arthur—of all people to be her father. Why Camelee? If he was real, and if he truly was the man those famous authors wrote about, then everything he told her was likely the truth. Giving her up nearly destroyed him and her mother, but they wouldn't have her killed on their account. She could understand that kind of love. She would give her own life for Hild. If her father hadn't found her when he did, she would have fought Leofric's men to the death to keep them from Hild. She understood. She could forgive her parents.

But what if none of it was real and she surrendered her anger and hatred to nothing?

"Our family should be here soon," the king told her. "Until then, tell me about your life."

"I would prefer not to think about it," she answered honestly. "It seems it's all I think about lately, so, I'd rather hear about your ordinary life, Mr. Lancaster."

He smiled and, for a moment, she fell, lost in the idea of having a loving father, who was handsome and easy to talk to. He wasn't stuffy with archaic ideas.

"I'm an archeologist. I spent this past fall in Egypt."

"Wow, that's pretty cool."

His smiled widened into a grin. "Yes, unless you're frying in the sun and covered in sand every day. Then it's not so cool."

"That's true," she agreed, daring to smile with him. No. If he wasn't real, she couldn't take it. "I was an actress," she told him, acting calm now. "Sometimes I used to think the people I was working with were bags of dry bones."

He laughed as if he had never heard anything so funny. Camelee had to admit liking him. It was hard not to.

She sipped apple wine from a cup made of frosted sapphire. "Wow, this is delicious."

Her father agreed. "You'll find that everything is just a little better here."

Nimue swept into the hall toting Hild by the hand. Hild looked like a little faery with all her flaxen curls piled on top of her head and silver dust coming off the gown Nim had made for her this morning.

When Hild saw her, she broke free and came running. "Lee!" She climbed into Camelee's lap and that was where she remained for the remainder of the afternoon, while Camelee told King Arthur which movies and shows she'd appeared in. He'd been living in NYC for the past twenty-six years. Maybe he'd seen her in something. She didn't mind that he didn't recognize any of them. He was more of a book person. And Viviane, who remained standing, didn't watch television or anything on an electronic devise.

The air shimmered around them for a moment and then Nim appeared with her arm looped with a man—was he a regular man? Camelee had never, in all her days, seen anyone like him. He was the kind of beautiful that drew one's eyes and kept them locked on him. He wore a black sweater that hugged his muscular body, with jeans that fit perfect.

"Father," he said, obviously having met the king before and knowing who he was. "Why am I here?"

The king smiled lovingly at him. "Mordred—"

Mordred. Isn't he the one who—

"Sebastian, please, Father."

He was her half-brother. He wore modern twenty-first century clothes. A knee-length wool coat, jeans covering long legs, and boots. He spoke with a British accent. She wondered where he was living. He was Morgan Le Fey's son, and one would have to be blind not to see the otherworldly beauty of him. He reminded her of a black stallion, wary and dangerous if not handled with care. He was 6'4" or 5" inches of pure male. His black hair reached his shoulders, and a few tendrils eclipsed his vivid green eyes. He had a strong jaw, darkened by a day or two of not shaving.

"Son, Morgan is free again—"

Sebastian's skin went pale, making him somehow even more striking. "Noelle!" He pulled away from Nim and lifted his hands. He began speaking. The air around him seemed to blur.

Magic, Camelee thought, mesmerized. There was no pretty shimmer, but a warped haze. He spoke more quickly, waving his hands with purpose and determination. But nothing happened. The air cleared, like a fizzled-out ember. He turned a hard glare on Nim—as if she, or the sisters, controlled Avalon. The king had no authority here.

His eyes changed from green to hot, molten gold. "Let me go back to her, Witch."

"Sebastian," their father said with a thread of warning in his voice. "Your beloved is safe. Please trust me. Merlin is taking care of everything in that realm. As for your magic, you know you cannot use it here."

"Father," his son pleaded but there was something so dangerous in his plea, Camelee wanted to leap in front of the king and keep Sebastian, aka Mordred, the king killer, away from him. "If you don't let me return to her, I will never forgive you."

"Sebastian, I can do nothing," Arthur vowed, "at least until Merlin returns. His magic is involved in keeping them safe."

"Why couldn't it keep us safe with them where we were?" Camelee turned to the king and asked.

"Who is this?" her half-brother demanded.

"*This*," she bit back, "is his daughter, Camelee."

"Oh," he said looking her over. "Yes, I can see the resemblance to Guinevere."

He said something after that, but Camelee didn't hear anything else. She resembled her mother. People often remarked that she resembled Genevra.

She felt ill and buried her nose in Hild's sweet, messy bun.

Could it be? Could Genevra be Guinevere? Wasn't the name Genevra Italian for…her mother…Guinevere?

Should she tell Arthur? She wanted to. In fact, it almost dropped right out of her mouth. But did she want to face Genevra as her mother right now? She had just found her father—and it was King-freaking-Arthur! Wasn't that enough for one day? For a lifetime? Would the king let her barter? Information about his beloved queen in exchange for Wolf to be brought here?

"Visions?" Sebastian asked, watching her.

"What? No," she replied, shaking her head. "Something you said—"

The air went silver again, and Camelee realized Viviane hadn't been there for the last few seconds. She returned now with another dark-haired beauty. This one, a woman in her early twenties. She was dressed in a bunch of skirts and a tight little bodice type of top with a square cut neckline. Fifteenth century maybe? She was about six months pregnant.

"Dad!" She ran down the hall and into the king's arms, where she remained weeping and clinging to him.

"Kestrel, my baby," Camelee heard her father say softly into his *other* daughter's neck. His baby. The way they reacted to each other made Camelee wonder how well they knew each other. Was Kestrel not sent away, as she had been?

"Elia—I mean Viviane told me everything," Kestrel told him. "It's all so crazy! You're King Arthur! Elia suspected it." She turned to gleam at Viviane and then back at her father. "Why did you keep it from me?"

"Everything will be made clear to you shorty, my love."

His love.

Camelee swallowed back something that burned like hellfire. She blinked away and caught Sebastian, aka Mordred, staring at her. She almost broke out into a sweat and looked away.

"Sebastian, Camelee, this is Kestrel, my daughter with my earthly wife, Cynthia." He turned to Kestrel and motioned the other way around. "Sebastian, my eldest son with Morgan, and Camelee, daughter with my beloved Guinevere."

Kestrel stared at her like a baby bird with huge eyes just waiting to be eaten by her predator. She smiled at Camelee. How did she do it? Was she so confident in her father's love that she wasn't threatened by the daughter born of his beloved?

"Okay, so, Dad," Kestrel said. "What's going on, because I have to tell you, I'm not feeling one hundred percent my best right now."

Instinctively, and for some reason, Camelee thought of Genevra. She put aside her jealousy and hurried to Kestrel's side and helped her into a chair.

"I know this is hard to accept and understand—"

Kestrel's lagoon-colored eyes opened larger, set on her father. "What do you mean hard to accept? What is hard to accept?" She spun around and stared at Camelee and Sebastian. "What?"

"You cannot return home at present because Morgan is once again on the loose. She will come after you with complete disregard for Nicholas or anyone else you love to get to me. If you are not there with him, she will not be able to find when or where he is. You are a danger to him. Do you understand?" The king looked at all of them. "You are dangers to those you love because of my blood flowing in you. I am sorry."

Kestrel covered her mouth with her hands and cried out. Camelee stepped back. He'd tried to tell her, but she hadn't heard.

"I don't know what you mean, I can't go back. Dad! I'm married and I'm having his child. I have to go back! You're responsible for my going back to him in the first place! I never wrote to you about this before, but I was transported right onto the battlefield, in the middle of the War of the Roses! Right in the middle of flying, bloody swords, Dad! I had a hard time. I don't care about Morgan! Let us worry about her!"

"Let us finally have our lives," Camelee added.

"Agreed," Sebastian said.

"Son, you know what Morgan is capable of. How do you expect your sisters to fight her?"

While father and son spoke, Camelee stared at Kestrel in her chair. She looked to be in shock.

"There now," Camelee heard herself say. A sister. She had a sister. Her traitorous heart melted within her. "We will find a solution to this."

Kestrel smiled at her. "I won't lie, I'm—hey, wait. Are you Camelee Pen—" she nodded. "Yes, Pendrey. Pendragon. I saw you in *Silver Buttons*, that cable series."

"Yes, before I was pulled back a millennium. How well do you know the king?"

"I grew up with him," Kestrel answered.

"Was he a good father?"

Kestrel nodded and then veiled her gaze. "I'm sorry you didn't have him."

"Thank you," Camelee told her softly, and then turned to glare at the king.

"Did we all not need to be kept safe?" she demanded of him.

"No. Not all of you did," he told her candidly. "Morgan would never find me. I would have to go to her. She would use those I love to get me to do that. Or use one of my dear children to kill me. Sebastian possesses more power than you, Kestrel, or Micajah, and he couldn't stop her from taking over his mind."

"More power? Camelee asked him. "We have power?"

"Of course you do" he replied. "I am a sorcerer. My mother, your grandmother, was Viviane and Nimue's sister before Morgan killed her."

It wasn't real. It wasn't real. It wasn't real. She was supposed to believe now that she had magic powers?

Something crashed above them on the second floor. They heard a man shouting, his voice deep and intimidating. "Somebody better start explaining before I take you all in!"

The king smiled, looking up. "That would be your brother, Michael."

Michael. Oh, it hurt to think she had a brother who'd been given up with her. She heard him pounding down the stairs. Coming closer. It still completely threw her off when she looked up at the glass ceiling and couldn't see upstairs through it.

Another beautiful woman appeared at the doorway, like Viviane and Nim, she wore a gown that appeared to be spun from the most gossamer gauzy threads. Her black hair cascaded down her back and, like the others, she wore a gold circlet over her brow.

Camelee had met her on her first night here. She was one of the sisters and her name was Gliten.

But Camelee's attention was on the man walking with her. If Sebastian was a stallion, Michael was a panther. An angry panther.

When he saw the king, he stopped in his tracks. "Mr. Lancaster...or should I saw King Arthur?"

"Dad will do fine," Arthur told him tenderly.

Michael didn't react. Except for the tightening of his jaw beneath a closely clipped mustache and beard.

Camelee saw the hurt behind the cool detachment. Yes. Michael had lost his family in this. Just like her.

Finally, he managed to say, "You sent a letter back in time to Judge Whimsey, telling him who you were."

"That's right," Arthur agreed. "We had met after Kestrel's disappearance. You were assigned to the case. Your name gave you away. There are not many Pendragons left."

Michael didn't react but slipped his sapphire gaze to Kestrel when the king pointed to her. "I remember your case. I wanted to find you."

"And you did," she said with a quirk of her mouth.

"Yeah," he said with a smile of his own, though it resembled hers. "Hi, Kestrel."

"Hi."

"So, you're my sister?"

"Half-sister," Arthur pointed out. "You've met Sebastian, your half-brother back in your time."

Michael stepped in front of the king. "Do you know who he is?"

"Yes. Mordred. But now he is Sebastian."

"I was hoping you did all right," Michael told his half-brother and allowed a smile to enhance his rugged good looks. Michael's mother may have been human, but his father was not.

After he spoke to Sebastian, his slightly glistening gaze went to her.

"This is Camelee," Arthur announced, "Like you, she is born of myself and Queen Guinevere."

Michael looked wide-eyed and a bit bewildered, but he understood one thing immediately. They had both been given up and their lives forever altered.

"I've seen you before." Michael narrowed his eyes on her. "On T.V.?"

She nodded, happier than she realized she would be that they recognized her. Not because of her ego, but because it solidified that this was real.

Still, she wondered what he thought.

"You believe all this? We're not imagining it? Not dead or something?"

"I'm not dead," he assured her, and she wondered if death was afraid of him. "And if I am, I don't want to go back to my life before my life with Charlotte. That isn't what this is about, is it?" He turned to Arthur. "Why are we all here, and where is my wife? I'm not going back to twenty nineteen."

"None of us are," Kestrel added.

"Let us go back to our loved ones," Sebastian warned. "We will deal with Morgan."

They looked at Camelee for agreement. Was she ready to declare that she didn't want to return to her life in front on the screen? Could the king or the sisters cast a spell on her to make her forget Wolf and Hild…her mother? If so, would she choose her future?

◆┄•　•┄◆

CHAPTER NINETEEN

WOLF SPENT HIS third night in the forest. He wouldn't give up. He'd heard Camelee weeping here. If she had truly gone into the future, the veil had to be thinnest here. He called out to her beneath the stars and the anguish in his voice made his companion cry silently on her pallet.

He'd taken Genevra with him because if she wasn't mad, and she truly was Queen Guinevere, Camelee's captor would come for her. And when he did, Wolf would get his woman back.

"Why do you think he has not come for you yet?" he asked Genevra the next morning while they sat around a small fire and broke their fast together.

"Mayhap he cannot find me."

"Or maybe you are wrong about all of this."

She stared at him boldly and frowned with insult. Something about her had changed over the last few days. She possessed an air of confidence and authority she did not have before. Each day, she displayed more royal demeanor. Either she was a true queen, or she was undeniably mad in her head.

"Do you accuse me of deceiving you?

"Not deliberately."

He studied her while she glared at him. "Tell me, what is happening to you? What is changing you?" He had to ask. If somehow Genevra was involved in all this, then she was his only connection to Camelee.

"I am remembering," she answered with gentle confidence.

"What are you remembering, Genevra, or…my queen."

Her smile was so unexpected and radiant he almost bowed his head. She was beautiful with her golden hair braided messily down her back. All the stray tendrils around her head were illuminated in the sun and made her countenance shine like someone kissed by God.

"I am remembering my past and my future."

She told him everything she'd remembered so far. The way she described the future was almost exactly the same as Camelee has described it.

"When you said King Arthur Pendragon is my husband, my heart leaped at the sound of his name. I know he is the man I love, have loved and longed for for almost thirty years. But I do not remember him. I do not know how he looks or smells, or what I love about him. I dream of him with Camelee, and he is mostly faceless."

"I do not think he will be for long."

At his words, tears paused at the rims of her eyes, and then fell down her wind-burned cheeks. He realized how cold she must be and yet she had not complained once.

He swept his cloak off his shoulders and wrapped her in it.

"No. You need it for yourself. I will fetch an extra cloak from the keep later. Keep it," he held out his palm to stop her from taking it off. "I am from the north. It is much colder in Denmark."

She nodded and smiled, and they were silent for a few moments. Then he looked at her and said. "You know how she feels about her mother?"

She nodded and swallowed, and Wolf hoped Camelee gave her a chance to make up for the lost years.

"She thinks I gave her up because I did not love her. But it almost killed me."

"You have much to tell her then," he said in a low voice.

"You are a good man, Chief. I will make certain the king knows."

He nodded, but he didn't care what anyone thought of him.

"What are your intentions with my daughter, Chief?" Genevra asked in the still of the morning.

"I wish to bring her back to Denmark and make her my wife."

"To Denmark? You would not prefer to go into the future with her? 'Tis much easier to live."

He shrugged his shoulders "We shall see. First, I must find a way to get to her. Unfortunately, we do not know anyone who practices magic."

"Hmm, aye," she agreed, then leaned in and whispered, "but mayhap, he knows, since he just appeared out of thin air." She motioned with her chin to a man weaving through the trees, coming toward them.

He had dark hair tied back and a beard just as long. He appeared of middle age and as he drew closer, Wolf unsheathed his sword. He was prepared to do what he must to get Camelee back.

"Guin! Guinevere! Is that you, my queen?" the man called out.

Wolf felt his hair rise off his skin. It was happening.

"Merlin?" she called back.

Who was Merlin? Wolf wondered as Gen—Guinevere's eyes filled to the brim with tears.

She flung off Wolf's cloak and took off running straight into the man's arms. "Oh, Merlin! Blessed friend! 'Tis good to see you…to remember you! Tell me, where is the king?"

"He searches for you each day, my queen. Nothing eases his pain, not even having his children back."

Wolf took a small step closer. The king had Camelee.

"Merlin, why have my memories returned and why were they taken from me at all?"

He explained about a witch called Morgan, who was free and looking for them. When Genevra heard the name, she gasped. This Morgan, thought Wolf, must be a formidable enemy if everyone was hiding from her.

"Take me to the witch," he demanded. "I will kill her!"

Merlin would hear nothing of it. His duty was to protect Wolf from her.

The insult was strong in Wolf's ears. Protect him? He didn't need anyone's protection!

"You are to wait here while I take her to the king. I will return to you shortly."

Wolf nodded his consent, but his plan had been to take hold of Camelee's captor and put a blade to his neck while he took Wolf to her.

But Genevra was about to go to her husband, a man whose love had kept her heart from all others, without even remembering him. She was going to be reunited with her daughter, whom she loved. Camelee needed that. She deserved to have a good mother, a mother like Genevra.

They began to disappear. Genevra's gaze caught his. "I will see to things."

He never trusted anything to anyone else but his own hands. He watched solemnly as he let his only link to Camelee go.

"Saints help us! Where did they go?"

Wolf spun on his heel and found seven Saxons there. All were armed.

"Men! You all saw them vanish. This Dane is in league with demons!"

The other six shouted their agreement.

Wolf drew his blade and held it ready to fight. He had so much fury in him, he was certain he could kill them all. He didn't see the small army deeper in the forest.

"YOUR MAJESTY," CAMELEE called out, finally ready to give the answer her siblings were waiting for. "Do you want to send me back to my future, in which I hated you and my mother?"

"No, Daughter," he was quick to tell her. "That isn't what I intend to do."

"What, then, did you intend to do?" she asked with her sister and brothers waiting for his answers to her.

"I want you all to remain in Avalon until Morgan is caught."

"Without Nicholas?"

"Noelle will not give up her career to come here."

"No," was all Michael said, but it carried much conviction. He wasn't staying.

"Morgan will go after the people you love if you are with them!" Arthur insisted. "Sebastian, you know I'm right. She went after you, and you almost took my life." He spread his potent gaze over each of them. "Do you want to see your beloved Noelle trying to kill you? And if she succeeds, she will live with it."

Sebastian didn't argue back but turned on his heel and pounded his fist on the door.

"I don't care about staying here, Dad," Kestrel told him. "Just bring Nicholas here. Please."

"I will speak to the sisters," he said. "I know there are exceptions to the rules. Maybe we can find one."

She nodded. They all did. There was nothing else they could do.

"Father...Dad...I'm not sure about any of this," Camelee told him. "But please consider what you've done. You have sent us by way of a brooch to the great loves of our lives, and now it's being snatched away. I know you have lost your love, as well. I now believe I know where—"

"I will see to things," the voice called out, interrupting Camelee. It was Genevra's voice. She was not in the great hall, and then she was. It was just like that. No silver sparkles. She was simply there...with a man who looked like he'd just come from a magic lamp.

"My king," the man said with a slight bow. "Please forgive

the interruption…"

"Guin?" the king choked out. He rose from his chair and rubbed his eyes. "Guin, are you real?"

Camelee felt her vision blur with tears while she watched Genevra cover her mouth to quiet her cries. She walked to him slowly, wiping her cheeks. When she reached the steps leading to the king, she knelt.

He was there to gently pull her to her feet.

"Guinevere, it's truly you," he cried, pulling her into his arms, where they wept, and kissed, and touched each other's faces in awe of being together again.

"Guin, our children…" The king turned her to look at them.

Michael went to her and swallowed her up in his embrace.

Genevra cried into her son's shoulder and Arthur cried into his hand. "I hated leaving you both at that orphanage. I try to imagine what the pain is like. Losing a part of my body? Losing a parent, your home, but there is nothing to compare with what I had to do."

She set her warm gaze on Camelee and then lifted her chin and turned to her husband. "I cannot stay."

"What?" the king's question boomed off the glass walls.

"My queen," said the man who arrived with her. "You can stay. This is where you belong now. There is no one back there for you."

"No, Merlin, but there is someone back there for *her*." She motioned to Camelee and then turned to Nim and Viviane, who had stayed though their sister Gliten had left. "My dear friends, my heart rejoices at seeing you again, but my happiness is only temporary. For when I think of the man I just left, I cannot partake and enjoy in what he needs to live and cannot find."

She speaks of Wolf, Camelee thought, ignoring the burning behind her eyes. Was he angry she'd left? Worried? Sad? From the sadness in Genevra's eyes while she looked at her, Camelee's heart ached to think his was aching for her.

"He does nothing but sit in the forest where you disappeared and call your name, hoping you will answer."

At Genevra's words, Camelee threw her hands to her face and wept. Was this what she had reduced a warrior to? No one ever cared for her this way. She wouldn't lose him. Genevra was trying to help her.

"You're her then," Camelee accused. "My mother."

Genevra shook her head and tears streamed down her face. "Not the woman you believe."

No. Genevra's memory had been taken. She'd been ripped away from her children, stripped of the memory of them because of Morgan. She'd lived in England as Genevra, mother to all because she wasn't mother to two. "I know…Mom."

They walked toward each other, crying. When Genevra reached her, she smiled. "What changed your mind about me?"

Camelee shrugged a shoulder. "My pain is real. It's so real. Why shouldn't my happiness be real, as well?"

"Pain for…?"

"Him," Camelee told her. "Wolf."

Her mother nodded. "I will do everything I can to help you."

Camelee never thought it would be so easy to forgive her mother. But she also never thought there was an evil faerie after them and in order to save their lives, her parents made the heart-wrenching decision to leave them. "I've missed you."

"And I've missed you, my cherished daughter. There was nothing left of me after I left you and Micajah. My heart and soul were with you. I welcomed Arthur and Merlin's spell to forget. If not for it, I would have given up my spirit as well."

Camelee threw her arms around Genevra and kissed her cheek. Her mother was forced, as explained several times by the king, to give up her children because she loved them, not because she didn't.

"We have so much to talk about, my queen."

"Aye, a lifetime," her mother agreed. "But first, I wish to know, is Hild well?"

"She's thriving and very happy here," Camelee answered.

"Would you like me to get her? She would love to see you."

"No," her mother said. "I do not want to see her and then have to leave again." She said the last words loud enough for her husband to hear.

"Guinevere," he shot, clearly offended by her words. "You know that here in Avalon, I have no authority in these matters."

"Avalon." Guinevere repeated with a poorly concealed smile. "Aye, I remember, Avalon."

"Viviane!" the king said with as much authority as he'd probably had in Camelot, startling the beautiful woman standing with Kestrel. "This has caused havoc in my family. Bring them their loved ones."

"Arthur," Viviane answered. "This is not a matter I can decide on my own. If I could, do you not think I would love to see my Nicholas and bring him here to Kes? I must discuss it with my sisters. You are asking us to bring four more people, mortals here to Avalon, and then, what? Return them to their normal lives when and if we ever catch Morgan again? Four timelines would be altered, not to mention these four coming from the twenty-first century."

He looked every part a king, standing tall and strong by his high crystal chair. "I understand what I'm asking. I'm pleading."

"Arthur." It was Nim talking now. "Come with us to the meeting room. Merlin, you come as well. We will summon Gliten and decide what to do."

Before anyone could reach out and stop them, the king and the sisters were gone.

"Does anyone know what his connection is to the sisters?" Michael turned around to ask them.

"He was brought here at birth by his mother, Igraine," Sebastian told them. "She is one of the original Nine."

"So, he's their nephew," Michael said. "Morgan slept with her nephew."

"And had me. Correct, Detective." Sebastian smiled.

"How do we know you won't go to her side when she

comes?"

"You do not," Sebastian answered lightly. "But I helped in her capture on Christmas Eve."

"Before or after your memories returned?" Guinevere put to him.

Sebastian didn't answer. Instead, he glared at Guinevere with molten anger. "I am not waiting for someone else to decide my fate. I am leaving now."

He lifted his hands to the air and began speaking. He didn't give up for ten more minutes. Twice, the rift in the air appeared, but it didn't last.

"If they say no," Kestrel said softly, "are we stuck here?"

"No. I know a way to leave," Guinevere let them know. "We need to go to the waterfalls of Alastra. Beside the pool, there is a tall rowan tree—"

The air began to ripple, but in a separate place from where Sebastian worked. They all heard a deep-throated roar, like that of an angry bear.

A hand appeared from the ripple, and then a short guttural cry and a face could be seen, as if it were squeezing through something no one else could see.

Wolf! Camelee saw his face. She went utterly still watching him break through time and space.

$$\diamond\!\!-\!\!\bullet \quad \bullet\!\!-\!\!\diamond$$

CHAPTER TWENTY

H E FOUGHT HARDER than he ever had in his life. Harder than a few moments ago when he was fighting and killing Saxons. He'd gone berserk and killed the seven Saxons in almost five swings of his blade. He didn't remember fighting them. As a berserker he was not in his right mind when it happened. Taken over by rage and fury, he'd gone into a trancelike state and destroyed everything in his path.

As he was hacking and tearing, he felt his blade go through something thicker than the air. His thoughts were jumbled and indistinguishable, still fighting in a trance. More men had arrived. Fin? Someplace inside him, someone called out to keep going. Keep slashing and cutting through. Do not stop!

He roared and shouted as he fought his way through. Growing weary but casting it aside. He could see something different. He was in the forest. He should have been looking at trees, but instead, he was looking into a cavernous room made of glass.

He pushed his arm through, but the air fought him, closed in on him. And then he caught a glimpse of Camelee standing at a table with others. With one more mighty roar that resounded off the walls, he pushed through and almost tumbled to the floor.

It took a moment for the cobwebs to leave his head and for him to realize what had happened. When he did, he was awestruck. What? He did it? He did it! He turned to Camelee and smiled. Before he blinked again, she ran to him and leaped into his arms.

"You came for me," she cried into his neck, held in his arms, her feet dangling off the floor. "How did you do it?"

"Do not move!"

A man's warning voice reminded Wolf that he was in a foreign place with potentially dangerous enemies. He pushed Camelee behind him and held his blade out before him.

The man who told him not to move stared at him with an unblinking gaze. "How do you still have your sword?"

"What?" Wolf asked, looking at his glistening blade.

The man held up his hands and began to chant.

"No, Sebastian!" Camelee moved in front of him. "Don't hurt him!"

Hurt him? Wolf scoffed. With what? His words? He almost laughed out loud.

"How did you get through?" the man...Sebastian demanded, lowering his hands.

"I fought my way through."

The man curled the corners of his mouth into a smile. "You cannot fight your way though. You are a sorcerer."

Ah, yes, this place was magic. It had to be. He looked around. He'd never seen anything like it. The walls, the ceiling, the floor, all of it was made of solid water. That's what it appeared to be to him. He wanted to touch it.

"No," he told Sebastian. "If I was, all this—" he pointing to the hall "—would be a broken ruin for taking her."

"Wolf," Genevra said. Was this her hall? "Do not threaten Avalon in the presence of the sisters or they *will* kill you. They will kill you with magic. You will not have a chance to defend yourself. Understand?"

He clenched his jaw and nodded. "Yes."

"I would not deceive you, Chief," she continued, "though I am uncertain of many things now that I see your sword in this place. Weapons are not permitted."

Wolf trusted what she said. He would not threaten

this…Avalon again. It was too beautiful to destroy anyway.

"I am taking her back," he told them all.

"Listen—Wolf is it?" Another dark-haired man stepped forward. "We're all kinda in this together, okay?"

Listening to him, Wolf's gaze fell to Camelee. This man spoke like her. He came from her future. Had they known each other? Had he taken her to his bed? No. Something about his eyes resembled Camelee's. Her brother or relative.

"None of us, including her," he continued, "wants to be here. The king is meeting with the sisters about allowing our loved ones to come here without screwing up the timeline.

"Chief Constable Michael Pendridge, by the way."

There were chiefs in her time? But that wasn't what was making his head spin. What did this man mean *screwing up the timeline*? It awakened something in him—a desire to make certain things were right in the timeline. He didn't know where the desire came from. Right now, he didn't care. He wasn't leaving without Camelee.

"I am Chief Ulf Kristiansen."

"What are you, a Viking?" Pendridge asked.

Pendridge, Pendrey, Pendragon. They were relatives. Her family.

"I am a Dane. High Commander of King Cnut." It was what he told anyone who asked. He didn't have to think about it. And he wasn't. Where was he? Was this real? Had he truly fought his way through the veil that separates realms? His instincts told him to take Camelee and run. But he reined in those rash desires and took control over them.

"King Cnut?" asked a dark-haired beauty with wide, sea-colored eyes. "I'm Kestrel. Kes." She smiled and gave him a little wave, then looked around him at Camelee. "You went to the eleventh century? Rough."

She spoke like Camelee, Wolf thought, listening. Another one of them from the same place. The same time?

"Oh, yes," Camelee agreed wholeheartedly.

A little too wholeheartedly for Wolf's comfort. He cut her a worried look.

"Where did you go?" she asked Kes, without looking at him. What was wrong? What was she afraid of?

"Fourteen eighty-five," Kes answered.

Wolf swallowed his thumping heart. Believing Camelee's story in theory was different than seeing all this magic unfolding before him. What could he do against it?

"Are these your children?" he asked Gen—the queen. He shook his head at himself. What was he to believe? His belly was tied in knots painful enough to give him proof that he was alive.

"Michael and Camelee are born from my womb," she answered gracefully. "I have always loved Mordred as my own and, today, I welcome Kestrel into my heart."

"Mordred," Sebastian held up his hand when Wolf asked who was Mordred. "I prefer Sebastian now."

"That is good name, Sebastian. I would like to meet the woman who captured your frolicsome heart."

He smiled and bowed. "I will be certain you do meet her." He turned to Wolf. "Tell me what you did."

"I do not know. I was fighting some Saxons in the forest where Camelee disappeared. I…I went berserk, as I sometimes do. I—"

They all asked for an explanation. He gave them one as best he could and then continued. "I felt a change in the air, and hoping it was the rift, I attacked it. I fought it for a few long moments because it did not want to let me through. I was unwavering in my purpose."

"So," Sebastian concluded, "this going berserk of yours pushes you into another realm, and there, *this* realm was vulnerable to you."

Wolf shrugged his shoulders and reached for Camelee's hand. Hers was small and damp in his. He wanted to tell her he loved her, and he wanted to stay with her for the rest of his days. He wanted to reassure her that all would be well, but he wasn't so sure it would be.

"Can you do it again?" Sebastian asked him.

"If I get angry enough," Wolf replied.

"I would suggest you hold your temper if you wish to live another instant."

At the sound of Genevra's friend, Merlin, they all turned to watch him make his way from the other end of the long table and come toward them. "How did you get here, Northman? And why is there a sword hanging from your belt? Do you possess magic?"

"He possesses no magic, Merlin," Genevra assured him. "He fought like a warrior to get to the woman he loves. That is all."

The man shook his head as if to clear it. "He fought to get here? What does that mean? And what do *you* mean, *that is all?*" He raised his voice slightly. "The meeting is over. They will all be retuning at any moment. When they see him—"

"Then hide him!" Camelee shouted at him.

"Mr. Simeon, do something!" Kestrel joined in.

"He cannot be hidden," Merlin said. raising his hands. "He will tell us how he arrived here. And then your father, the king, will tell you their decision."

Wolf had no idea what was going to happen, and he hated the feeling. He decided he didn't like magic. It may fashion beautiful objects like the castle, but it held too much power over a man.

"Camelee," he said as he turned to her while everyone was questioning Merlin. "Forgive me if you do not share my sentiments and I seem like a madman—"

"I do. I do share them," she vowed, reaching her free hand to his. "I'll be mad with you."

He smiled, and meant it, for the first time since she'd left, he felt lighter and kissed both her hands.

They heard the king's footsteps before he entered the hall. When they did see him, Wolf thought he would have known in a moment who was the king among the servants walking with him, for he carried himself with the same confidence and authority as King Cnut.

He looked more like Kestrel and Michael than he did Camelee. When his blue gaze found Wolf, he stopped dead in his tracks. "Who is this?"

"I am Chief Ulf—"

"How did you come here?" the king demanded, and then without giving Wolf a chance to reply, he called for someone called Viviane.

"Father, wait!" Camelee cried out and clung to Wolf as if she could stop harm from coming to him "I love him! He's not here to hurt anyone. He wants to be with me. Don't you take that from me!"

The king immediately stopped and gave her a sorrowful look. Wolf guessed the meeting Merlin had mentioned did not go well. His fears were conformed a moment later when two women entered the hall.

Wolf thought they were almost too beautiful to be real.

"What is this?" one demanded.

"Who are you?" asked the other on a shaky voice.

"I am Ch—"

"How did you get here?"

"Merlin," they said in unison, "did you bring him?"

"I fought my way here," Wolf told them on a wave of authority. He was tired of being ignored. "I ripped open the veil with my sword." He remembered what Genevra had warned him about threatening Avalon, so he controlled his words by ending them there.

The two women were not as pale when they entered the hall as they were now. Wolf could see and sense their fear. Who was this man who could tear through time and other realms to get here? What else could he do? They had no idea. For that matter, neither did he.

"I came for her, and only her." He reached his hand out to Camelee and hoped he wasn't struck dead. He couldn't help but slip his gaze to Genevra for any clue as to how he was doing.

"Uf! Uf!" Like a little drop from heaven sent to save him, Hild barreled into the hall with two other little girls. When she saw him and Genevra, she squealed with glee and ran into his arms first.

"Uf, you come back!"

He held her and closed his eyes. She'd lost her mother…twice. He couldn't let her lose anyone else.

The two women watched, one with a smile curving her mouth, the other, wide-eyed, and looking like some sort of faerie with her hair cascading around her face.

"Aye, my lady. I told you, I will always come back."

He smiled and kissed her head before he let her down to run to Genevra. He heard a sniffle and looked down to see Camelee wiping her eyes and smiling at her mother.

"Uf," one of the women called out.

"Wolf," he corrected and felt a glint of hope course through him when they both turned to Hild and smiled warmly at her.

"Explain *how* you tore through time."

"I was fighting Saxons and felt my blade rip through something other than flesh. I swung again and again, seeing nothing but white fog or smoke, thinking of nothing but Camelee, and still I hacked my way through."

Their dainty hands trembled. One of them covered her mouth and whispered to the other, whom Wolf suspected by now, was her sister.

"Queen Guinevere, please remove the children," the other one asked.

"May I ask why?" the queen requested, squaring her shoulders.

"We must test his power."

Test? Power? Wolf turned to Camelee, but she had no idea what was happening either.

He was grateful that they had thought of Hild and the other two girls and sent them way first. If they meant to harm him, they would have used his weakness against him. He would not have fought back in front of Hild.

When the children were gone, he turned to the sisters and drew his blade. They looked at each other. The king and Merlin looked wary and a little afraid.

Everyone else was still, breathless, waiting for what was to come. Camelee stepped out of the way.

The two women raised their hands and began a low chant.

Magic. He couldn't fight magic.

As if reading his mind, the sisters turned their hands toward Camelee. The king leaped forward and was stopped with one swipe of a sister's hand in his direction.

All right then, they did indeed try for his weakness. The air around their hands began to sparkle and billow outward toward Camelee. The first vaporous finger touched Camelee and wound around her wrists.

"Hey, what are you doing?"

Wolf watched the next five fingers coming at her and put all his strength into a swipe of his blade. He felt the thickened, sparkling air and swung at it again. The vapors dropped to the floor and faded away.

The sisters gasped and sent more, but his blade sliced through all of them.

They stopped, released Camelee and the king with Wolf's permission, and stared at him.

"I am Nimue of the Nine Sisters of Avalon," said the short-haired woman. "This is Viviane, one of my sisters. Who are you?"

"Chief Ulf Kristiansen of the north, High Commander of King Cnut."

"It is foretold," Viviane told him and the rest, "a man would come and be able to leave and return at will, without using magic. His power comes from the Creator. His purpose is to stop others from changing the timeline from Avalon."

"I know nothing about any of that," he told them. "I came for her alone."

"You cannot take her from Avalon," the king spoke up. His tone was strong and authoritative. "Morgan will find her. I won't let you put her in danger after I took her from her mother for her entire life!"

What was Wolf to say to that? He swallowed and shifted his gaze to Camelee. She was all that mattered to him in any world. If this witch called Morgan was a danger to her, he would find her and kill her. He could stop a spell and destroy it, but he had to be quick and not distracted.

And though he was an esteemed warrior in the earthly realm, he doubted he could take on Morgan and her magic there. He could only fight her in Avalon.

"We allow very few men here, and only for a short time."

"Good," he corrected and returned his sword to the scabbard. If he could come and go as he pleased, there was no reason to fight. "I do not plan on staying long."

CHAPTER TWENTY-ONE

"I SAW HIM step through the air and disappear. He did not turn to consider you, his brother, but left. He left you to your enemies. To me." Leofric smiled close to Fin's face. His breath was like old fish and ale.

Fin gagged a little. Other than that, he couldn't move. He felt no restraints and, after a moment, he realized he was wounded.

He was in a clearing in the forest, tossed on the cold ground. He tried to sit up. Pain shot through his stomach. His chest felt as if it were on fire. He had been stabbed multiple times. If he knew any better, and being a warrior for many years he did, he'd say his wounds were fatal. He had escaped death many times, but not this time. And hell, Wolf had left him.

They'd been fighting the Saxons. Wolf had already killed seven or eight in his savage rage. But then he stopped fighting their enemies and fought the air in front of him instead. Fin kept as many of them that he could off his brother for as long as he could. He didn't think Wolf even knew he was there.

He didn't think Wolf would disappear. He didn't know what Wolf was doing. But he stood by him and made sure he didn't get killed while he did whatever he was doing.

But he hadn't stood for long. Leofric showed up and came straight for him. They fought. Wolf didn't stop fighting the air while Leofric and ten other men fought Fin and brought him down. In the end, sheer exhaustion had done him in. Wolf was gone. He'd disappeared as if there were a slice in the air. He remembered calling out. But nothing else after that. He wasn't angry with Wolf...or he hadn't thought he was until Leofric got into his ear. Instead of killing him, he'd kept Fin alive to torment him about his brother.

"Greetings, Fin." He opened his eyes at the sound of a woman. What he saw made his heart batter against his ribs. She was beautiful, with raven hair cascading down her back. A silver veil covered it. Her skin was pale white. Her eyes were as green as summer blades of grass.

She wore a gown of blood red, as tight as a second skin. Her body was sensual, voluptuous, with curvy hips and a perfectly round arse. He immediately wanted to take her to his bed. He suspected he was under some kind of spell because he was half-dead and hard as granite.

She stroked her fingers over him, making him shudder. "I can make you better, Fin. Do you want to get better? Do you want to live?"

He nodded. He must be dreaming. Where had she come from?

"Who are you?"

"I am Morgan." She leaned closer and whispered in his ear, "Say my name and live. You do want to live, don't you, Fin?"

He felt lightheaded and weak. Yes. He wanted to live. "Did Leofric send you to seduce me?"

"Who is Leofric but a mere servant? Forget him for now and kill him later. Now it is my time."

He watched her lips as she spoke. They were painted red, a sharp contrast to her white teeth. Did he want to kiss her and possibly get bitten? He stared into her beautiful eyes. She...she was evil. It dripped out of every pore and he wasn't about to give up his soul so easily after keeping his body alive for so long.

"Who needs to live anyway?"

Her eyes went from green to topaz flames. "You're correct!" She balled her hands into fists and was about to fling her words at him.

He held her glare. In fact, he matched it in strength. This wasn't the first time he'd looked death in the face. If she was waiting to see fear in his eyes, she would be here until *her* death.

Finally, being overpowered by his fearless audacity, she opened her hands, cupped his face in them, and lowered her mouth to his.

He didn't resist. He could have, but he felt his body rejuvenating, so he let her kiss him. He didn't owe her anything since he hadn't asked her for anything. This was free.

He licked his tongue across her teeth in a daring dance, hoping she didn't bite it off. She didn't. She was enjoying herself, filling him with strength, so he could use it on her.

He deepened their kiss and roved his bold hands over her luscious rump. He would move atop her and then flip her over and take her from behind—

She broke free and backed away. Her hair was falling around her face and her breath came hard and heavy.

He sat up and looked at his healed wounds. "You are a witch."

"Put away your human words," she scoffed. "I will teach you new ones."

"You will teach me nothing." He looked down at the hard rod poorly confined in his pants. "It is I who will teach you."

She smiled but her eyes blazed like molten fire. He nodded to drive the point home. "Get me a sword so I can kill Leofric."

"No. We are leaving."

"We?"

"That's correct. You will tell me where your brother went and how he was able to open a rift. Is he a sorcerer? What is he called?"

"His name is Ulf Kristiansen, and he is called Wolf. He's not a sorcerer. I do not know how he did it."

"Do you know the man who was with him? Merlin?"

"Who?" Fin asked, watching his erection go down. Just as

well. "There was no one here with him."

She looked around when they heard approaching footsteps. "Do you want to kill him?"

He knew she meant Leofric. "Yes."

She tossed him her own blade and disappeared into the trees.

Fin threw himself down and lay on his back, eyes closed.

"Wake up, Devil. We are heading out." He smirked. "You will have to walk."

Fin groaned low and muttered something that could barely be heard.

Wanting to hear, Leofric leaned his ear to Wolf's mouth.

"My brother…wants you dead." He pulled back and stared Leofric in the eyes. "And I am loyal to my brother."

He used the woman's dagger and thrust it into Leofric's belly until the hilt almost disappeared into him. He dragged the blade upward, spilling the Saxon's guts, never taking his eyes off Leofric's.

Fin pushed him off, leaped to his feet, and started out of the camp through the back woods. He left the king's enemy gurgling on the ground.

"I can kill them all, if you like," Morgan said as she picked up her steps and came up beside him.

Yes. He would like it very much. But he owed her nothing. "I want you to go away."

Her red lips snaked into the smile. "Oh, I cannot do that. I need you to help me find your brother."

"Why do you want him? Is he in danger?"

"Fin." She looked at him as if he were simple-minded. "He went through a rift in time. Of course, he's in danger. Are you not worried about him?"

He stared down at her. "Witch, my brother went through a rift in time. He can obviously take care of himself."

But Fin did worry about where of was. Was he coming back? What if he couldn't? "How can we find him?"

She smiled. "Tell me everything going on in his life for the last few weeks. Leave nothing out."

He didn't want to tell her anything, but he wanted to find Wolf.

"There isn't really much to tell," he murmured. But he proceeded to tell her whatever he knew or suspected.

"So, Arthur and that mortal have another child," Morgan said, scowling. "He hid them from me well."

"How did you heal me?" Fin asked. He didn't care about some king of another realm, or whoever this king was. He wasn't sure he believed her, but she'd healed him. He felt better than new.

"With magic."

"And why did you?"

"So you could help me," she answered.

"But I have not helped you. And yet, you still have not killed me."

She looked up into his verdant eyes while they walked. "I still might after I have my way with you."

He tossed his head back and laughed. "Woman, when I am done with you, you will be done for any other man."

"You're quite confident and bold."

"And you like it," he said, his laughter fading into a smile. He aimed it at her.

"I do. She returned his smile, though hers was sweeter. "Keep it up or I'll dispose of you."

He believed she would try.

He paused for an instant, letting her step ahead, then he slipped behind her, took her neck in one hand. He held her dagger to her throat with the other. Pressing his body to hers, he whispered in her ear, "I like a good challenge. Keep it up or I will be the one doing the disposing." He lowered his hand from her throat and moved it over her left breast and then beneath it. "Your heart has accelerated. Are you afraid, Witch?"

She turned in his hands and looped her arms around his neck. He watched her close her eyes and part her ruby lips. She wanted a kiss. He would give it.

But he would be careful not to give her anything more than his flesh. Of that, she could have all she could take.

He dipped his head and kissed her and while he was kissing her, she faded in his embrace and appeared in solid form behind him—with her dagger in her possession once again. She didn't threaten him but stabbed him in the back.

He went down in front of her, crashing to his knees.

Bitch.

⋙⋘

CAMELEE WATCHED WOLF reach his hand out and touch the glass wall along the long hallway. Everywhere they looked walls glistened and glimmered around them. They had set off to find Genevra and Hild, but they were more interested in each other…and the glass walls.

"What did you say this is called?" Wolf asked, turning his grin on her.

"Glass."

"It is wondrous!"

She smiled, looking at him. He'd come for her. Like some knight on a charging horse come to save her from a dragon. She'd never seen anything like it. Neither had anyone else, apparently. A man in braids and furs, fighting and breaking through time. And doing it to be with her. "It's common in my time, except I've never seen glass that wasn't trans—see-though."

His eyes opened wider. "You can see through your glass?"

"Yes."

He gave the wall one more pat and then removed his hand. "I wish we had glass in Denmark."

She was quiet, still unsure about living in the barbaric eleventh century.

"Camelee, I do not blame you for not wanting to leave Avalon," he said, sensing the change in her tone. "This place is beautiful, and Denmark is cold."

He was right, she didn't want to leave. But not because Avalon was beautiful. She had just found her mother and father. She'd been wrong about them her entire life. They had left her because they loved her. It changed everything. She wanted to get to know them and to get to know herself.

"But I love you, Camelee, and I want to spend my days with you. Do not be afraid to come with me. We will live. We will travel, and the seas may get rough. But we will always be together to get through it. I will keep you warm on cold winter nights, and I will keep you and Hild well fed in the days to come. I will not leave or abandon you. I am even ready to cease fighting. I want to be with you. I just want you to know that."

No one in her life had ever promised her such things. She was glad it was Wolf because she wanted to spend her days and nights with him, too. She wanted to cry to him, to beg him never to abandon her, or stop loving her. But she let herself trust him. He would always do all he could to stay with her. It was such a trumpeting affirmation of his heart for her. It belonged to her, and she would cherish it.

"And I want to make you as happy as you make me, so I guess this will work out. But I wonder if you would want to come to the twenty-first century with me for a little while."

He smiled and drew her in for more kisses. "It sounds like a good adventure."

Yes. An adventure. That's what he liked. Apparently, Wolf could travel to any time, any realm to stop someone from creating a glitch in time. She wondered if, being the king's daughter, she could hitch a ride with whom the sisters called *The Timekeeper*.

"We can stay here for as long as you like," he went on. "I overheard Merlin telling Viviane that Morgan was on earth using her powers, trying to find any of you. You are safest here."

"That's perfect. You make everything perfect."

"Me?" he laughed. "I have done nothing."

"You have done everything," she corrected, looping her arm through his as they began to walk again.

"Then you agree to become my wife today?"

She stopped and gazed at him. "Wolf."

"Say yes, love."

"Yes. Yes! Is this real? Now I *really* doubt it!" She leaped into his waiting arms and kissed his hungry mouth. He kissed her until she felt lightheaded. When he slipped his hands over the mounds of her buns, she groaned. "I'm glad this glass isn't see-through."

He looked around, suddenly distracted, and frowned. "We must not mention glass when we return to England."

"What?"

"Glass. They do not know of it yet. We cannot contaminate the timeline."

"I know, but since when do you care about such things?"

"Since I learned of them." He grinned, dragged her in with one arm, and kissed her parted lips when she looked at him. "Let us go find your father so he can get us wed."

"Eager, are you?" she said, snuggling her face into his shoulder and taking in the scent of him.

"I am eager to have you to myself. Your brothers and sister are fascinating, all coming from a different time, but I want to be alone with you."

"Yes, my love. They are fascinating, aren't they? Kestrel went back to—well, for you, she went forward to the time of the famous War of the Roses. I don't know much about it but they made a movie about it in my time. A tragic comedy. A great movie with three great actors."

She thought about her siblings and smiled. She went from having nothing real in her life to traveling back in time, meeting the love of her life, and finding out she was the beloved daughter of King Arthur and Queen Guinevere! And this all felt more real than anything she'd had before.

"Kes is pregnant. I'm going to be an aunt. I think she and I will get along very well. Michael didn't live far from me my whole life." She glanced at him and widened her eyes. "Isn't that nuts? I would have liked having a brother, and Michael seems nice. Sebastian seems like a bit of a handful, though."

"Yes," Wolf agreed, "But there is also something very dangerous about him. I am happy he cannot use magic here."

"Yes." She told him what she knew from earthly authors about Mordred and how it was his hand that killed or came close to killing King Arthur. "But here, I see a spoiled lord who loves his father very much."

"I like that you can see the good in people," he told her, leaning in to smile a hair's breadth from her face.

It was a new thing. She'd been too disinterested in others to see anything but what they showed the rest of the world. She never looked deeper. She was sure she wouldn't like what she saw anyway, so she never thought twice about it. But at times, it hurt. Like when she was feeling lonely in her beautiful penthouse in New York and there was no one to call for comfort. No one.

Now she had many.

She closed her eyes and smiled like a satisfied cat. She was happy.

"What else do you like about me, my lord? What?" she added when she opened her eyes to see his expression on her change.

"That is only the second time you have ever called me your lord. Now, when I want to be so much more than that."

How could she not fall in love with him? What did the future hold for them? Which future would be best for them?

"I don't mind you being my earthly lord," she smiled playfully, zoning in on his gloriously handsome face instead of the hundreds of questions vying for answers in her head. "Not when you love me the way you do."

Thousands of years or miles or whatever, wherever she had to travel to find him…how could she ever let him go? But there were so many obstacles.

When he swooped down to lift her in his arms, she didn't fight him.

When he told her that he didn't think he could wait until they wed, she giggled against his ear like an eleventh-century milkmaid. She loved having this power over such a warrior. "Have you so quickly run out of things you like about me?"

He laughed and she thought of a wolf, hungry and ready to hunt. "I love that you are bold, but not foolish. That is a trait I admire."

He admired. She liked that very much.

"You are compassionate and protective over your child—"

She was going to correct him, but she did love Hild as a mother would. She deepened her smile on him for seeing that in her before she did.

"Excuse me," came a man's resonating voice. She smiled when Michael appeared around a bend. He smiled, blushed a little, and then went back to being emotionless. "I was looking for my room, but these walls are really confusing."

"Yes," Wolf answered him. "We have been walking for two hours now."

Camelee gasped a little. "Has it been that long?"

He nodded and put his arm around her.

Michael smiled ever so slightly. "To be honest, the rest of us are pretty envious that you two are together and our loved ones can't be here. I know it's selfish, but it's a fact."

Camelee nodded, understanding. "We are doing everything we can to help."

Wolf held up his finger. "If I am correct, the reason they give for not bringing them here is that it will affect the timeline. I can tell you that it will not. Avalon is not part of the normal timeline. You should bring it up. I will confirm it."

Michael stared at him for a moment and then smiled and nodded. "Thank you." He turned to his sister. "I'm glad you found someone who makes you happy, Camelee. The brooch worked despite being burned and charred."

"I'm happy for you, too, Michael. I would love to catch up with you."

"I'd like that, too. But we need to know where we're going in this place." His voice grew a little louder as his sentence ended.

"Lord Micajah."

Nim appeared in a spray of silver through the air. "We sense your frustration. You should have told us you were having difficulty navigating the palace."

Before he confessed or denied, she turned to Camelee and Wolf. "How about you?"

"We've been lost for two hours," Camelee told her.

"Oh, my," Nim said, shaking her head and lifting her hand through the air. "Imagine what you prefer until the glass changes." She moved her eyes over Camelee and her brother. "You have the power. The glass can be changed into any vision you like. Each of you will only see his or her own vision. Do you understand?"

"Yes," they both said, looking at each other and then around the hall.

"Lady Camelee, the queen is in the yard with the child. Two lefts and three rights. You will come to three windows and a door. Go outside.

"Lord Micajah, your room is in the west hall—this is the north. So, that way." She pointed west with a smile. "You will go to the second floor, where the rooms are. Yours is the first door on the right, across from your brother. My lady," she went on, turning to Camelee. "You will follow the same direction as my lord. But your room is the second door on the right, across from your sister. Timekeeper, you will sleep on the—"

"I will sleep with my wife tonight," he corrected her. "Now that we can find our way around better, please point us to where the king is, so I can ask him for his daughter."

Nim's radiant face appeared even more beautiful when she gave them both an excited smile. "A wedding in Avalon! How exciting!"

"No. We do not want anything—"

"We will need at least a year to plan everything."

"Nim," Camelee pleaded. "Really, we just want to—"

"Of course, anything you both want!"

But she didn't sound convincing. Her happy grin remained as if she were telling them what they wanted to hear, but her plans continued.

"I must go and tell my sisters!"

"I want to tell my father first."

"Of course—"

"Nimue!" Camelee stopped pleading and said in a much firmer voice. "I mean it!"

Nim bowed and nodded, appearing more somber, then disappeared.

"She's not going to wait." Michael pointed out, then pointed down the long hall, now paneled in polished red mahogany walls. "I just came from talking to him—okay," he held up his hands and gave her an incredulous look. "King Arthur is our father…"

CHAPTER TWENTY-TWO

WOLF AND CAMELEE waited for the king in his private solar. They had arrived after being directed by one of the women who lived here. They had just missed him. He had gone to get his wife and bring her here so that she could be with him. It was perfect. They would both be here when he asked them for their daughter.

He had not been fidgety or dry-mouthed until now. Who was he that he should think the king would even consider him for the beloved daughter with whom he had just been reunited?

Now, he felt sick to his stomach. So what if he, the *Viking*, loved her? It was not enough to keep her alive the instant she left Avalon. What would he say to the king? What was he doing here?

The dark wood door opened. It was a pretty young woman with long dark hair, and a flower wreath around her brow. "Excuse me, Your Highness, the king and queen have returned. They have been told of your presence."

"Thank you," Camelee said and turned to Wolf as if she knew what he was thinking. That he wanted to run away. Get out of here while there was still time. But what did something done in fear ever accomplish?

He stayed in his chair, reining in his fears. Her only threat was Morgan. Once he killed her, that threat would end. He would kill Leofric and the threat to his own life would end.

They could go home to Denmark, at least for a while until

they traveled again. He wanted a life on the farm and on the water. And he wanted it with her.

"Are you nervous?" she asked him.

"Nervous?"

"You know, anxious about talking to him. I don't think you should be. He seems very nice."

Her voice was like music playing in his head, soothing him, calming him. He remembered why he was here. To have her in his bed, in his life forever.

They couldn't hear any footsteps since, in Camelee's palace, which he chose to see with her, the floors were covered in something she called *carpet*. It kept the halls warm in the winter years. Yes, years. Winter came every four years and stayed for three, here in Avalon.

The palace and the rooms within were lit by candles on walls in metal sconces and on long candlestands in the rooms, as well as grand fireplaces. It gave the place a comfortable, inviting feeling. His longhouse in Denmark wasn't as big as Avalon, but if she liked glowing candlelight and wood walls, she would like his house.

"Are you sure you want to do this?" she asked him across the small space that separated his chair from hers.

Looking into her worried eyes, he knew with certainty that this was exactly what he wanted to do. "I am sure. I belong to you, Camelee. It is not the other way around. In case you have not noticed, I do everything you ask." His smile grew wider when she realized he spoke true, and she pouted.

"No. Do not lose your good mood," he said gently as the door opened again.

Wolf stood to his feet as the king and his queen entered the solar. Genevra smiled at him.

He bowed to them both and remained quiet until he was permitted to speak. They didn't make him wait long but opened their arms to their daughter and to him and invited him to speak. Before he knew it, they had spent the afternoon with the royal couple, one of whom was his servant not so long ago.

"My wife has reminded me," King Arthur announced, "that she is acquainted with the Chief of the North. Your men killed her lord?"

"Yes. That is true," Wolf confessed. He saw no reason to lie to the king.

After another short length of time spent talking, Arthur gave them his blessing and then almost took it back when Wolf swept his smile over them in the solar and requested a priest next. He had no intention of waiting a year, six months, or one week. He wanted to marry Camelee now, today, and he wanted to be in her bed tonight.

Thankfully, if it was their daughter's will, they would do anything to help her.

And so, Wolf found himself facing a priest beneath the vaulted ceiling of the chapel.

Camelee's family was there, looking deeply troubled but keeping their troubles to themselves.

When the priest announced them husband and wife, he kissed her and the intensity of it shook the glass walls of Avalon.

They were given one of Avalon's best rooms as long as they gave the sisters approval on most everything they wanted.

They spent an hour with Hild in her room and promised in private that they would always come back. And speaking of coming back, she would spend the night in Queen Genevra's room and they would see her in the morning. Thankfully, the little girl loved Genevra and went without a quarrel.

"Do you both not want baths?" Viviane asked them as they tried to hurry away from her.

"We will take one together," he called out.

Camelee laughed and slapped his arm. "You are a barbarian!"

They found the rooms they'd been given for the night easily enough now that every corner didn't look like a thousand others.

Wolf carried her into the front room and kissed her as he set her down on the oversized velvet chair. He dropped to his knees between hers. Who needed a bed?

He lifted her skirts to her thighs and kissed her bare kneecaps. They both groaned, hungry for each other. He tore his lips from her so that he could bask at her for just a moment, willing his touch, desiring it. In that moment, he wondered if things were done differently a thousand years from now.

Someone knocked at the door. He scowled at it.

"It could be about Hild," his beloved offered softly.

He hadn't thought of that and rose to answer it.

"Yes?" he asked, scowling once again, this time at the woman at the door and the row of women behind her all carrying buckets of water. "No!" he refused, holding his hands up to stop their entry. "Not now. Later." He had no problem giving orders. He wasn't accustomed to women sizing him up and down as if he were some despicable, filthy thing. He remembered there were no men here.

"But, my lord," she choked out. "They will have to carry the water back down the stairs, dump it, and boil more when your order comes."

He could tell she was controlling herself not to say much more.

He nodded and allowed her and the others entry. He turned to Camelee to toss her an apologetic look, but she was smiling at him, her legs tucked under her, elbow perched on the armrest, her chin in her hand.

He smiled back while the women filled the bath in the adjoining room.

"What are you called?" he asked the head of this little army.

"You may call me Beth, my lord," she answered while keeping her eyes on the other women. "Or do you wish to know who I am so you can complain about me to Lady Viviane?"

"I have nothing to complain about, Beth. If anything, I will be sure to compliment her on your service and the control of temper you possess."

She blushed a pale shade of red against her alabaster skin at being caught.

"In that case, forgive me for intruding upon you and Princess Camelee."

He had forgotten his wife's royal title. How could he?

"It is no intrusion," the princess assured her.

Beth beamed at her and bowed. "May this night bring you a healthy daughter," she said, standing up.

Wolf threw his wife a half-grin. "What happens if she has a son?"

Beth turned to frown at him. He exercised his own control by not laughing.

"Thank you, Beth." He clearly stunned her by offering his appreciation.

Camelee came to his side in a show of unity and took his hand. "Yes, thank you."

They waited for all the women to leave. There was an endless line of fourteen of them. But the door finally closed. Wolf leaped forward and slammed the bolt home, locking them in.

Camelee tossed him a playful smile and dashed off. He gave chase and stopped, facing her when she reached the steamy bath. She kicked off her shoes. He did the same with his boots.

He gazed at her face, into her eyes. She gazed into his. He never thought it would matter if his wife loved him very much. But he found that he never wanted Camelee to gaze at him with anything less than what she exuded at this moment.

He moved in to kiss her, but she held him back and began to pull off his léine. She wanted to delight in him, too. It fired his blood. He lifted his arms while she stripped him. He moved closer when his chest was bare and settled his upstretched arms around her.

He untied the laces of her gown behind her back and dipped his face to kiss her while he pulled the gown off her shoulders. He scraped his teeth down her chin and throat to her shoulder. When he tugged her gown lower and exposed her round breasts, she lowered her gaze. He smiled. "Come now, Wife. You should be staring boldly at me, sure in the fact that you are more beautiful than anyone my eyes have ever seen."

"As are you, Wolf." She stroked her fingertips across the flat of his lower abdomen, below the crooks and hills everywhere else.

She pulled at his belt and loosened it until it slipped from his hips. Then she started on the laces of his pants. He pulled her gown down around her ankles and came back up with his lips pressed to her thigh, her hip, and the hollow above it. He straightened and kicked off his pants, and then, wanting to make certain the water wasn't too hot for her, he stepped into the bath first then held her by her waist and helped her in near him.

Holding hands, they sank in and smiled at each other. The water was perfect. She went willingly when he slipped her around and sat her between his legs with her back resting against his chest.

"Camelee?" he said against her ear.

"Yes, my love?"

He smiled at her endearment behind her. "I do not want to make you live in my longhouse in Denmark."

"What?" she asked, sounding surprised and turning to look at him. "Wolf, have you been worried about this?"

"No. I simply realize that a princess should live in…someplace bigger than what I have."

She slapped his arm softly and turned her back to him. "I'm willing to try it. I like the idea of you keeping me warm in bed every night." She stiffened in his embrace. "You do have a bed, don't you?"

"Yes, I have a bed, Wench."

"Oh, now I'm Wench, not Wife?" she asked with a playful—maybe—warning in her voice.

"You are both," he growled like a bear and began roving his soapy hands over her body. He hardened at the way her nipples grew taut at his touch. He widened his legs and she fit perfectly between them, except for one thing.

He wanted to wait and play with her a little, but he felt as if he were on fire. The instant her body touched him he almost lost himself. He lifted her and set her down atop him under the warm water. He used his fingers to gently massage her hard nub. She squirmed going down, enflaming his blood, his flesh further, hotter. He pressed her down and rubbed until she tightened around him and made him spend himself deep within her.

The more she gasped out his name in her pleasure, the more he filled her. It was as if he filled her with years' worth of himself.

He sat with her cradled in his arms. They breathed and laughed softly at nothing, or about everything. He wasn't sure which. He didn't care. He was expecting things to happen quickly since he hadn't been with a woman in years. But not that quick!

"I would like to live in your longhouse, Wolf. Tell me, what's a longhouse?"

He smiled and leaned in to smell her hair. He loved her. It surprised and frightened him how much. He turned her in his arms so that they faced each other in the still warm water. "I like it here."

"You mean to live?"

He shrugged. "For as long as we like. We do not age here. You cannot tell me that does not appeal to you."

She smiled, turning away. But there was nowhere to hide. "We could stay for a little while. With all the magic going on, we might hate it here."

He grinned at her and shook his head. He passed her the small, silver bowl of liquid soap and lathered up his hands. She felt irresistible in his hands, slippery and sensitive to his touch. As he was to hers. When she gripped him in her small hand and pumped him almost to overflowing, he snatched her up and set her down, impaling her to the hilt.

She rode hard, bringing him to his peak twice more, and just when he thought he had nothing more to give, she swallowed him up from head to hilt until he cried out, sure he had died and gone to...heaven?

They left the bath and used fresh water left in two basins to clean off.

"What do you think of Morgan?" he asked, lying beside her in a comfortable bed. He knew Camelee knew as little as he did. But what if, like Genevra, her memory was coming back slowly? What if she remembered something?

"She's Sebastian's mother and one of Viviane and Nimue's sisters."

"A sorceress," he muttered.

"And you're not a sorcerer?" she challenged.

He didn't know what he was he told her honestly.

"It doesn't matter, Wolf. I don't care what we are as long as we are what we are together."

"Yes. I agree." He kissed her one last time before she fell asleep. He watched her for a little while, thanking God for bringing her into his life.

He wondered if Fin had found and killed Leofric. He should return to their time, their world and check on his brother. He would do it in the morning. Though there was coming a time when Fin was going to have to get along without him. He thought that time was now.

CHAPTER TWENTY-THREE

ORGAN WANTED TO possess him forever. But there were obstacles and the first one was getting him to Avalon. She would have to imprison or kill the remainder of her sisters. All three of them that were left. She trusted no one. Not even her son, Mordred, anymore. They all loved Arthur. She didn't mind capturing them and holding them forever, just as they had intended to do to her.

But here was a loyal servant, a skillful warrior. Fin Kristiansen—dreadful name—who made her smile, even chuckle in the daylight and groan and pant every night. Yes, she had to stab him a few times, but she always healed him before he died.

She watched him bending to the stream for a drink of the cold water, his yellow braids hanging between his wide shoulder blades. His facial hair was a bit darker around his jaw. He was cut to perfection. His mouth, his body, everything. She wanted to rise and go to him and run her fingertips over his scars.

When he straightened and turned, sensing her gaze, she took in the glorious sight of his whipcord-tight belly. She wet her lips while she took in her fill. She had to be careful or she'd end up in love with him, when she didn't want to kill him, that is.

"I can feel your gaze on me from here, Witch."

She didn't like when he called her that. She didn't care if she was a witch. It was the way he said it. Like it was the worst thing someone could be.

"Are you falling in love with me?" he asked playfully.

"Do not flatter yourself, Mortal," she said with the same disdain when he grew closer. "I would rather slice my own throat than love a rogue like you."

He pouted, scoffing at her. Damn him for being so handsome, so masculine. She didn't worry that she was in love already. But she could come to be, later.

"Those villagers said they saw your brother twice. He traveled with a woman."

"I know what they said," he told her walking ahead. "I was with you."

He spoke with a frustrated tone. As if she were an annoyance. She should kill him sooner rather than later. But she would miss the rough way he handled her. He never hurt her. He wasn't a fool. For she would surely kill him if he did. He was just rough enough to make her wet. Besides that, his stamina outdid many fae men she had taken to her bed.

"How do I know who my brother is fu—"

She held up her hand. "Is that what it is to you?"

"Yes," he told her. "That is what it is. What do you call what we do?"

He was correct. It was raw and brash, and she loved it. "Foolish."

"Ah, Woman, have more faith in yourself than that."

"It is you I am concerned about," she let him know.

"Poor sorceress. Forgive me for stealing your heart. It has been a burden I carry with me every day. I cannot help but make women fall in love with me."

She pulled an arrow out of thin air and flung it at him like a spear. He threw back his head and laughed, and she watched, cursing the way he made her feel.

It was time to stop whatever was happening between them. She was forgetting her mission. To hate Arthur for deciding she wasn't good enough for him. She was far from the standards of his precious honor, including seeking after wonders, injuring no one, defending the rights of the weak. She almost laughed out loud. There were more. Endless more rules Arthur invoked upon his men—and his women. She'd been his first lover. The one who taught him what he knew about pleasuring a woman. He cast her away from his home, Camelot, in the earthly realm. He didn't know he'd cast out his son, as well. Mordred had lived with her in Avalon. Until, curious about his father, he left Avalon and went to Camelot. She'd lost her son there. The only way to get him back had been to enchant him. So that was what she did. His mission to kill Arthur would not have failed if not for Viviane and her other sisters, who'd taken Arthur to Avalon to save his life.

Her sisters joined forces and cast her from Avalon and broke the spell she'd had over Mordred. They imprisoned her on *Jezmel*, an island with magical waters surrounding it. In the water lived the *Azurel*, a predator with blue hair and green skin on the top and scales and a tail on the bottom. Their mouths opened to reveal rows of sharp angular teeth, which they used to eat you. They ate through wood, so boats were useless. Magic had no effect on them. There was no way off the island.

But she had found a way. It had cost her five of her sisters. But she'd let nothing stop her. Ending their lives had been difficult. They were her sisters, after all. But killing one gave her some of that sister's power and strength. Killing four more made her stronger than the three that were left.

She could have found Arthur if that stupid brooch worked the way it was designed to work. But fortune was ever in her favor, and on Christmas Eve she found Arthur *and* her beloved Mordred living on earth.

But her son rejected her for Arthur's sake and trapped her in an unbreakable web while her mortal enemy, Merlin, prepared to bring her to another prison.

"Fin?" she called out to him now.

He went to her, as if he couldn't stop himself. He was lean and powerful, and he had a streak of bad in him all the way down to his bones. She might need him when she found his brother. If she could mine that streak with precision, he could bring havoc to Avalon.

"I'm afraid my sisters might come after me. But I must find my son. I fear they already have him in Avalon. Now, they have your brother as well. They will cast their spells and our loved ones will try to kill us."

"Wolf would never try to kill me," Fin argued.

"Under the power of their magic, he will not be able to stop himself."

Fin stared at her and then looked around. "I sincerely do not know where my brother went. He disappeared into…into a hole in the air."

"So that's the way in. We must create a hole. How did your brother do it?"

"I do not know. He was fighting and then he fought with the air."

Morgan held her finger to her chin. "I will have to create a spell that will show us where the rifts occur. I will find a hole and we will go to Avalon to save our loved ones."

He nodded, smiling when she wound herself around him, heading for his hungry mouth. "Make love to me," she whispered against his lips when he lifted her off her feet to kiss her.

He laughed at her refusal to use his more meaningless term. What did it say of him?

She didn't care an instant later when he dragged her in closer for a more intimate kiss.

"Do you want to lay in the snow?" he asked with a salacious smile.

She murmured an enchantment and they appeared in a small cottage with two windows, one on either side of the roof. Through each window came a tree branch. They snaked around Fin's wrists and snatched him off his feet. Morgan smiled at him hanging by his wrists before her. She spoke some ancient words and moved her hands. His clothes ripped from his body.

He laughed, enjoying the challenge of being completely vulnerable to her. "I could kill you right now," she warned.

His laughter faded into a mocking smile. He looked down at himself, hard and jutting upward, then he lifted his hooded gaze to her. "Let me see you give it a try."

He thrilled her. He set her blood to boiling. Her clothes came off as quickly as his. She looked at him dangling a few inches off the floor, muscular arms giving strength to his body. He was swollen and ready. She thought she could come to a climax just looking at him.

But she wanted more than to feast her eyes. She wanted some of everything. She wanted to possess him. He was the perfect man for her. If he could find his brother and hand him over to her, she would grant him anything he wanted. But Fin was frustratingly loyal.

She knew what she had to do for him to be hers. She went to him and took him into her mouth. He groaned and promised her pleasure beyond her control while she had her way.

She didn't let him find release yet. She whispered a string of words and climbed up onto him. She wrapped her thighs around his waist and rode hard while he cried out…cried out through clenched teeth while he filled her. "Yes. Yes, my love. All that I have is yours."

⇒⟫⟩❌⟨⟪⇐

"Come in," Camelee called to whoever was behind the door to her and Wolf's room. They were both dressed and almost ready to go to the meeting her father had called for all to attend.

"Genevra, I mean…Your Highness, Majesty, Grace…Mom?"

"Mom is nice," her older twin said with a smile.

Camelee recognized it all now. Genevra's expressions, the way she quirked her mouth at certain things…Genevra, Queen Guinevere Pendragon was her mother! It couldn't get any bigger than that, she thought.

"I'm sorry for bothering you. I know you're getting ready to see your father—"

"You're not bothering us," Camelee assured her with a smile, turning away from the mirror. She didn't want to wear too much make-up. It all suddenly felt like a mask. Of course, the sisters provided the best make-up, dewy soft, as sheer as their breath. Like everything in Avalon, it was all perfect.

But nothing is perfect, she heard in her heart.

"Camelee, I wanted to—"

"Please, excuse me," Wolf came forward. "I will wait in the other room."

Genevra tried to stop him, but he told her they had things between them—as mother and daughter—that was for them to speak of alone. He would wait in the other room.

"I told your father what a good man Wolf is," Genevra told her, watching him leave.

"Yes," Camelee agreed. "He is." She pulled a chair closer to hers and patted the seat.

Genevra spread the billowy skirts of her beautiful crimson velvet gown over the chair and sat.

"I love the gown you chose," Camelee complimented.

"I wanted something simple. What about you? What are you wearing? I love that deep blue on you. It accentuates the golden light of your face."

As simple at that, Camelee felt as if they were back in the keep, giggling about something Wolf or Hild said or did.

"I let Wolf choose what I wore, and I chose his creation," Camelee looked down and smiled at herself. Her gown was simply cut in the color of moonlight. One of the other wonderful things about Avalon was that you could use your thoughts to create almost anything you wanted, as long as it wasn't a weapon of any kind. It was considered a useless magic by most who lived here. Why did any need all the clutter? She had to confess that her husband looked quite handsome in his jeans and boots and the tight navy sweater. She's almost jumped on him three times while he was dressing. Two of those times, he'd caught her and pinned her down on the bed. They laughed and kissed while they—

"Oh, aye!" Genevra remarked. "He looked very handsome. Dearest, I wanted to speak with you alone about…everything. We haven't done that."

Camelee nodded. What could she reply? She'd forgiven her mother, but the remnants of that wound were not yet healed. Was she just supposed to be ready to be a mother now? Could she find that elusive switch to forget everything she knew about love and mistrust and abandonment? She hadn't been abandoned by her biological parents. Knowing that helped greatly and she hoped that, with time, she would heal completely. This was the person she needed to recover with. They talked and cried a little when Genevra told her about poor Arthur and what he'd gone through.

"He remembered us. He didn't know who or where…or when we were, but he remembered that he loved us. Can you imagine? I have never remembered him, and his love still changed my life. I cannot fathom remembering us all and living without us."

Camelee was glad her father had Guinevere in his life. Now, Camelee had her, too.

When they were ready to go, they called Wolf to them, and exchanged warm smiles on the way to the hall.

A short while later, Camelee sat at a large round table with her siblings and her parents, along with Viviane, Nimue, and Gliten. It wasn't *the* round table. This one was here for smaller gatherings. As for its shape, she'd read long ago that King Arthur liked round tables because it made him equal to his men. With no king at the head, no one felt less important. Her father was a good man. That was important to her because she'd always imagined him as being mean and hateful. How else, she had thought, could you give up your baby if you weren't heartless? But her father had a tremendous heart. To give up everyone he loved.

Now, he was giving everyone a voice. That was good because her brothers and sister had things to say to their father and they would be heard. It was mainly about their husband or wives.

"No one is tampering with the timeline if our spouses come here," her brother, Michael, charged. "Avalon is not in the earthly timeline, so they can come here."

"Truthfully, Aunt Viviane," Sebastian said from his chair at the table. His green eyes blazing as if he were on fire within. There was a hint of gold in them, but it grew as he spoke. "I have waited my whole, long life for Noelle, and days after I finally win her heart, you snatch me from her. Now, she is alone if Morgan goes to her. Someone better bring her here or I'll find a way back and get her myself and no magic you can conjure will stop me."

"My child needs its father," Kestrel added with less threat in her beautiful blue-green gaze. "If Sebastian can find a way out, I will go with him."

Camelee's father turned to cast an anxious look at the sisters. They spoke quietly among themselves and then finally looked up at Wolf.

"Timekeeper, is it true? Are we *not* tampering with the time-line?"

"No," Wolf answered as if he were the man in charge, and comfortable with the position. "I do not believe any tampering is taking place."

"Very well, then," Viviane said. "We will allow Sir Nicholas—" she paused and smiled as if she couldn't help it. "Lady Charlotte, and Noelle to come to Avalon. They must never speak of it. If they do, they will be brought back here, where they will remain for the remainder of their days. You who love them are responsible for this. Do you accept?"

They all did, though Sebastian, with eyes blazing like molten lava, muttered something about them trying to take Noelle from him and how he would smash every wall down until the palace was a pile of sharp debris.

Viviane stood. "We will go to Merlin. He knows where everyone is. I will bring Nicholas here. Nim, you bring Noelle, and Gliten, Lady Charlotte.

The sisters nodded and disappeared before anyone had time to speak.

Camelee was glad for them. She thought they should all be together.

She moved her gaze and caught her father staring at her.

She smiled at him. She knew if it were up to him, he would have given them what they wanted without all the fuss. He'd been deprived of being a father because of Morgan.

"We have a lot to learn about each other, Dad."

He smiled and breathed out a breath that almost bent him over. "Yes. I agree. Let's take our time. I know you want to go back to…wherever, but it can wait a little. Can't it?"

How could she refuse him? Why would she ever want to? She'd found her father. "Yes. It can wait."

She reached for Wolf's hand on the table. He angled his head to set his gaze on her when she glanced his way. He smiled and she saw the weakness for her in his eyes. It frightened her. If they ever ran into Morgan…

"Camelee," her father said softly, pulling her attention back to him. "I know this is all difficult to accept."

Yes. Having her parents back. She looked at Genevra. Her mother, who had poured out her heart to many others to compensate for the two she'd lost. Her father, who had sacrificed everything in his life to save his family.

"I will do everything I can to protect you, Daughter," he continued. "I always have. I always will. I will keep you both safe." He looked at Wolf, who smiled at him.

"We hope you can forgive us for leaving you," her mother told her, her golden brow creased with guilt. "We wanted you to have a safe life. But we wanted you to be happy and to want for nothing."

"I had everything—" Camelee told them, looking away. But it

had all been smoke and ashes. It was all insubstantial. None of it mattered. When the smoke settled, the only thing left was her, alone and bitter at six years old. It had only gotten worse from there. "—and nothing at all." She lifted her gaze to them. To her mother first, and then her father, and let her warm smile shine on them both. "But I understand why you gave me up. We were all robbed of a life together. It's just nice to have you both now."

Genevra left her chair and hurried to her. "Oh, my darling girl, before I knew I was your mother, I wished I was."

"I wished you were, too."

Camelee closed her eyes and smiled when her mother put her arms around her and embraced her where she sat. She wiped her eyes and smiled at Wolf while her mother returned to her seat.

"I'm glad you found them, Camelee," he told her and lifted her hand to his lips.

"Nicholas!" Kes shouted and bolted forward into the arms of a handsome man dressed in a tailored longcoat, pants and military boots. He received his pregnant wife tenderly. After making sure she wasn't hurt, and kissing her senseless, he looked around at the others then at the king. "Are you truly King Arthur?" The king verified that he was and then went to him and embraced him. "I've heard much about you from Viviane. She speaks highly of you."

Nicholas slipped his gaze to Viviane and smiled. "Still, Elia, I would prefer to have my sword."

Noelle came next and it was a good thing because Sebastian appeared ready to start breaking down walls.

"Sebastian!" She hurried to him, her russet waves flowing behind her. "What's going on? Do I want to know? That woman said it was better if you told me. Told me what?"

Camelee was shocked to see her half-brother's expression go from deadly to temperate in a single moment. Mordred had a heart. A good one as far as Camelee could tell.

"Aren't you Noelle Upton from the news?" she asked, recognizing her.

"Yes. Oh, wow, you're Camelee Pendrey! I saw *Silver Buttons*. I loved you in it."

Camelee smiled and thanked her. She knew she and Noelle were going to be good friends.

Michael's wife, Charlotte, appeared noble in her scarlet riding coat and matching skirts and hat, with a delicate veil over her face and dark hair.

She pulled the hat, and the veil with it off her head and threw her arms around Michael. "We have been out searching for you for the last week. Oh, thank God, you are alive!"

"Week?" Camelee asked, looking at Arthur while her brother and his wife kissed.

"Time moves differently in most other realms," the king explained. "Usually much faster than Avalon."

She noticed after a few minutes that Wolf was quiet. "Is something wrong?"

He blinked, as if his thoughts had taken him somewhere else. "Fin. After a week, he probably thinks I'm dead somewhere."

Her belly sank. What if he wanted to go back and show his brother that he was okay? What if he died there?

She smiled and spoke to her new family around the table of King Arthur. She wanted to remember this forever, and push negative thoughts out of her head.

They remained in the great hall and had an extravagant array of fruit cut, sliced, and diced. If anyone wanted bread or meat, it was served. Even Kestrel's request for mashed potatoes with butter, pickles, and pancakes with lots of syrup was granted.

"Genevra—I mean, my queen," Wolf stumbled over his words a moment and then spread his warm gaze over the faces around him. "What stops Morgan from coming here?"

"Magic. Avalon is locked to any magic but ours—" she pointed to the sisters,"—and Merlin's."

"And Wolf's?" Camelee asked.

"Not exactly," said Viviane. "Wolf is a Timekeeper. He is to stop anyone from corrupting the timeline."

"His kind—in their time—" Nim told them, "—were almost dispatched twice for Kestrel and Michael, but they did not corrupt time, so they were saved from the sword."

"The sword?" Kestrel gasped and moved a little closer to her husband, who asked why Wolf was allowed to have a sword.

"Was I under the spell to forget, as well?" Wolf asked Nim, his jaw clenched.

"No. Timekeepers live regular lives until they are dispatched."

"So, I was dispatched?"

Nim nodded. "It would seem so."

"By whom?" he demanded.

"By the One we all obey." She smiled at him and bit into a peach.

Camelee tugged his sleeve. "Do you have any memories of your past?"

"Yes," he told her. "Of Fin and my longhouse in Denmark. That's my past that I remember. Nothing else. But I *do* have this new sense of keeping things moving along as they should. It is strange. I feel…watchful."

She couldn't help but giggle at the thought of watches keeping time in the future.

"Let's just hope you're not called upon to *put your sword* to anyone."

He agreed with a worried look.

"So, why all the Morgan hate?" Kestrel asked their father. "Why does she want to hurt you enough to be a danger to us? What did you do to her?" She turned he gaze to the sisters. "Why do you keep her out of her home?"

"She killed five of our sisters," Nimue told her. "She should be thankful we didn't destroy her for eternity or give her boils." Nim turned the two sisters she had left. "Why didn't we give her boils?"

"We were…together," the king told her. "Many centuries ago. I was young and naïve. She was…enchanting. But I saw the evil in her here so I left her and Avalon and built Camelot on earth. The home of my heart. I never knew she and I had a child until Mordred came to me."

"I'm sorry I asked," Kestrel whispered. "I'm sorry about your sisters, and for you, Dad. It's tough being in a relationship with a nutcase."

Camelee and Michael smiled at her and Camelee suspected her brother also missed future slang.

"I came here," Wolf reminded them.

"What?" Camelee asked him.

"They said Morgan couldn't come here because no magic, other than theirs is allowed here. But I came here."

"Not with magic," Vivian pointed out. "You were fighting, going berserk, as you call it. You are human. As we said, you are a Timekeeper, most likely alerted to all this movement and dispatched. You found the rift and must have opened it between the realms, where magic is weakest."

"So, anyone can do what I did as long as he is human and a little out of his mind?" Wolf asked, putting it all together.

Viviane shifted her eyes to Nim and they both looked at Gliten. "No," the first one said. "The fact is, we do not know why certain people are called. Only that they are ruthless and cold—"

"Not all," Wolf softened his smile on the sisters. "Surely not all."

"They are wrong," Camelee told him when the sisters nodded. She pulled him out of his chair and dragged him away. "They aren't God. They don't know everything. They are wrong about you. Come with me, my darling. Come away with me."

$$\blacklozenge\cdots\bullet\quad\bullet\cdots\blacklozenge$$

CHAPTER TWENTY-FOUR

ONLY CAMELEE COULD lure Wolf away from all his troubles, his duties, his family.

He was cold in battle. It was true. But one either becomes cold or suffers a sorrowful death.

But he wasn't cold with her. Not anymore. He understood why she defended him, and he was thankful that she enjoyed his warmer side enough to stand up for it.

She was everything to him. How had he become so hopelessly in love with her? Was he always meant to love her? Did he believe such things? He looked into her sparkling blue-gray eyes as they reached the door to their room. Yes. Yes, he believed something was at work. Whatever it was, it melted the cold.

They undressed each other, eager to comfort and soothe with kisses and long, intimate strokes.

He carried her to their bed, kissing her neck, her chin, her mouth. He set her down on the soft mattress and laid on top of her.

Stretching her out beneath him, he looked down at her with a smirk. "Now I have you where I want you." His breath fell on her lips. "What will you do?"

He hadn't expected an answer.

She shifted in one swift motion and kneed him in the groin. Not hard, just a touch to let him know how close he came. Without pausing for a breath, she pushed him off while he was trying to cover his groin. He rolled over and grasped her wrists, stopping her from pummeling him with her fists.

They stared into each other's eyes and laughed softly. He pulled her in for a kiss. He wanted nothing more than to stay here with her forever. Denmark could wait.

She sat up and undressed herself, teasing him with glimpses of her creamy skin, until he tore away her clothes and feasted on her body. She was perfection, with a small brown mole on her left breast, and one on her hip. He pulled her down on the bed and kissed each one. He didn't remember how or when he removed his clothes. Or she did. He only remembered being so hard he hurt.

"I love you, Camelee." He remembered telling her often.

"And I love you, Wolf," she replied every time, entwining his fingers in hers and wrapping her legs around his waist.

When she bit his lip and rolled over so that she was atop him, she rose up and drove him to the edge of madness.

Later, she lay in his arms, where he believed she was meant to be. "Wolf, you know you are more than what they say, don't you?"

"I do not care what they say, love. My service is to you."

She smiled and pressed down to his hilt. She was grateful that he was dedicated to her and would do what she asked.

"Camelee?" he asked as the wind howled outside.

"Hmm?"

"I must go back and find my brother."

WOLF DRESSED IN a fresh pair of pants, a clean, tan léine, and a leather belt with scabbards of various sizes. He sat in a chair in their room and pulled on his boots. His beautiful wife stood behind him, braiding his hair, kissing his neck, trying to tempt him into not going.

But not in this. He couldn't just leave his brother with no trace, no word. He had the ability to travel back and forth, so why not use it?

He stood up when it was time to go and took Camelee in his arms. "Remember, tell no one where I went. I will return to you, my love."

"You better, Wolf. No. Really," she added when he laughed.

She walked out of the palace with him and into the inner grounds. It was dark and late in the night, quiet, and perfect for sneaking away.

He kissed her, then kissed and embraced her again. Then he drew his sword and began slicing at the air. After an hour, exhaustion hit him and he had to pause for a rest. They hadn't realized it right away, but Merlin was observing them in the shadows.

Camelee spotted him first, when he moved to keep the direction of his gaze on Wolf's movements. His hair was as dark as the shadows, straight and long, as were his mustache and beard. When he was caught, he stepped out into the light with boldness.

"Why are you trying to leave?"

"Are you telling me I cannot go?" Wolf asked.

"I think my question was plain enough."

"I want to find my brother and tell him I am well."

Merlin folded one arm across his chest and stroked his beard with his other hand. "You shouldn't do this."

"And you all should not have pulled all these people out of their lives. Something is bound to go wrong in the timeline You took three people from the twenty-first century and dropped them into three different times, possibly changing all those timelines. Not to mention Sebastian, an eighteenth-century lord, who used to be a first-century sorcerer, now living in twenty nineteen. You are truly going to judge me on this?"

"No," Merlin conceded, looking at Camelee then veiling his gaze for a moment behind long, black lashes. "But for the record, I had nothing to do with any of that. I have recently discovered that it was all Morgan's doing. She was using the brooch for its intended purpose to find Arthur. It found his children instead—and guided them—as Arthur intended—to their true loves." He smiled at Camelee and Wolf.

Wolf cast him a doubtful look when he met his gaze again. "What is a record?"

Merlin curled his lips into a smile that softened his angular features. "Forgive me, Wolf. I lose track of where everyone is from. I cannot remember how everyone speaks."

Wolf finally smiled back. The sorcerer was difficult not to like. "I imagine it is quite difficult."

"More than I hope you will ever know," Merlin said in a solemn voice. "Do not meet more people than you need." He turned a handsome smile on Camelee. "When this is over, take your husband home and live your lives. Don't allow him to flit around from time to time because he can." He set his dark eyes on Wolf again. "You will lose yourself."

"Did that happen to you?" Wolf asked him and felt Camelee's hand searching for his. He caught her and closed his fingers around hers.

"I could never stay long enough in any one place to form serious attachments to others. The choice was not my own. It still isn't. If I wasn't doing this for as long as I have, I would never have learned anything from the timeline. I still sometimes get mixed up when speaking of certain kings and their eras." He smiled and then it faded. "One day it will end. I hope my day and your day are the same in the timeline."

"Do you think I will kill you?" Wolf asked, growing tired of being some prophesied cold killer of people he liked. He would find the chapel here and go to it when he returned from finding Fin.

"Let's hope not, eh?" He placed his hands on their shoulders, one on Wolf's and one on Camelee's. "Tell me why you have not been able to leave."

"I think I am not passionate about it. Feverish."

"I will go to your brother," Merlin told him. "I will tell him—"

"No. I have a feeling I am going to be here for a while. I want to tell him."

Merlin cast Camelee an understanding look. Then closed his eyes and tossed back his head.

"What are you doing?" Wolf demanded and stepped in front of Camelee, blocking her from the sorcerer.

Another moment passed with Merlin crying out. Wolf was about to give him a shake, but Camelee stopped him. An instant later, Merlin opened his eyes and stared at Wolf. All the color drained from his face and left him gaunt and hollow-looking.

"Your brother," he gasped as air and life returned to him. "Your brother might be in trouble. There is an evil force around him. I don't know what it is. I fear it might be Morgan, but I did not see her."

"Morgan?" Wolf repeated quietly, then lifted his sword and turned toward the darkness.

"Wolf, please don't go!" Camelee begged him. "It's most likely a trap."

"Wolf," Merlin cautioned. I'm not sure you should go. In fact, I advise against it. If it is Morgan, you will die. You cannot beat her. You don't even have magic. Besides, all the magic in Avalon cannot beat her."

All the magic in Avalon…Wolf set his gleaming gaze on Merlin. "If she is allowed back in Avalon, can the sisters stop her from using her magic, as they stopped Sebastian and the king?"

"We are unsure. We have never had to try it."

"Now is the time. Tell the others."

Merlin blinked. "What?"

"Let her in, Merlin. Open the gates to her. Take her power, if possible. If not, I will have to find another way."

"Another way to what?"

"To kill her. What else. Every spell will be broken. Will it not? She is the one who brought all of them back. It is my duty to stop her. The threat to everyone here and to the timeline will be gone."

Merlin nodded.

"I can stop her if she is here. My sword…"

"Yes." Merlin's eyes opened a little wider. "Yes. Of course!"

They blinked and he was gone.

Camelee stared at Wolf and then threw herself into his arms. "This is all real. She's real. I'm not ashamed to say I'm afraid of her."

"She will not be victorious, Camelee. I'm on the right side." He grinned and closed his arms around her. "What can we do until she gets here?" He dipped his head and kissed her neck, letting her know what he wanted to do.

"Let's go back inside for starters," she said. "I'm freezing."

"There you two are," Sir Nicholas called out when they entered the palace. "Kestrel wants me to hear her music. We have gathered in the great hall to dance. The king sent me to look for you."

"So, what is it like being a knight?" Camelee asked her brother-by-marriage while they followed the knight through the long corridors leading to the hall.

"The same as any warrior I would imagine. I fight for my king and country as your husband does."

"Depending on the country," Wolf murmured, walking.

"Aye, after meeting you," Nicholas answered him as they turned a corner and came to the king waiting at the doors, "'twas easy to forget that your people are conquerors."

There was no judgment in his eyes, only the truth. Wolf thought King Arthur must have been happy that Kestrel had found a man who could likely sit at the Round Table.

Come to think of it—"Where are Sirs Gawaine and Lucan?" he asked, turning to the king.

Arthur greeted his daughter with open arms. Wolf's heart swelled with happiness over what she had found.

"Most of my men are human," the king answered him, sending his daughter inside where the sounds of her family waited.

Wolf brought her hand to his lips and smiled after he kissed it. "I will be in shortly."

"That's right, you will!" she called back over her shoulder. "I'm going to teach you how to dance."

"I do not know why that feels like a threat," he leaned in and told her father.

Arthur laughed softly. "Because it is, Son."

Wolf liked King Arthur. He liked the things that Arthur stood for, according to Genevra—the mother he never had, and who had not changed despite the change of her name.

He looked over the king's shoulder to see Nicholas nodding his head at him.

The three of them laughed, and then the king cleared his throat.

"There is nothing better than the sound of happy men, unless two of them are the men married to your daughters, then, it is better.

"Now, as for my knights," the king continued while they lingered at the entrance. "The sisters don't like having men here, especially human men. I sent them off to protect your loved ones and try to find Morgan."

"Speaking of Morgan, Sire. We think she is with my brother. Merlin informs me that Fin is in great danger. I wanted to return to him and help but Merlin said that would be a bad idea on earth. But I can fight her here." He told Arthur their plan and then his belly tightened in a knot when Arthur refused to let Morgan come here.

"I forbid it, Wolf," the king warned. "Do not bring her near my children."

That was all he said and then walked inside and joined his wife. Nicholas gave his arm a pat, and then he, too, left to join his wife.

Wolf stood alone at the doors. He was going to have to disobey the king. Bringing Morgan here was the only way to stop her. And he was going to stop her.

He didn't want to go inside and dance. He wanted to go home to Denmark and live his life, as Merlin had said. Forget all this. Forget...

Kestrel stood in the center of the hall with her finger on the button of some kind of contraption he was sure wasn't supposed to be here. But the same rules didn't apply to Avalon, did they? If anyone spoke of what they saw here, they would be brought back and never allowed to leave again, so the timeline was safe.

She pushed the button and the soul-soothing sound of a woman's voice mixed with blessed instruments, the likes of which Wolf had never heard before, filled the air. The melody was haunting as she sang about the first time she saw her beloved's face.

Each husband and wife embraced and swayed to the sound.

Wolf looked through them and found his beautiful wife waiting for him. He wanted to go to her. He moved his foot—

The air crackled behind him. Viviane, Nim, and Gliten appeared with Merlin in front of the king. They each whispered words that blended, sparkling the air, making Wolf's hair rise off his skin.

"No!" the king suddenly shouted. He let go of his wife and glared at Wolf. The music stopped. "I don't want her allowed to come here! Are you mad? I've kept them all away from her and now you want to bring her to the middle of them? No. I forbid it!"

"Arthur," Merlin pleaded. "He can stop her."

Wolf cast his wife a calm, confident smile and then took one last look over his shoulder to make certain everyone was behind him. His gaze found Merlin's. The sorcerer nodded slightly while the king cursed behind him. They had opened the gates. She was coming.

Wolf pulled his sword free of its sheath and held it ready. Yes, he was ready. This was what he was born to do.

He watched the rift opening. Morgan wasted no time in getting here. Well, let her come. Let her—

"Wolf! Help me!"

Fin!

Wolf's heart froze for an instant—and that was all the time Morgan needed to strike. She fired a force of power at him that knocked him across the hall. The last thing he heard before everything went black was laughter.

CHAPTER TWENTY-FIVE

MORGAN LET THE full extent of her rage flow freely toward her sisters and that bastard Merlin. It was the only way to stop their enchantment against her using her magic.

So, she used it, wrapping her sisters and their sorcerer in a web of gossamer tendrils, their arms pinned at their sides, and then she tossed them aside with a brush of her hand.

When she saw Arthur, she laughed. She laughed at all of them. Their ridiculously weak men coming at her with their swords. She flung them aside, too.

"Mordred," she growled, in front of him, "you have chosen their side, I see."

"You know," Sebastian said silkily, "I already killed the man who finished raising me, and I tried to kill my real father. Your odds are bad. I suggest you forget I'm your son."

She wanted to kill him. She wanted to smash him like a snail beneath her foot. But she couldn't. Not her child. Her eyes slid to the woman behind him—and then to his father. She was too delighted that she had them all, all his children, including Mordred—under her power, to let her son's hateful words affect her.

"Which one of you should I kill first?"

"Morgan," Arthur ground out. "I'm going to end you."

She laughed. "You can't even move, you fool. You are not going to do a thing but watch as I destroy everyone you love, beginning with your wife."

"No!" more than one of them screamed, proving the queen was well-loved.

It made Morgan hate her even more. She pulled an arrow out of the air and threw it at Guinevere. She turned to Mordred's woman next. She heard a sound behind her, the *clink* of metal against metal. She looked over her shoulder to find her arrow on the floor a foot away from Guinevere, and a savage-looking man standing in her defense. His sword was long and there was a hint of illumination to it. Who was he?

The one she'd flung across the hall.

She fired another burst of power at him, but he sliced at it and it burst into a dark vapor, no longer dangerous. She fired another. She tried an incantation to bind him, to blind him, to cook him from the inside out. He stopped every spell, breaking them apart, moving toward her as he swung.

Who was he? How was he stopping her magic? Was he going to kill her? Could he? Well, first she would make Arthur pay for all this. She snapped her wrist and the son he had with his queen grasped his throat and fell to his knees.

She was going to kill them all! Let her assailant stop all this! She waved her hand across the entire hall and everyone began to choke to death.

But like a pesky insect, the man with the sword slashed and smashed her spells to pieces before anyone died.

Oh! She'd had enough of him! She produced ropes and wound them around everyone's necks at the same time.

They were dying. Some stopped writhing. A woman screamed mournfully. Guinevere. Morgan smiled.

And then she stopped, and everyone fell loose when Morgan felt the cold blade going through her warm body. She felt every inch of it. He was trying to reach her heart.

But it stopped short.

"Brother," she heard Fin's voice above her, "withdraw or I will kill your wife."

He held a bow, arrow nocked, and aimed at the king's daughter, Camelee. Morgan smiled at him. Yes, kill the one named after his beloved home.

"Fin!" his brother shouted. "What are doing? You are under her spell."

Fin pulled back the string.

"Please, Brother! Look at me!"

Fin did. "I'm going to kill her."

It didn't work! Noooo! The sword plunged deeper, piercing her heart, ending her spells.

Fin dropped his weapon and covered his face with his hands.

Wolf pulled him into a tight embrace and then yanked his sword from Morgan's body.

"Is anyone hurt?" he called out.

"You killed her," Arthur said with awe in his voice. "It's really over."

"No," Nim told them as a hush fell over the hall. "Her heart needs to be removed."

Morgan listened. Nimue was right. She wasn't dead. She sat up and turned to Fin, her spell over him broken. Did she not fulfill his dreams? Was there nothing tender in him toward her? "Which one of you is cold enough to do it?"

"I am," her lover proclaimed and flung the sword at her.

She caught it in her hand, blade first, ignoring the injury. But he was on her in seconds. He fell atop her and looked into her eyes. She cursed herself. Did she love this human savage?

"Fin."

He pushed the metal inside her with all his weight. "Farewell, Witch." His words were tender and familiar, not insulting.

He cared. He wasn't going to—

The blade went through her heart. He stayed where he was and cut it out of her chest and held it up.

The last thing Morgan heard before she was ended was a collective sigh of relief.

⇒⇒⇒⇐⇐⇐

NO ONE HAD to stay. They were free to leave Avalon and go back to their original century alone, or back with their loved ones to their century. They all chose to stay with their partners.

Wolf vowed that he would help his wife grow accustomed to the rugged mountains of his home. He would make certain she was happy, and safe.

Hild would be staying on in Avalon, with the queen and the sisters. She was happy there and would grow strong. Wolf and Camelee would always be there for her whenever she needed them.

Fin swore his fealty to the queen and though he was not permitted to remain in Avalon, he would come to her side if ever she called upon him. He also swore to look after Alric and to teach him well.

Kestrel and Nicholas promised to send word to the sisters when she gave birth.

Michael and his sister didn't want to part and Camelee swore she wouldn't let them go unless the sisters promised to bring them together once every year. Maybe at Christmastime, she suggested.

The sisters agreed and sent Michael and Charlotte, Nicholas and Kes home first.

Sebastian took a bit of time leaving his father. It was clear to see that things were different between them.

"I'm looking after everything in New York," he told Arthur. "I will see you then, at Christmas."

"Yes," the king agreed and pulled his son into a tight embrace. "Son of my youth. I'm sorry about your mother."

"Her end was her own doing, Father," Sebastian said into his father's neck. "I'm just thankful I didn't kill you."

"So am I."

They laughed and Arthur patted his son's shoulders. "You are strong, Sebastian. More than you were ever taught, for you resisted her power. Well done."

Sebastian pulled back and smiled, then nodded and returned to Noelle. He faced her and held their hands between them. And then they, too, were gone.

"Ulf," the king said, "I trust you with my daughter's life."

Wolf bowed his head. The honor was too great to speak of. "I will never disappoint you, my lord."

The king and his wife and daughter smiled at him.

"As a way of thanking you for saving those I love," the king continued. "I will ask the sisters to grant you one thing, but remember, you can only have it here in Avalon."

Wolf nodded and looked down at the woman who burrowed her way under his skin and laid waste to his heart. He leaned in and whispered in her ear. Her smile widened and she nodded her approval.

"We want a night of music and dancing. Slow music," he added, remembering how his new family had danced with each other.

"Fast music, too," his wife corrected quickly and with a smile. "Some rock and roll. Don't worry. You'll love it. The louder the better."

He turned a worried look at her father. Had he chosen the wrong thing? He had anything to pick from, after all. He chose a night of music and dancing.

And then Camelee smiled at him, and he knew whatever they chose would be perfect.

Certainly, he would learn how to dance if it made his wife happy.

Wasn't that what husbands were supposed to do?

The End

About the Author

Paula Quinn is a New York Times bestselling author and a sappy romantic moved by music, beautiful words, and the sight of a really nice pen. She lives in New York with her three beautiful children, six over-protective chihuahuas, and three adorable parrots. She loves to read romance and science fiction and has been writing since she was eleven. She's a faithful believer in God and thanks Him daily for all the blessings in her life. She loves all things medieval, but it is her love for Scotland that pulls at her heartstrings.

To date, four of her books have garnered Starred reviews from Publishers Weekly. She has been nominated as Historical Storyteller of the Year by RT Book Reviews, and all the books in her MacGregor and Children of the Mist series have received Top Picks from RT Book Reviews. Her work has also been honored as Amazons Best of the Year in Romance, and in 2008 she won the Gayle Wilson Award of Excellence for Historical Romance.

Website:
pa0854.wixsite.com/paulaquinn

www.ingramcontent.com/pod-product-compliance
Lightning Source LLC
Chambersburg PA
CBHW070921190726
48292CB00004B/1045